Once a
Duchess

Once a Duchess

Elizabeth Boyce

Author of *Once an Heiress* and *Once an Innocent*

CRIMSON
ROMANCE

F+W Media, Inc.

Crimson Romance
an imprint of F+W Media, Inc.
10151 Carver Road, Suite 200
Blue Ash, Ohio 45242
www.crimsonromance.com

ISBN 10: 1-4405-7345-X
ISBN 13: 978-1-4405-7345-3
eISBN 10: 1-4405-5738-1
eISBN 13: 978-1-4405-5738-5

Printed in the United States of America.

10 9 8 7 6 5 4 3 2 1

Cover image © 123rf.com.

*This book is available at quantity discounts for bulk purchases.
For information, please call 1-800-289-0963.*

Dedication

For Jason. Thanks for keeping me high on support.

Acknowledgments

My heartfelt thanks to Michelle Grass and Sarah Zuba, my dear friends and tireless companions on this journey. To Catherine Milne, thanks for helping me kill the horse. *Merci*, Oasis, for cheering me on. Many thanks to the wonderful writing community of SCWW Columbia I for helping me grow from fumbling novice to published author. Particular thanks to the incomparable C. Hope Clark for your guidance and advice.

I'd like to express my appreciation to everyone at Crimson Romance, to my editors Jennifer Lawler and Julie Sturgeon, and to my fellow authors for holding my hand, calming my fears, and kicking my tootkus as needed.

More thanks go to Tara Gelsomino and J.C. Kosloff for bringing this novel further than I ever dreamed.

Thank you, Amanda and Debbie, the world's best sisters and sometimes ruthless beta readers.

Finally, thank you, Mom. You believed in me, and that made all the difference.

Chapter One
1813

Isabelle Jocelyn Fairfax Lockwood, the former Duchess of Monthwaite, knelt on the stone hearth and prodded the weak fire in the grate of her small cottage in southern Leicestershire. The flames gave a half-hearted attempt to brighten before they settled back to a feeble glow. She blew into the coals. Again, the flames briefly intensified. She held her hands out for warmth, their cracked skin pained by the January chill.

"Another bit o' peat, do you think, Mrs. Smith?" asked Bessie, Isabelle's lone servant and companion.

The middle-aged woman's round cheeks were pink from cold, she noted with a pang of conscience. Bessie wore stout wool stockings under her dress, a shawl, cap, and fingerless gloves. Isabelle wore much the same; her attire was of only marginally better quality. She felt chilled, but she knew the cold did not seep into her bones the way it did Bessie's. It wasn't fair to make the woman suffer on account of Isabelle's thriftiness. "Certainly."

She rose from the hearth and picked up the dress lying across the back of a chair in the cottage's parlor. It was a fine gown at odds with the humble abode: sky blue silk with silver embroidery down the long sleeves and around the bottom hem, and seed pearls adorning the neckline. It was a heaven of luxurious elegance, a dress fit for a duchess, and it had several small moth-eaten holes in the skirt. Isabelle had cursed under her breath when she discovered the damage this morning. She had so few nice things left to her name, she'd be damned if this dress would feed those insidious creatures.

She settled into the chair near the fire, took up needle and thread, and began carefully repairing the fabric.

"Wouldn't you like me to do that for you, ma'am?" Bessie hovered beside her, one hand extended. "Such a lovely thing. Where've you been keeping it?"

Isabelle flinched inwardly. It was foolish of her to have the dress out where Bessie could see it. She ran the risk of spoiling the false identity she'd cultivated to escape notoriety. "Mrs. Smith," the parson's widow, had no business owning such an extravagant gown.

She should have sold it with the rest, she chided herself. Goodness knew she needed the blunt. Alexander was late with her allowance— again. The last money her brother sent in October was nearly gone.

But sentimentality had gotten the best of her. Everything she owned now was simple, serviceable, sensible. She had precious little left to remind her that she was a gentleman's daughter and, for a short time, a noblewoman.

"No, thank you," she said, pulling the gown against her stomach. Isabelle cast around the immaculate cottage for something to occupy the maid. "Do you have any mending of your own?" she asked.

Bessie frowned thoughtfully, deep lines marking her cheeks. "My nephew did drop off a few shirts when he brought the peat on Monday."

"There you are." Isabelle smiled brightly. "Go ahead and see about them." She watched the maid disappear into her small bedchamber. The door shut.

Foolish, stupid girl, she chided herself. If she weren't cautious, Bessie would discover Isabelle's true identity. The past year had passed in peaceful anonymity. Her only correspondents were her brother and her last remaining friend, Lily. They both knew to address their letters to Mrs. Jocelyn Smith.

Isabelle stroked her hand down the gown's limp sleeve, the embroidery's ridges a textural contrast to the slippery silk beneath. She'd never worn the dress. It was a winter gown, suited for a fête in London. That party never came.

What had come was her mother-in-law Caro, hurling accusations of adultery against Isabelle and Justin—while Isabelle was still bedridden with a broken rib.

What had come was Justin's disappearance. She never saw or heard from her friend again after Caro came to Hamhurst.

What had come was Marshall, confused and angry. He asked her over and over whether she had betrayed him. But what was the word of his wife of only months, compared to the wisdom of the woman he'd known all his life? He believed the worst: that Isabelle was the fortune-hunting, title-hungry jezebel his mother had always known her to be.

What finally came, after months of agonizing uncertainty, was the divorce.

* * *

Isabelle stood on the walk in front of the village's little posting office, clutching the letter from her brother. Finally, her allowance. She tore it open as she started toward the mercantile where the owner would exchange a bank draft for currency. There remained no money to purchase peat for the fireplace, nor tallow candles, or Bessie's wages—or much food, for that matter.

With fingers aching in the cold, she unfolded the letter and blinked in surprise. Instead of a bank draft tucked inside, there were only a few lines in her brother's hand. She stopped and read the note in the middle of the walk:

> *Having given the matter due consideration, I find I must discontinue my financial support. While I was obligated to look after your welfare when you were unmarried, and would be again if you were widowed and destitute, I simply cannot afford to maintain you further in your present situation. My own circumstances no longer allow for such an expense, as I'm sure you understand.*
> *A. Fairfax*

Cut off. Alexander had finally done it. She'd wondered, with her pittance of an allowance coming later and later every quarter, whether this was where it was headed. She scanned the letter again, searching for any sign of filial affection. There was none. Rather, she detected anger behind his words. Her *present situation* could only refer to her being divorced. If he truly felt no obligation to support his divorced sister, why had it taken him nearly three years to say so?

Isabelle reversed direction and trudged back to her cottage with her brother's letter buried in the pocket of her heavy wool coat. There was nothing remotely feminine or decorous about her outerwear, but neither was there anything refined about the bitter wind that lifted last night's snowfall from the ground in swirling clouds that stung her eyes.

The mile-long walk would not have been so burdensome if she had money in her pocket, instead of the cruel letter. Twice she lost her footing on snow-covered ice.

"All it needs is a broken ankle to complete the Gothic tragedy," she muttered.

She passed the rest of the trip home playing out the novel in her mind: the ill-used maiden, broken in body and heart, taken to bed with consumption. The doctor shaking his head sadly. No hope for it, he'd say, nothing more to be done. Alexander, contrite, kneeling beside her bed, clutching her hand and weeping, begging her forgiveness and promising all the peat she could burn, if only she'd recover. She would turn her fevered eyes upon him, open her mouth as if to speak, and then sigh her last. Her brother would gnash his teeth, and pull out clumps of hair in his despair, cursing himself for being such a fool.

She opened the cottage door no richer, but a little lighter in spirits.

* * *

The following Saturday, a visitor arrived to alleviate the winter doldrums. Though the cottage door opened into the front hall just off the parlor, Bessie took the unnecessary step of announcing the identity of the new arrival.

"Miss Bachman to see you, Mrs. Smith."

Isabelle was already on her feet, flinging her needlework aside to embrace her friend.

"Lily!" she exclaimed. "Whatever are you doing here?"

Lily's abigail sidled in behind her mistress, carrying a valise. She scrutinized her surroundings with a dismayed expression on her face.

Both women sported bright pink cheeks. "Never say you walked in this inclement weather!"

"Nothing like a bracing bit of exercise to shake off a post chaise trip," Lily said.

She divested herself of her fashionable bonnet and cloak, revealing a fetching red traveling costume. Isabelle took the items and passed them off to Bessie.

"You must be freezing," Isabelle said. "Can I offer you some—"

Behind Lily, Bessie emphatically shook her head. No tea.

"That is, perhaps you would care for some coff—"

Bessie shook her head again.

Isabelle's face burned. Oh, this was low. She silently cursed her brother and the Duke of bloody Monthwaite, but most of all, she cursed herself for being in this predicament.

Lily patted her lovely chestnut coiffure and pretended not to notice Isabelle's discomfiture. Her brown eyes lit up.

"I just remembered." She gestured to her maid who pulled a small wooden box from her own coat pocket and handed it to Lily. "I brought some tea. It's a new blend I haven't tried." The container was about the size of her palm and a couple inches deep. "I know you probably have your own favorite," she said apologetically, "but if it's not too much trouble, would you try this one with me?"

Isabelle blinked back the tears burning her eyes. Only Lily could come bearing charity and make it sound as though Isabelle would be doing her a favor by accepting.

She took the proffered gift, her fingers cradling the box. "Of course," she said, her voice thick. "Tea, please, Bessie." Her mouth twisted into an ironic half-smile. "In the good service." She only had the one.

Bessie gave the faintest of curtsies and bustled off, carrying Lily's outerwear and the tea. Isabelle directed Lily's Abigail to take her bag to Isabelle's own bedchamber. They would have to share a room, as they'd done when they were girls.

When the maids left, Lily started to sink onto the faded couch, but Isabelle scooped her up again in a fierce hug. "Thank you," she whispered against her friend's ear. They sat down and Isabelle took in her friend's lovely ensemble. "It's so good to see you in a cheerful color," she said kindly. "The black never suited you."

Lily nodded. "Believe you me, you cannot be happier to see me in a color than I am to be wearing it. What an odd thing it was, to mourn a man I scarcely knew—to be a widow before I'd even wed. I'm glad the year is over, but neither do I quite look forward to being thrust onto the marriage mart. My whole life, I never had to wonder who I'd marry; I always knew. But now my future husband is an enigma. Which makes me like every other female in England, I suppose," she finished matter-of-factly.

Isabelle smiled sympathetically. Through the designs of all parents involved, Lily had been born with her wedding date already set. She was to marry her betrothed the first of June, 1811, when she was twenty years of age. January of that year, however, Ensign Charles Handford and the rest of the Nineteenth Lancers were sent to reinforce Wellington's Peninsular force. Charles didn't make it home for the summer wedding, and in November 1811, he'd been killed in battle. Isabelle knew her dear friend did not truly grieve him, but neither was she glad to have escaped the match at the cost of the groom's life.

These dreary thoughts occupied her mind until Bessie brought the tea tray. While Isabelle poured, Lily pulled Bessie aside and murmured to her in a low voice. The maid nodded and collected Lily's abigail. The women donned cloaks and departed through the front door.

"What was that about?" Isabelle asked wryly, hoping to put aside the somber atmosphere. "You haven't sacked Bessie, have you? No one else worth a salt will work for such a miserable pittance. I shall never find another like her." She passed a cup and saucer to Lily.

"I've sent them to the butcher." Lily shrugged guiltily. "You know how particular I am about food. I'm a horrible guest."

Isabelle shook her head. Again, Lily made her gifts sound like a nuisance.

"Besides," Lily continued with the spark of the devil in her eyes, "I wanted your dear Bessie out from under our feet. I live in fear of slipping up and calling you Isabelle, instead of Jocelyn or Mrs. Smith."

Isabelle nodded. "Fair enough." A strand of her blond hair fell down alongside her cheek. She hooked it behind her ear. She couldn't remember the last time her hair had been styled by a lady's maid. "Why have you come, Lily?" She touched her friend's arm lightly. "Not that I'm not delighted to see you, of course, but I don't get many surprise visitors."

Lily set her tea on the small table beside the sofa. "I've come to issue an invitation."

Isabelle's ears perked. "To what? No one's invited me anywhere in years."

"A wedding," Lily answered. "My cousin, Freddy Bachman, is returned from Spain. He's getting married in a week. I hoped you'd come as my guest. It will be my first outing in quite a long time, too."

A wedding? Isabelle wrinkled her brow and buried her face in her teacup. A wedding was so respectable. Two people standing before God, pledging their lives to one another—surely they wouldn't want a divorcée there. She'd be like a leper at a garden party—completely out of place, abnormal, despised.

"Isabelle?" Lily ventured.

She raised her eyes over the rim of her cup.

"Shall I pour, dear?" Lily asked. "Your cup was empty before you lifted it."

Isabelle quickly lowered the vacant china. "Ah, so it is. Yes, please," she said with tight gaiety. She forced a laugh. "Who on earth is married in the dead of winter?"

"My cousin, for one," Lily said while she poured Isabelle a fresh cup. "His fiancée has been waiting these several years for his discharge from the army."

Isabelle's smile faltered. "She waited for him to come home from the war? For years?" Such a testament of devotion was humbling. Isabelle shook her head. "I can't. It wouldn't be right."

Lily's finely arched brows drew together and she tilted her head to the side. One gleaming curl rested prettily on the shoulder of her red dress. "Don't be ridiculous."

Isabelle shook her head again. "No."

"Why not?" Lily took Isabelle's cup and set it aside, then scooped both of Isabelle's hands in her own. "You must stop thinking of yourself as some kind of pariah. You're divorced, not diseased. No one else is going to . . . catch it." Her full lips turned up in a sympathetic smile. "You've been in exile long enough," Lily continued. "I assure you, no one is talking about you at all anymore."

Isabelle regarded her warily. "Really?"

Lily nodded. "You're not nearly as interesting as you think you are."

Isabelle laughed, then drew a nervous breath. "Oh, I just don't know. I would feel so conspicuous."

"It's just a family affair," Lily assured her. "You wouldn't know anyone there, and they don't know you, either—except for my parents, of course, and they adore you. It will be a perfect first step."

Isabelle sighed. "It does sound like an ideal reintroduction to respectable company. But, something has happened that may delay my plans." She went into her bedchamber to retrieve Alexander's letter and handed it to her friend.

Lily scanned the page, then clicked her tongue. "The absolute gall of the man." Her fist closed around an edge of the page. She shook it in front of her. "How dare he? Punishing you yet again? What does he hope to accomplish by cutting you off?"

"I don't know." Isabelle pulled her shawl tighter around her shoulders. "But you see, now is not the time for me to try to go back into society. I'll have to work first, save a little money—"

"Work?" The word fell from Lily's mouth like a bite of rotten egg. "What do you mean?"

"I have to earn money," Isabelle explained calmly. "I've given it a great deal of thought. I'll do something small to start, perhaps take in mending. I can't rely upon unexpected visitors to keep me in tea."

Lily blushed.

Isabelle stood and paced the length of the small room. "I should like to open a shop, eventually. Perhaps a millinery."

"You don't make hats," Lily pointed out.

"There is that," Isabelle agreed. "Perhaps I could import them. From Paris."

Lily's eyes widened. "Smuggled bonnets? I really can't imagine you mingling with the criminal element. Not at all a respectable endeavor."

"I suppose not." Isabelle tapped her chin. "There must be something!"

"We'll think about it this week, all right?" Lily reassured her. "I wonder, though, if you won't be in your dotage by the time you have enough money to launch yourself again."

Isabelle sighed and plopped back onto the couch in a rather unladylike fashion. "I just want a family, Lily. Is that really too much to ask? A respectable husband and a few children of my own?"

The familiar emptiness in her heart ached. Childbirth had taken both Isabelle's mother and the infant girl who would have been her little sister. Her father then fell into a melancholy from which he'd never recovered. Fairfax Hall went without the attention of its master for a decade. Isabelle had likewise gone neglected. Left to the care of doting servants and a tutor, she'd been permitted to do as she pleased.

Her treasured friendship with Justin Miller should never have gone on as long as it did, she now knew. It was not at all the thing for a young lady to be on such close terms with a young man, but no one bothered to put a stop to it. Justin was the one constant source of affection and amusement in her life.

Lily's family came from their home in Brighton only a couple times a year to visit Mrs. Bachman's parents, who were neighbors to Fairfax Hall.

Alexander had gone to Oxford, and Isabelle's papa spent his time in solitude—in the library, in his study, or wandering the estate. Several times, she and Justin had found him lying on the ground, sleeping beside the white marble tomb he'd built for his wife and child. There was room inside for him, too. It seemed to Isabelle as though he wanted to crawl inside and join her.

Isabelle sometimes wondered how her life would have been different if he had been dead in truth, rather than absent only in mind and spirit. She would have been properly provided for, she supposed, not allowed to develop such hoydenish tendencies. It had been painful, too. As a child, she tried and tried to cheer her father. She danced and sang silly songs. He smiled wanly with eyes devoid of humor and patted her head. Isabelle wondered why she and Alexander weren't good enough. She missed Mama, too, but there were still people she loved around her. Didn't Papa love her? She was certain there was something—some one thing—that would make him better. Isabelle spent countless hours trying to find it.

In time, when she was twelve, Papa did the only thing that would end his suffering. Isabelle heard the shot and got to his study first. He'd fallen sideways on the leather sofa, and what she noticed most was not the blood, but the peaceful expression on his face.

Isabelle returned to herself. She blinked a few times and said in a low voice, "I've never *had* a family, Lily. Is it too selfish of me to want one of my own?"

"Of course not," Lily cooed. "We'll get you there, Isa, never you fear." She straightened to a businesslike posture. "As much as I dislike the idea, I agree you must do something to generate income. I'll save up my pin money, too, and maybe in a few months—"

"No," Isabelle interjected vehemently. She clutched her skirt in her fists. "I'll take your tea, but I cannot accept your money." Lily started to protest, but Isabelle raised a hand to stop her. "Please. I have endured this situation for several years. This is just a new obstacle, and I *shall* overcome it. But not with your allowance."

Lily sighed. "All right, then. Do say you'll come to the wedding, though. I should dearly love your company."

The allure of polite society warred with Isabelle's practical concerns. At last, she shook her head. "I'm sorry, but I just can't, Lily. Not with things so tight here. The days I'd spend away are days I could be earning money to keep this place heated."

Worry lines bracketed Lily's mouth. "I wish you would let me do something for you, dear. Your bleak circumstances cannot persist."

A half-smile tugged Isabelle's mouth. "Things will improve. And I'll tell you something," she said, pulling her shoulders back. "It will be nice to have reliable income, rather than depend on a man's whim."

"Hmm." A thoughtful expression crossed Lily's pretty features. "I didn't think of that, but you're right. What a novel idea. Since you won't come to the wedding with me, I'll do what I can to help you find a position."

"Maybe it will even be fun," Isabelle said, her mood brightening. "This is a chance to make a new start. I've been living a kind of half-life ever since the divorce. Now I can start over."

Lily raised her chipped teacup. "To new beginnings."

Isabelle lifted hers to join the toast. "To new beginnings. *And*, to the devil with men."

* * *

Lily's brows shot to her hairline. "A cook? Really, Isabelle, what are you thinking?"

A week after her arrival, the maids bustled to prepare for Miss Bachman's departure to her cousin's wedding. In that time, Isabelle had approached every business in the area at which she might be at all useful.

Isabelle playfully swatted her friend's arm. "Yes, a cook. I'll have you know, I'm a reasonable hand in the kitchen. At home, Cook taught me out of Mother's French recipe books."

The taller woman cast her a dubious look. "Be that as it may, inns are frequently rather seedy."

"Oh, no, the George is a very clean establishment. Mr. Davies was so impressed with the stew I made, I was even able to negotiate a higher wage."

"Wage negotiations?" Lily's shoulders rose and fell with her sigh. "All right, Isabelle, you've impressed me. Go ahead and tumble into the working class. I suppose you're ready as you'll ever be."

Isabelle grasped her friend in a tight hug. "Thank you for everything."

Lily held her back at arm's length. "You can do anything you put your mind to, Isabelle. Your dreams of a husband and children—you *can* have those, you know. Go and cook for your villagers if you must, but you're still hiding. Come back to the world and take your proper place."

Isabelle's lips curved in a wistful smile. "This *is* my proper place now, Lily. This is the life I must live."

Chapter Two

"On the matter of Thomas Gerald, Your Grace, there has been no progress."

Marshall Trevelyan Bruckner Lockwood, Duke of Monthwaite, looked up from the folding desk in his traveling chaise where he was reviewing the annual expenditure summaries he'd collected from his various stewards over the past month.

His secretary, Perkins, sat opposite, with papers strewn across his lap and the seat. The pale, bespectacled man had a mind as strong as a steel trap. He'd been in Marshall's employ for several years now, and had become invaluable in keeping Marshall's dealings sorted out.

"Nothing?" Marshall asked, raising a brow.

Perkins scanned the parchment in his hand. He pressed a handkerchief to his lips, squeezed his eyes shut, and shook his head. "No, sir, nothing." He cleared his throat. "Thomas Gerald's name appears on the manifest of the *Destiny*, which sailed from Van Diemen's Land August 17, 1809. He worked as a deck hand to pay his passage. All told, the voyage took the better part of a year, with stops for provisions, and repairs in the Caribbean islands. He could have disembarked at any one of these locations, rather than return to England. His name is not mentioned again, either in the manifest or the captain's log. There is nothing more." Perkins dabbed at the sheen of sweat that had popped out on his forehead as he spoke.

"How does a man just disappear for years?" He muttered to himself. "Are you all right?" he asked Perkins. "You're looking a touch green."

"Apologies, sir," the secretary said through clenched teeth. "Reading in a moving vehicle causes a mild indisposition. I'm quite well, though, I assure you." Marshall watched his fastidious secretary run a finger under his neck cloth, loosening it. "Shall we continue?"

"No, that will do for now," Marshall said. "I'd rather you not cast your accounts on my boots."

Perkins scowled.

"Take a rest," Marshall suggested. "We'll soon be stopping for the night."

"Thank you, sir." Perkins looked decidedly peaked, but neatly stowed away all the papers before leaning his head back against the squabs.

Marshall took up the Thomas Gerald file and flipped through it. He once again scanned the sole report his investigator had been able to generate about Gerald's departure from the penal colony, having fulfilled his ten-year sentence for the willful destruction of Marshall's father's property—his prize mare and her foal. The information was now several years old. He could be anywhere, Marshall thought in frustration— Brazil, or Haiti . . . or England.

He closed his eyes, and the whole horrible scene was there, as though the incident had been yesterday, not twelve years ago. In his mind's eye, he saw the mare, Priscilla, past due for her foaling, and the grooms worried about her. He saw Thomas Gerald, a young man just a couple years older than Marshall, laughing and jovial as he joked with the other grooms, tender and concerned when he looked after the ailing Priscilla.

And then Marshall saw himself: a boy of thirteen, bored with the confines of the schoolroom, desperate to prove his maturity, and longing to earn his father's approval. His newfound interest in botany consumed his adolescent mind. He'd read a few books and had begun helping the gardener in the greenhouse, observing the way the man planted seeds in different fashions and watching carefully as he grafted one plant onto another. In short order, Marshall became the embodiment of the phrase about a little knowledge being a dangerous thing.

Priscilla's swollen belly had the stable in a tizzy, and the duke on tenterhooks. But Marshall remembered the midwife's words he'd once overheard to the blacksmith, offering the man's wife a tincture of mugwort and juniper berries to help ease her birthing, and an idea took shape in his mind.

Then Priscilla ate from Thomas Gerald's gentle hands. The mare convulsed. And then she screamed. Marshall pressed his hands to his eyes—dear *God*, he could still hear that horse's scream. Marshall had never been so scared in all his young life. He squeezed himself into a corner, where he remained unnoticed as every hand in the stable came running.

So much blood. At first, Priscilla had thrashed and protested against the restraining hands that held her down while she was examined in her stall. Marshall heard the head groom yelling for a towel—he was going to try to pull the foal free. Gradually, Priscilla's cries gave way to piteous whinnies, until even those declined into gentle moans, and then silence. Horrible, heavy silence.

They sent for His Grace, and explained to Marshall's father that Priscilla's womb had ruptured. Both mare and foal had been lost.

His father was terribly distraught. Marshall remembered his pale face, the concerned crease of his brow as he looked into the poor mare's stall, how he pressed a handkerchief to his lips and then quickly walked away.

Marshall himself slipped out of the stable a short time later. He spent the rest of the afternoon and well into the evening wandering through the woods, throwing accusatory looks at every herb he encountered. They were supposed to help, not hurt! His beloved flora had betrayed him.

The next morning, Marshall awoke to a house in an uproar. When the mare's body had been removed and the stall cleaned, a jar had been discovered under a layer of straw, containing the remains of an unknown sticky substance.

Someone had fed Priscilla poison. Someone had deliberately killed His Grace's favorite mare. If there was one thing in the world the Duke of Monthwaite was passionate about, it was his horses. The gruesome way in which his most prized bit of horseflesh had met her demise was beyond all reckoning. The criminal would be punished. Severely.

Another groom said he recalled seeing Thomas Gerald feeding the horse by hand, but never imagined he'd do something so heinous. Sticky stains found on Gerald's shirt cuffs gave weight to the accusation. For his atrocious crime, the fifteen-year-old groom was transported to Van Diemen's Land for ten years on the labor gangs.

The carriage pulled to a stop. Marshall opened his eyes and drew a shuddering breath. Somewhere in the world, possibly even in England, roamed a man who could rightfully blame Marshall for ruining his life. Such a man was dangerous and had to be found before he attempted something foolish. Marshall scrawled a note on the report to remind Perkins to call in yet another investigator, since this one had lost the trail.

* * *

In Leicestershire, Marshall stopped at the estate of David Hornsby, the younger son of an earl. He had the good fortune of a sire who'd acquired a spare estate to give his youngest offspring.

As a result, the estate's master epitomized the idle rich. Mr. Hornsby was of an age with Marshall, and lived well off the income of his land. With a competent steward taking care of the estate's day-to-day operations, Hornsby had no purpose in life other than pursuing pleasure and fulfilling his own whims.

One of his few redeeming qualities was a kindred leaning toward botany. They had attended lectures together at the Royal Society and struck up something of a friendship, founded only on their shared intellectual pursuits. The botany community was a small one, and Marshall would not turn his nose up at a man who was as eager as he was to see progress in the field.

Marshall was shown into Hornsby's library, the walls of which were adorned with framed prints of local wildflowers.

"Monthwaite!" Hornsby sprang from the leather chair in which he'd been ensconced with a book and a bottle of brandy. Marshall noted this last item with distaste, considering it was just past noon. Hornsby extended his hand for Marshall's greeting and pumped the duke's arm vigorously. "Good to see you, Monty, good to see you. How fare the great swaths of the kingdom in your possession?" The man's face, flushed with drink, clashed against his yellow-checked jacket.

Hornsby had no sooner returned to his seat than he sprang up again. Most men as far into their cups as he appeared to be—judging by the alarmingly low level in the brandy decanter—would have been half-asleep by now. However, Marshall's host appeared as energetic as if he'd just awoken from a refreshing night's sleep.

Hornsby strode on thick legs to an oak table standing near a large picture window overlooking the expansive gardens on the back of the house. He unrolled a map and gestured for Marshall to join him at the table. He jabbed a chubby finger into the map. "I believe I've located a suitable site for the herbarium."

"Coventry?"

Hornsby nodded. "London would be the obvious choice, of course, but land there is dear and hard to come by. I thought," he said, turning his glassy brown eyes on Marshall, "a centralized location would be a nice gesture."

"To whom?" Marshall asked.

Hornsby shrugged and smiled like the spoiled little boy he was. "Everyone."

Everyone Marshall took to mean the entire population of Britain, and indeed the world, to whom their proposed herbarium would be open.

For a long moment, he held Hornsby's gaze. His eager face seemed desperate for Marshall's approval. Though they had been born the same year and Marshall only a few months before Hornsby, Marshall still felt as though Hornsby looked to him for guidance, like an older brother. He regarded the map again. His lips turned up in a slow, lazy smile.

"You might be on to something," he drawled. He nodded, affirming his statement. "Yes, let's go have a look at the land you have in mind."

A wide grin broke across Hornsby's face. "Really?" he breathed rapturously.

Marshall took a step back and away from the fumes rolling off his friend.

"I'll have my bags ready in a trice," Hornsby said. As he hurried from the room he called over his shoulder, "I know a good inn where we can stay tonight."

Chapter Three

Isabelle gave the stew a stir. She wiped her palms against the faded linen apron around her waist, then peeked into the oven to check on the roasting chickens. Everything was coming along nicely, but a few customers had been kept waiting longer than she—or they—liked.

In the month she'd been working in the kitchen at the George, word of the inn's uncommonly good cook quickly spread beyond the village. The inn now often saw customers who came just to dine, rather than to stay the night or spend the evening drinking in the common room.

The first dish to win the locals' acclaim had been her savory beef stew. Initially, Isabelle made use of the last bit of ale in the barrels as the base for her concoction. The dish had become so popular, however, Mr. Davies now purchased ale specifically for cooking.

A serving girl stuck her head in the kitchen. "Is the stew ready yet, Miz Smith? Some of the blokes are startin' to grumble."

"Almost, Gretchen." Isabelle fished out a slice of carrot and bit it. Still a touch too firm in the center. "Ten more minutes," she told the girl. At the servant's harried expression, Isabelle snapped, "I could give it to them raw, but they wouldn't like that, either."

"I s'pose not," Gretchen muttered. "But they're 'plainin', and I'm the one has to hear it."

Isabelle's annoyance fell away, and she gave the girl a sympathetic smile. "Why don't you hide in here with me for a few minutes?" She blew at a wayward strand of hair that had fallen loose from the cap containing her unruly tresses.

The serving girl gave her an appreciative look and stepped farther into the kitchen. It was a large room, but cramped for all that.

A brick oven was set into one wall, pouring out heat as a steady supply of bread went in and came out. Beside the oven was a long counter on which the dough was mixed, kneaded, and set aside to rise.

A large table for preparing meats and vegetables dominated the center of the room. Above it hung a black iron rack covered with saucepans, stockpots, and skillets. Beside the pantry, a door opened on stairs leading to the modest wine cellar.

Another wall had a sink and scullery counter. The fourth side of the room held the massive stove and roasting oven where Isabelle toiled her hours away.

Isabelle directed Gretchen to pull fresh loaves from the brick oven with the long bread paddle, while she cubed a cut of beef for another pot of stew. A boy came in carrying dirty plates. The omnipresent rumble of talking and laughter was momentarily bright and clear until the door swung shut again, dampening the noise.

"Sammy," Isabelle said to the boy, "run to the larder and fetch me some suet." The boy dropped the dishes to the counter with a clatter and scampered out the door.

Isabelle dumped the beef cubes into a hot skillet to brown. She washed her hands, wiped them on her apron, and checked the stew again. Perfect.

"Gretchen," she called, "stew's ready." She glanced over to where the girl had set the steaming, fresh loaves on the bread counter and was struggling to get an unbaked loaf into the oven.

"Bollocks! I forgot to flour the paddle," Gretchen exclaimed.

"Do you need help?" Isabelle ladled up a bowl of stew, set it on the counter, and reached for another empty dish.

"I can manage." The serving girl gave up trying to shake the dough free of the paddle and moved right to the oven, where she attempted to force the loaf off with her hand.

She shouldn't do that, Isabelle thought with trepidation. "Careful," she called. "Pull the whole thing back out and I'll—"

Too late.

"Yeouch!" Gretchen snatched her hand back and grabbed it with the other. The paddle clattered to the floor and the stubborn loaf of dough rolled traitorously onto the stones.

Isabelle hurried to the girl. Three of Gretchen's fingers were red and one was already blistering. The serving girl kept up a steady stream of cries and curses. Isabelle dragged her to the washing station and plunged her hand into the basin of rinse water.

Gretchen yowled.

Isabelle made a shushing sound. "The water will cool the skin."

"What is going on in here?"

Isabelle looked up. Mr. Davies, her employer and the proprietor of the George, cast a look of wide-eyed alarm over the chaotic disarray in his usually orderly kitchen. His balding pate glistened with sweat. He grabbed a dishtowel from the counter and ran it over his head and mutton-chopped cheeks.

"Gretchen burned her hand," Isabelle explained.

He huffed in annoyance, pressing his massive fists to his hips. Mr. Davies was a large man, but Isabelle would never have called him fat. He gave one the impression of a rock-filled sack. "Well, get it out of the basin and get that food to the customers!" Mr. Davies ordered.

Isabelle shot her employer a disapproving look, but released Gretchen. The girl gingerly patted her burned hand dry, lifted a bowl of stew, and set it down again, howling with pain.

"Would you shut it?" Mr. Davies hissed. "We've got gents out there. You want them to think there's a murder going on?"

Isabelle drew the weeping Gretchen back to the basin and once again plunged her hand into the water. Mr. Davies was usually a jovial man and was not an unkind master of his establishment. There was a larger-than-usual crowd out there tonight, though, so Isabelle tried to ignore his insensitivity to Gretchen's predicament. "She can't work anymore tonight," Isabelle said in a reasonable tone.

"Who's going to do the serving, then?" the man asked. His dark blue eyes were wide and his gray brows shot up into his forehead. "I'm already short-handed. Gretchen's the only girl in tonight, as is. We've got honest-to-God blue bloods in the private dining room who need seeing to, and half the common room's going to die of barrel fever on me if we don't get food into their bellies to sop up the ale."

"My sister would come help!" Sammy, the dish boy, piped up. "She needs a few shillings for a bit o' ribbon she's got her eye on."

"Go get her, then," Mr. Davies instructed. The boy dashed out. "In the meantime," he said, turning to Isabelle, "you do the serving."

Nerves grabbed at Isabelle's middle. She was happy in the kitchen, working with only a few other employees. She did not relish the idea of plunging into the morass in the common room. "Who's going to mind the kitchen, then?" she asked.

"You are!" Mr. Davies barked. "Do both until Sammy's sainted sister gets here to save us."

Isabelle gritted her teeth, pulled Gretchen's hand from the water, and wrapped it in a towel a little more roughly than she'd intended. Gretchen yelped. "All right," Isabelle muttered. "Who's first?"

"Get that stew out there to the common room. Once they've got spoons in their mouths, they won't be hollerin', and we'll all be able to hear ourselves think. The nobs down the hall want stew, too, and a chicken with the sides."

Isabelle nodded. Gretchen gave her a pained look and bit her lip. "I'm sorry," she mouthed.

"Don't worry about it," Isabelle said.

She finished wrapping the girl's hand and sent her on her way, with instructions to keep the burn clean and wrapped.

Then Isabelle loaded a tray with bowls of stew and loaves of bread. Mr. Davies held the door for her, and she walked down a short hall that opened into the common room.

Twenty tables stood in the spacious room, every one occupied. When the crowd spotted Isabelle and her tray, a cheer went up around the room. She smiled in spite of herself. Most of the patrons were good-natured villagers. There were a few ribald comments from men deep in their tankards, but she began enjoying herself as she served the hard-working folk their suppers. In turn, the men and women seemed to appreciate being able to personally thank the woman who so satisfactorily filled their stomachs.

A shilling landed on her tray when Isabelle delivered food to the table where Mr. Barnaby, a village carpenter, and his wife were dining.

"Excellent, as usual, Mrs. Smith!" the man boomed. His wife nodded her agreement.

Isabelle's heart swelled with pride and delight at the extra coin. "Thank you kindly, sir." She bobbed a curtsy in her giddiness.

As she returned to the kitchen to reload her tray, heat crept up her neck as she realized what she'd done. She was a gently born woman who had just curtsied to a carpenter.

Never did Isabelle think she'd see the day where she'd make a cake of herself over a few pennies tossed in her direction, but that was before she was a ruined woman, before her brother had cast her aside. She might have been born to a softer life, but that life was long gone. She slammed open the kitchen door and filled more bowls.

This was her life now. She cooked in the kitchen of a middle-of-nowhere inn to keep a roof over her head and food on her and Bessie's plates. Fortunately, Mr. Davies didn't mind if she took home some of the leftovers from her evening's efforts. She'd eaten more beef stew and mutton than she cared to think about, but at least she could count on having one hearty meal at night and a bit of bread in the morning.

With her tray once again laden, she made another round through the common room. Her smile was not as bright this time, but she still collected some coins from the jolly patrons.

On her next return trip to the kitchen, Mr. Davies ran her to ground. "Get the food down the hall for the gentlemen now," he said. His voice was still clipped, but his relaxed posture indicated that he felt better about the state of the common room. The grumbles had given way to convivial laughter as neighbors broke bread with one another.

Isabelle loaded down a wheeled cart for the patrons in the private dining room. She felt not the least bit concerned about encountering someone who might know her. First of all, though Marshall had introduced her to a few of his friends, she had encountered only a tiny portion of the *haut ton*. Those she had not met would have known her only by name, not on sight, and Isabelle used a false name here. Further, if by some remote chance there was someone she'd met before in that dining room, she understood the way the privileged class operated. A nobleman might pay attention to the servants in his own house, but he never took notice of the servants in someone else's home, much less a simple serving girl in a country inn. Her position was the perfect disguise.

She filled a covered serving dish with her beef stew and set a ladle alongside. A roasted chicken, along with an assortment of roasted vegetables, asparagus in crème sauce, two loaves of bread, fresh butter, and a slab of cheese also made their way to the tray, along with a bottle of Madeira, another of port, and a decanter of brandy. She then found room for the dishes, utensils, and glasses the meal required, and rolled the heavy cart down the hall.

The noise of the common room faded as she moved toward the dining room. She knocked on the door, waited for the perfunctory, "Enter," opened the door, and pushed in the cart. Warm air rolled out. While the dining room afforded the upper class the privacy they demanded, there were drawbacks to the enclosed space—namely, its oppressive stuffiness. The dishes on the cart tinkled and rattled against each other, a sound that had been previously drowned out by the multitude of voices outside.

Two men sat close together at the far end of the gleaming table, their heads bent over maps and other papers.

One had a commanding air that captured her attention at once. Broad shoulders, straight back, black hair, a firm jaw, and strong nose. He did not so much as look in her direction, but Isabelle instantly recognized the chiseled profile.

Marshall.

Shock numbed her face and limbs, while her heart launched into a panicked gallop. Her fists tightened around the cart handle, white knuckles threatening to burst through her skin.

What was he doing here? *Stay calm,* she ordered herself. She took in great gulps of air and concentrated on acting like a serving girl. Her position was her disguise, she reminded herself.

Marshall's companion, a ginger-haired fellow Isabelle did not recognize, groaned when she came in. "Finally! We're famished. I thought we were being starved out."

"Apologies, m'lord," Isabelle said. It was a wonder she could talk with her heart in her throat. "There's a dreadful crush of people wanting supper tonight." She forced her limbs into motion, lifting the dishes from the cart to set the near end of the table for two.

"Still, it was bloody inconsiderate of you to leave us neglected." The man's lips pursed in a petulant, effeminate fashion.

"Give over, Hornsby," Marshall said in a flat tone. "Mr. Davies told us there would be a wait."

A flash of tenderness unexpectedly tugged at her heart at the sound of his voice. He was tired, she realized. She remembered that tone in his voice after he'd spent many hours in the greenhouse with his plants or working at his desk.

As quickly as she detected the sensation, she fought to squash it out. He didn't need or deserve her pity. It was idiotic to feel badly for the pampered duke, while she—thanks to *his* wrongful divorce—worked long hours in a hot, steamy kitchen to survive.

Isabelle kept her face lowered and turned away from the men as much as possible. Still, she identified Marshall's movements by sound. That Hornsby person flailed around. He sounded messy. By contrast, Marshall made careful, deliberate motions. She heard the tap of a stack of papers being made neat, followed by the light, smooth scrape of his chair moving back from the table. His even footsteps came her way. Her heart pounded, and she dropped the ladle onto the table. She winced at the clatter.

"Something smells delicious," Marshall said.

Isabelle paused. Should she say anything? No, she decided. Probably not. Servants shouldn't engage in conversation with their betters.

"Is this the famous stew we heard so much about?" he asked. Marshall stood close beside her to examine the tureen's contents. His imposing presence seemed to make the air heavier and more difficult to inhale.

Isabelle noted with another pang that he even looked as though he'd been working for hours. His coat was slung over the back of a chair. The sleeves of his cream-colored shirt were rolled up his forearms. He did that when he wrote a lot. An image sprung to mind of an afternoon at Hamhurst, shortly after they were married. She'd spent most of the day alone while he took care of estate work, and when she went to find him in his study, he had been sitting at his desk, looking much the way he did just now.

She also remembered what happened when she found him in the study, how she'd come to stand behind his chair and put her fingers into the soft hair at his nape, rubbing his neck, trying to distract him. And it had worked. Her cheeks burned at the brief memory.

"Is this not the famous stew?" Marshall's voice held a note of teasing. He turned his head to look over his shoulder at her.

Isabelle sucked her breath and whirled away. "Ah, yes. Yes, my lord, it is," she stammered. *Stupid!* She should have answered him right away. If she'd done that, he wouldn't have paid her any attention whatsoever. Now she'd turned her back on a peer of the realm. She tried to cover the blunder by hastily setting out the rest of the food.

Hornsby moved around the table to the other side and looked first at the spread and then at her. "There's a tasty dish," he said, dragging his eyes over her. Isabelle pretended not to notice. She could not imagine *any* man finding her attractive in her shapeless wool dress and stained apron. She'd been working for hours and probably smelled as much like beef stew as the food itself.

Marshall caught his friend's entendre. "That will do, miss," he said softly. "We'll take care of ourselves from here. Madeira, Hornsby?"

How smoothly he redirected his friend's attention, she thought, grateful for his intervention—and then annoyed at herself for feeling gratitude. The longer she stayed in his presence, the more eager she was to be away. Keeping her face ducked, she bobbed a curtsy. Just another moment and she'd be free. With shaking hands, she collected the cart and pushed.

And crashed into the door. The cart handle drove into her middle, pushing her breath out audibly.

Embarrassment washed over her. What an imbecilic blunder!

"What the devil?" Hornsby said.

She would not turn around and see how *he* reacted. "Apologies, my lords," she said to the door. "I'm used to the swinging kitchen door. Terribly sorry." Isabelle leaned across the cart to the doorknob, but couldn't quite reach. She felt two pairs of aristocratic eyes on her, watching her make a buffoon of herself. She tried again, leaning farther. If she got up on her toes . . .

"Allow me." Marshall's hand landed on the knob a split-second after hers, pinning hers underneath its warmth.

A tingle coursed up her arm at his touch.

His eyes flew to her face. Isabelle kept her own resolutely downcast. Her gaze fell on his middle. He wore a maroon waistcoat with gold buttons. She followed them down to where waistcoat ended and his close-fitting brown trousers began, and instantly wished she hadn't allowed her gaze to wander. The sight of his well-muscled thighs did nothing to ease her discomfiture.

"Look at me," he said.

She shook her head, shame suffusing her entire being. She didn't *have* to look at him. He knew, damn him. He knew. The least he could do was leave her with a scrap of her shredded pride and let her go without making a scene.

"Isabelle," he said in a low voice meant only for her ears.

She took a steadying breath and shook her head again, but this time it was a quick gesture of resolve as she gathered her courage. Then she raised her eyes.

The shock on his face at positively identifying her was most gratifying, she decided. His mouth fell open, but no words came out. A storm of emotion roiled in his dark eyes.

She met his gaze boldly and raised her chin, *daring* him to expose her.

"I told you she was a tasty one," Hornsby said.

The interruption brought Marshall back to his senses. He blinked. His brown eyes went strangely flat as he stepped back and returned to the table without another word.

Isabelle got the door open, wrestled the cart through, and closed the door behind her. She took several deep breaths, waiting for her heart to stop racing before returning to the kitchen.

The cacophony of the common room was welcome after the debacle in the dining room. She wished the noise would envelop her so she could disappear into it. She suddenly felt very tired as she pushed into the kitchen.

Mr. Davies was in the kitchen again, trying to calm Sammy, who stood in front of him, hopping from foot to foot.

"Start over," Mr. Davies said. "I couldn't understand a word!"

With visible effort, Sammy fought to still himself, though his feet in their scuffed, oversized shoes continued to tap anxiously.

"I said," he began, his huge eyes intent, "Sally can't come. Pa just found out she's got a belly full, and now he's hollering and swearing to kill the man what did it. And me mam is hollering, trying to get Pa to be quiet. Sally's crying, and says Pa had best not hurt a hair on her beau's head, because she reckons she's in love, and wants to marry him. So, Sally can't come. She's either planning a wedding or a funeral now. I don't know which. I cut out of there."

Mr. Davies growled. "So much for your sainted sister."

For a moment, Isabelle forgot all about the insufferable man she used to be married to, who happened to be sitting in the dining room down the hall. She clamped a hand over her mouth, stifling a laugh at the precocious boy's animated recitation. She let out an undignified snort, which drew Mr. Davies' attention.

"Just you tonight, then," he said.

Isabelle clucked her tongue and rolled the cart to its spot in the corner.

"I could ask Doris," Sammy said.

"Here, who's that, then?" Mr. Davies asked.

"Me other sister," the boy explained.

Mr. Davies looked ready to spit. "Why didn't you ask her while you were home?"

"Didn't think about it." Sammy's chest puffed out. He proudly tapped it with a fist. "I just found out I'm going to be an uncle. That's a big 'sponsibility." He fixed first Mr. Davies and then Isabelle with a quelling look. "And didn't neither of you offer your felicitations."

"How remiss of us!" Isabelle inclined her head in a stately fashion. "Please accept my congratulations for your impending happiness, Uncle Samuel."

"Cor, you go on, Miz Smith," Sammy said, blushing furiously. "You sound just like them lady nobs."

Isabelle winked at the boy. "Anyone else need stew, Mr. Davies?" she asked.

He stroked his hand first down one muttonchop sideburn and then the other. "Yeh," he finally said. "New table o' blokes in the middle. And the apothecary came in. He and his missus want supper, too."

She loaded her tray with food and headed to the common room, hoping her former husband wouldn't venture this way. Marshall showing up in the George's private dining room in no way fit into her plans of a fresh start in life.

* * *

Several hours later, the supper crowd in the common dining room had finally begun to disperse. Those remaining had set about the more serious endeavor of becoming thoroughly sotted. Mr. Davies took over the trips up and down the cellar stairs to keep his customers in a steady stream of intoxicants.

The pots and pans had all been washed, dried, and hung on the rack over the butcher block. Now she sliced a roasted leg of mutton and another roast of beef for cold plates. The chambermaids could easily assemble a simple supper for any overnight guests coming in from the road after the kitchen was closed for the night.

The door swung inward to admit her employer. "About done there?" Mr. Davies asked. At Isabelle's nod, he said, "Don't forget the private dining room. Those dishes need collecting."

"Yes, sir," Isabelle said, her heart sinking in unease. She had kept herself industrious in the hopes that Mr. Davies would take care of the gentlemen himself. It had been hours since she first delivered supper to Marshall and his companion, though. They must have long since retired to their rooms.

She wheeled the cart down the hall again, accompanied by the tearful rendition of "My Bonnie Lies Over the Ocean" a lone patron sang to a stupefied audience. His lilting voice rose and fell, shaping the lyrics into the ocean waves that had carried away the narrator's love. A few more voices rose up to join in the chorus.

The melody followed her down the hall. Isabelle opened the dining room door without knocking. To her surprise, Marshall and his friend were still in the room. They had moved to armchairs facing the fireplace, with their backs to the door. The men were deep in conversation and did not notice her entrance. Judging by the impressive collection of empty bottles on the table, it would seem quite a few of Mr. Davies' trips to the cellar had been on their behalf.

"Wha' was this you started saying 'bout an expedition, old man?" Hornsby said.

"South America," Marshall replied. "I'm going to take an expedition to the Brazilian jungle. D'you know, Hornsby, we have, in just the last few years, discovered *thousands* of new species in the South American jungle. And we've only scratched the surface. There is much work to be done." His voice dropped. "I'd like to see it myself. Maybe discover a species or two."

In the silence that followed, both men drank from their brandies. Isabelle felt another insidious twinge of tenderness for this man who had tossed her aside. She would feel that way for anyone who spoke with such obvious fervor for a passion, she reminded herself. It wasn't just Marshall who could evoke such feelings.

"Sounds marvelous," Hornsby said. He reached for the bottle on the small table between them to refill his glass and, finding it empty, stood and turned on unsteady feet. "Hullo," he said, catching sight of Isabelle. "I din' realize we had a guest."

Marshall turned. Whatever warmth he might have felt in discussing his dreams of a botanical expedition drained away at the sight of her.

Isabelle flinched under the force of his withering expression. "Forgive the intrusion, my lords," she said. "I'm just clearing away the dishes." She began to do just that, all the while painfully aware of both men watching her. Had Marshall told his friend who she was?

Her rattled nerves evidenced themselves in short order. The moment she picked up a stack of plates, the lot of them clattered against one another, thanks to her trembling hands. Her cheeks burned. She lowered the stack to the cart and turned around to collect more dishes. Marshall was just in front of her.

"You're not very good at this, are you?" He stood with his arms crossed, leaning casually with one thigh against the table, looking every inch the cool, aloof aristocrat. His expression was as perfectly bland as his drawl.

Isabelle's tongue flicked over her lower lip. "No, I'm not," she said frankly. "Waiting on spoiled noblemen is not how I usually spend my time. But I do thank Your Grace for highlighting my deficiencies."

Marshall's eyes narrowed dangerously.

"Oh, ho!" Hornsby exclaimed. He moved to stand a short distance from her right side, effectively boxing her in, with Marshall to her front, the table to her side, and the wall behind. "This one's got a mouth, don't she?"

Marshall paid no attention to his companion swaying drunkenly on his feet. "How, pray tell," he said, clipping his words, "*do* you spend your time? Usually."

"I could hazard a guess," Hornsby said. Again, neither Isabelle nor Marshall deigned to notice him. They were wrapped up in their own, private exchange, with no room for a third party.

Isabelle met Marshall's scathing expression with a small smile. She slipped into parlor mode to answer his question, her tone as light as if they were sipping tea on the settee. "Thank you for asking, Your Grace," she said with a slight nod. "I am chiefly employed by Mr. Davies in the capacity of supper cook. This evening, however, our serving girl suffered an unfortunate accident that left her with an injured hand. Young Sammy," she continued, "meant to bring his sister in to help; however," her voice lowered as though she were sharing the tastiest new *on dit*, not village gossip, "the young lady seems to have found herself *enceinte*."

Marshall continued to regard her in stony silence.

"As she was preoccupied with her own imbroglio and unable to come to our aid, I took over serving duties tonight." Isabelle tilted her head to the side and quirked a brow, hoping her face betrayed none of the heart-racing nerves she felt.

A muscle in Marshall's jaw twitched. "Are you quite finished?"

"Oh!" Isabelle said, blithely ignoring his black mood. "The serving girl's name is Gretchen, and her hand was quite badly burned. Please remember her in your prayers tonight."

Hornsby barked a laugh. Isabelle turned just as he slipped an arm around her waist.

"What a delightful creature," he said, hugging her to his side. The man's bloodshot eyes roved boldly over her figure. "I daresay, Monthwaite, put a gown on this one, and she could pass muster at most any rout, don't you think?"

"I daresay," Marshall drawled.

Hornsby's soft body emanated clammy heat. Isabelle tried to create some distance from the man, but he held her in an iron grip. "What is your name?" Hornsby asked. "I must know."

"Mrs. Jocelyn Smith," Isabelle said, reflexively giving her assumed name. The man's arm slackened. She started to edge away from him.

"Married, then?" Hornsby regarded her with droopy eyes reminiscent of a bloodhound.

"I used to be," Isabelle said. Marshall straightened. "My husband died several years ago."

Hornsby's face brightened with a wide grin. "A widow! Some of our favorite people are widows, aren't they, Monty?" He clutched her tightly again, this time bringing his other arm around her waist, as well.

Isabelle struggled against his crushing embrace. His sickly sweet aroma filled her nostrils. She turned her head to escape it.

"I'm sure the nights have been lonely, m'love," Hornsby slurred against her ear.

Isabelle cast a desperate look at Marshall. Fury blasted from every line of his being. He made no move toward intervening on her behalf.

"Actually, no," Isabelle said, casting daggers at the tall, silent man, "not at all. I don't miss my husband in the least."

"He must not have been man enough for you." Hornsby's hands slid down her back.

Isabelle answered him while Marshall's intense black eyes held hers captive. "No, I don't suppose he was."

Three things happened in quick succession: Hornsby grabbed hold of her derrière; Isabelle yelped and pushed against his chest; and Marshall bellowed, "Enough!"

Hornsby released Isabelle, who made a dash for the door, only to have Marshall's hands close around her upper arms in a vise grip.

"You will come with me now," he said through clenched teeth.

"Now, see here, Monthwaite," Hornsby said, indignantly wagging a finger, "I should like to point out that I laid claim upon Mrs. Smith's attentions first. If she is going to go with anyone, in the spirit of fair play, it should be me."

"Shut up, Hornsby," Marshall snapped. "*Mrs. Smith* and I," he said, dripping sarcasm all over her assumed name, "have some things to discuss." He pushed, steering her out the door and toward the stairwell.

"I really don't have time for a chat just now," Isabelle said, futilely attempting to twist free of his steely hold. "Mr. Davies expects me to clear the dishes." She leaned her back against him, pressing her feet into the floor in an attempt to force him to stop.

His hands tightened almost painfully around her arms. "If you continue to resist, I will pick you up and carry you."

"I'll scream if you do," she ground out.

"And I will throttle you." The low, seething tone dragged down her spine like a glacier.

Would he actually strike her? She cast wildly about for assistance, but the corridor was deserted but for the two of them. "You'll be tossed out. Maybe arrested."

Marshall snorted. "It would be worth it," his voice rumbled against her neck. She shivered.

"All right," she hissed. Isabelle snatched her arms out of his grip and mounted the stairs under her own power, excruciatingly aware of his looming presence behind her.

He guided her to his room toward the back of the inn. He opened the door, and a raspy, masculine voice said, "Good evening, Your Grace. I've laid out your nightshirt—"

Isabelle followed Marshall into the room. His valet stopped speaking the instant he clapped eyes on her. At first, he gave his master a disapproving frown. Then he looked at Isabelle again. "You!" His mouth pinched, pulling his thin nose downward.

"Good evening, Clayton." She gave Marshall's valet a cool nod.

A glance around the bedchamber revealed a fine room. A double-mattressed bed occupied one corner, with a porcelain ewer and basin on a stand beside it. Marshall's grooming implements had been arranged on top of a bureau next to the basin. There was a sitting area in front of the fireplace, and a smaller room off to the side to house his valet and trunks. Isabelle felt even more conspicuous in her cook's garb in this lovely chamber, standing in front of the duke and his impeccably dressed servant. "Go have a drink," Marshall said.

"Sir," Clayton started, casting a frosty look at Isabelle, "if I may say so—"

"You may not," Marshall interrupted. "Not this time."

Master and valet exchanged a silent communication. At last, Clayton acquiesced. Isabelle stepped back to allow him to pass, but he still managed to clip her with his shoulder on his way out.

Marshall crossed to a sideboard and splashed whiskey into a glass for himself, but offered her nothing. The light from the candelabra on the sideboard cast flickering shadows across the hard planes of his face. "I'm waiting, Isabelle," he said.

"For what, Your Grace?" she asked. She smoothed the front of her skirt with her palms and took a turn around the sitting area, nervously taking in her surroundings. She'd never been in the guest chambers before; Mr. Davies made sure his moneyed customers had well-appointed rooms, she observed. The chairs and settee were arranged around an Oriental rug with a navy and crimson medallion in the center. Twin lamps with fluted glass covers stood on either end of the mantle, illuminating the area in a soft glow.

"An explanation," Marshall said. "What is this ridiculous charade about, *Mrs. Smith*?"

Isabelle flinched as though struck. "Charade?" she scoffed. "Do you think I'm *playing* at being a cook? Like Marie Antoinette, the shepherdess?" She shook her head. "You're blind, Marshall. You always have been."

Marshall slammed his glass to the sideboard. "What is that supposed to mean?" He crossed to where she stood. Isabelle quavered. "And take that off. It's obscene." He yanked the humble servant's mobcap from her head and tossed it to the floor. Isabelle's long hair unwound from its unpinned twist and fell down her back.

"I mean exactly what I say, Marshall. You are blind to the truth." She turned away from him and stared into the fire rather than continue exposing herself to his searching eyes. "At least when it comes to me."

"Oh, yes. You and the truth. Old bosom bows," Marshall said, gesturing widely with a hand. "How could I forget?"

Exhaustion and hunger wrapped tentacles around her. She still had to clean up after her former husband and his amorous friend before she could walk a mile through the cold February night to share a bowl of stew with Bessie. She could think of no good reason to put up with Marshall's abuse. "I'm leaving," Isabelle said wearily. "You're completely foxed. Go to bed." She stooped to pick up her cap, but Marshall got there first and snatched it up.

"You're right," he said. "I'm foxed. I got foxed because I'm angry and embarrassed."

Isabelle drew herself up. "What reason do you have for anger and embarrassment? If you are referring to my position here—"

"It's degrading," Marshall said, wringing her cap in his fists. "A woman of your birth—my former wife, I might add—"

"'Former' being the key word," she interrupted. "My actions in no way reflect upon you."

"Like hell they don't!" He raked one hand through his dark, wavy hair and gave her an imploring look. "Isabelle, if you were recognized, I would be the laughing stock of the *ton*. Again."

She bristled at his words. "Poor little duke," she mocked, flinging her arms wide. "Suffering the slings and arrows of outrageous fortune. At least you don't have to work in an inn." Isabelle shook her head and turned.

"Talk to me," he said in a more moderate tone. "Why must you work in this inn?"

"Because the one the next village over wasn't hiring," she quipped.

Marshall chuckled. His hand was on her shoulder then, gently turning her around. He tipped her chin with his thumb and forefinger. Isabelle looked into his eyes. She wasn't sure what she saw there—

compassion? Pity, perhaps? At least it wasn't anger. She was too tired to confront his anger again.

"Has your brother cut you off?" he asked. His thumb lightly stroked her jaw.

The gentleness of his words and touch utterly crumbled Isabelle's defenses. The strong, capable facade she'd been carefully building ever since receiving Alexander's letter could not withstand his kindness. She squeezed her eyes shut and nodded. He cupped her cheek in his hand. One hot tear slid down her face and over his fingers.

"That was not well done of him," Marshall said quietly.

Isabelle turned her face into his palm, unable to contain the tears she'd been holding at bay for weeks. In the next moment, his other hand was on her back, drawing her forward. Isabelle stepped into his arms and cried against his chest. Her own arms wound around his torso. Marshall stroked her hair and murmured against the top of her head, but she could not make out his words for her crying. Still, the rumble inside his chest as he spoke soothed her.

"I'm sorry." She sniffed and wiped at her eyes with the back of her hand. "I'm making an absolute cake of myself." Marshall produced a handkerchief and pressed it into her hand, while keeping his other arm firmly around her.

The scent of freshly starched linen almost set her off again, but Isabelle managed to restrain herself.

"I think," Marshall said, "you're awfully brave."

Isabelle pulled back in his arms, searching his face for a sign of mockery, but found none. "You do?"

He nodded. "It's not every woman who could take care of herself when times got hard."

She smiled weakly.

His eyes dropped to her lips. "You always had," he said, stroking her bottom lip with his thumb, "the prettiest smile."

He lowered his head and Isabelle stiffened. But what would it matter if she shared one kiss with him? Just this one. The last time she'd kissed him, she hadn't known it was the last. This time, she did. It would be good, she told herself, to have this final kiss. A kiss of farewell.

Suddenly, Marshall broke away before his lips touched hers. Isabelle, in a disoriented, dreamy state, slowly opened her eyes and looked into his. It was like being doused with a bucket of cold water. His dark eyes were once more hard. Pained.

Isabelle blinked, feeling confused and bereft.

"Forgive me," Marshall said, stepping back. "It was ill done to treat you with such disregard."

"No need to apologize," Isabelle said. She ran her palms up her arms, the wool of her dress coarse beneath her fingers. No doubt, Marshall realized he'd almost kissed a servant. She cautiously laid a hand on his forearm. "I know I'm out of practice, but I haven't forgotten how it's done."

He jerked his arm away from her and took several steps backward. "Mr. Miller hasn't kept you in practice?"

Isabelle's jaw dropped.

"I cannot touch you," he said, bracketing his hands around his face, "without remembering what you did with that man and being cuckolded all over again."

An icy fist grabbed her innards. "How dare you?" she seethed. "I never betrayed you!" She stalked forward, hands on her hips. "Justin never did anything wrong. He tended me when I broke my rib in a riding accident, and for that both he and I have been ruined!" She stood in front of her tormentor, shaking with the force of her anger.

Marshall held out a staying hand. "Spare me those tired old excuses. My father *died*, Isabelle." He jabbed a finger into his chest. "And while I was gone settling his affairs, you brought that man into my house. My mother saw your disgusting tryst in the cottage. I suppose I can only be grateful you didn't bring him into my own bed. Do you expect me to believe she was mistaken? Or that she lied?"

"No," Isabelle hissed. "I don't." Something deep inside snapped. He would never listen to reason all those years ago. Swamped with grief over his father's passing, Marshall was called home to deal with his wife's supposed infidelity. Nothing Isabelle said would convince him she and Justin had done nothing wrong.

Her hands balled into white, bloodless fists. Her voice was steely quiet when she spoke. "Of course I don't expect you to believe me. You never did. I apologized for inviting Justin to stay while you were gone, but for mercy's sake, Marshall, you knew when we married that he was a close friend. He came to dinner the very day we met!"

His lip curled in a sneer. Marshall circled her slowly, a wolf waiting to make the killing blow. "Oh, yes, your *friend*. Tell me, Isabelle, what kind of *friend* accepts an invitation to a newlywed woman's home while her husband is away? Hmm?" He stopped in front of her, his hands clasped behind his back. "And then runs for the hills as soon as he's been caught taking advantage of his host's . . . hospitality," he finished suggestively.

She raised a fist in front of her chest in a challenging stance, and in that moment, if she could have, she would have consented to a round at Gentleman Jackson's to settle things between them. "Your vile insinuations and your evil divorce were the betrayal. Not me, Marshall. It was never me. You trumped up your petition on the flimsiest of reasons, based only on the filth your mother fed you."

Marshall's eyes blazed with a fury as strong as her own. "Your memory fails you, my dear."

Isabelle scoffed.

"The servants confirmed you invited Mr. Miller to Hamhurst after my departure. You rode together every day, disappearing for hours at a time. And when my mother—whom I sent to keep you company, by the by, knowing you would be in need of company—found you in *flagrante delicto*, you start spinning yarns about broken bones and friendly teas."

"How can you say that?" Isabelle grabbed the hair at her scalp and bent forward. The room seemed to have gone askew. "Are you mad? My ribs were still wrapped by the time you came home. I tried to show you the bandages."

He exhaled slowly and rubbed his hands over his face. "You're wasting your breath, Isabelle."

The flat, disinterested tone of his voice made her heart feel sick. She didn't know why it even mattered to her anymore what he believed.

"We were young, and I was foolish and you were—" He gestured with a hand. "Well, I was warned."

By his mother.

His mother, alarmed by Isabelle from the first, insisting to anyone who would listen that her son's intended was only after his fortune and title.

His mother, whose protests could only be silenced by Marshall's father.

His mother, crying at their wedding for the proper match her son had failed to make.

His mother, newly widowed, standing over Isabelle while she was laid up in bed with a broken rib, calling her a whore.

His mother, telling her a divorce was only what an overreaching nobody like her deserved.

A dozen memories tumbled through her mind, each and every one of them pointing to a single, horrible conclusion.

Isabelle didn't feel her knees give way. Marshall was suddenly crouched beside her on the floor, rubbing his hand across her back. Then she became aware of her position, on her knees, curled into a ball.

"Have you fainted?" Marshall asked, his annoyed tone tinged with concern.

"No," Isabelle said into the rug. "I rarely faint. You know that."

"It looked for all the world like you fainted," Marshall said. "Your face went ghastly white, and you fell to the floor. What does that sound like to you?"

Isabelle straightened to sit on her heels. "Listen to us," she said smiling sadly, "arguing over whether or not I fainted." Marshall regarded her with a bemused expression. She looked at her hands in her lap and concentrated on keeping them still. "Just as well your mother had us divorced."

She could have recited the first three pages of *The Mirror of Graces* in the ensuing silence.

At last, Marshall said in a carefully even voice, "That's quite an accusation, Isabelle."

She lifted her chin. "I do not make it lightly."

"On what evidence do you base such claims?"

Isabelle shook her head. "There is no evidence. The dowager duchess always hated me, because I committed the sin of being born to a man without a title and a French peasant. No evidence, as you say. There was only the word of the woman who hated me, and the word of your wife." She shrugged. "You chose to believe her."

Marshall sat down on the floor with his arms resting on his knees. He looked at Isabelle for a long moment, searching her face. After a while, his eyes were still settled on her, but she could tell he was no longer *looking* at her. She saw anger and hurt in his expression, but also introspection.

The clock on the mantle chimed one o'clock in the morning. She'd been in his room for almost an hour. Mr. Davies would be furious with her for neglecting the kitchen for so long, especially if he found out she'd gone to a bedchamber with a guest.

"I have to go," Isabelle said. Marshall seemed not to hear her. She retrieved her cap from the floor, twisted her hair into a hasty knot, and pulled the cap over it. She crossed to the door, but the sound of his voice stayed her hand.

"Even if what you say is true," he said, "what do you expect me to do about it?"

He looked disarmingly charming sitting on the floor—nothing at all like the forbidding aristocrat he'd been downstairs.

She had no idea what sort of answer he wanted. She hadn't thought that far ahead herself. "Nothing. What's transpired is done."

He nodded slowly.

They exchanged one last gaze—Isabelle in her cook's garb and Marshall a disheveled duke sitting on the floor—and then she walked through the door and back to her duties. She still had dishes to do before she could have her own supper.

* * *

For a long time, Marshall remained sitting on the floor. He didn't know why—perhaps it had something to do with his affinity for being close to the earth. Whatever the reason, sitting on the floor had always been his preferred posture for serious thinking. He didn't do it often, for reasons of propriety, but at a time like this, a chair was too confining for the large, troubling thoughts lumbering through his mind. A field would have been even better, but the open expanse of the sitting area floor would have to do.

Several truths had made themselves evident this evening. First, his former wife was living in anonymous exile and poverty, working to support herself. She was also an excellent cook, which he hadn't known when they were married. It bothered him that he had not known this about his wife. She was well aware of his love affair with botany and the work he was involved in with the scientific community. Why hadn't he taken the time to discover her talents and passions?

He shoved that bit of self-criticism aside to further ponder tonight's observations. Isabelle had continued to deny that any wrongdoing transpired between herself and Justin Miller.

This troubled Marshall. If he were honest with himself, he had to admit she had always been a forthright woman, and had never given him cause to doubt her intentions or word, until the fateful day he learned she'd played him false. However, he could not discount the scene his mother witnessed at Hamhurst, especially when combined with Isabelle's admission of inviting Miller to Hamhurst behind Marshall's back.

Of course, there was her accusation that his mother manipulated both of them into divorcing. This was certainly an alarming prospect. Yet, when Marshall thought back to his courtship of Isabelle, their wedding, and the brief time in which they had lived together as husband and wife, he could not disregard her accusation out of hand. Caro, dowager Duchess of Monthwaite, had indeed distrusted Isabelle from the first. She had pleaded with Marshall not to marry her, certain the young Miss Fairfax was interested only in her son's title and fortune. Only Marshall's father had finally convinced her to keep her mouth closed on the subject. Her tears at the wedding were an unusual display of emotion from a woman who typically kept her reactions on a tight rein.

Caro was nothing if not a strong woman, with a firm sense of what was best for her children. As much as it pained him to think so, it would not be beyond her to have done what Isabelle suggested, particularly if she had good reason, such as proof of adultery.

Finally, Marshall turned his attention to the kiss he and Isabelle had almost shared. It had been there in his mind, the elephant in the room he had tried to think his way around without acknowledging. The Isabelle Marshall encountered tonight was in need of several good meals and a bath. Her dress was the most unbecoming woolen sack Marshall had ever laid eyes on. She smelled like a kitchen, herbs and yeast and lye soap. And she had intoxicated his senses more surely than all the alcohol he'd been steadily consuming since he saw her earlier this evening.

She had wronged him. She had lain with another man. Because of her actions, he'd been forced to air his private grievances in the most public forum imaginable, a divorce trial. He had spent years avoiding her and replacing whatever silly, juvenile tenderness he'd harbored for her with a sophisticated cynicism toward females.

And yet, he'd still been powerless against her artless charms. He'd unwillingly pitied her predicament, and simultaneously admired the gumption she had displayed by taking on employment. Worst of all, he had been painfully aroused. It was as bad as, or worse than, the passion he remembered from their marriage. If he had felt only a passing attraction for Isabelle, enough to beget his heir and little beyond, her betrayal would not have struck the blow that it had. But he had been strongly, deeply attracted to his young wife. She had awakened passion in him that no other woman before or since had come close to realizing. It was that he could not forgive, the way she had him nearly eating from the palm of her pretty hand and then turned to another man for what Marshall had so freely given her.

Still, he thought, pulling himself to his feet and retrieving his portable writing desk, however she had wronged him, she was a gentlewoman who did not deserve the circumstances to which she had been reduced. He seated himself at the table in the corner of the sitting area and took out a fresh sheet of paper.

Mr. Fairfax, he began,

I have recently discovered a matter that may cause you a degree of concern. Though we no longer share a familial connection, it is my sincere hope that you will take my words in the manner with which they are intended. You have my assurance, as a gentleman, of discretion. In return, I suggest in the strongest terms that you take every measure at your disposal to rectify the problem.

The matter to which I refer concerns your sister . . .

Chapter Four

In the middle of March, a letter arrived from Fairfax Hall with a summons from Alexander for Isabelle to return home. Her brother included with his letter a bank draft with more than enough money for her to hire a post-chaise for the trip. He also said she should plan on an extended absence from her cottage, and should, therefore, make arrangements for its care while she was away.

When she went to the George to deliver her resignation, Mr. Davies met the news with dismay. "What do you mean you're leaving us, Mrs. Smith?" He ran a rag over his sweat-sheened pate. "Is it a higher wage you're after?" His eyes narrowed suspiciously. "Is that blighter at the Fox and Glen trying to steal you away?"

Isabelle shook her hand. "No, sir, nothing like that. My brother has offered me a place to live, so I'm going home." Her stomach flipped at the fib. She could dream of such a positive reception, but had little hope of it actually happening.

That business concluded, she returned home to deal with Bessie. It pained Isabelle to leave her behind to fend for herself, but she couldn't very well bring her to Fairfax Hall and insist Alexander give her a place.

Instead, Isabelle offered Bessie the position of stewardess of the cottage. She gave Bessie most of Alexander's bank draft, keeping out just enough for the post-chaise. The money she left with the woman was more than they had seen in the last six months, and Isabelle promised to send more in a month, provided Alexander was reconciling with her, and not bringing her home just to inform her she was cut from the family for good.

Finally, Isabelle packed her meager belongings into a single trunk and set out. As the countryside rolled by, Isabelle felt a mounting sense of nervous anticipation. Thankfully, it wasn't a long journey. Alexander's own coach met her at the posting house nearest her brother's estate.

The sun was setting as the coach carried her down the drive, through the home woods, past a lake full of noisy ducks set in a modest park, to the manor house. Though the rambling Grecian-style structure was young by most standards—only a hundred years old—Isabelle thought the stuccoed construction was perfect. She loved every inch of it, though she knew most of the *ton* would have scoffed at its insignificant twenty-seven rooms.

Sweat beaded on her upper lip as the coach drew to a stop in front of the broad steps leading down from the door. The footman hopped down and assisted her.

The door swung wide open. "Miss Isabelle!" the butler cried joyously. "Here you are at last. Come in."

"Hello, Iverson," Isabelle said, nearly weak with relief at not having the door slammed in her face by the aged retainer. One of the butler's eyes was clear blue, the other cloudy and blind, yet his face had a stately quality unimpeded by his handicap.

"Welcome home," he said, smiling warmly.

She stepped into the front hall. The parquet floor gleamed from a fresh waxing. Two footmen passed Isabelle, carrying her trunk to her room. "Where's Alexander?"

"Mr. Fairfax is going over some business affairs with the bailiff," the butler answered. "He asks not to be disturbed."

"Oh," Isabelle said, deflated. Perhaps this was not the warm homecoming she had hoped for, after all.

"He bade me tell you he would see you at supper tonight and asks that you join him in the parlor to dine *en famille*."

"Seven o'clock?" Isabelle asked, recalling the time her brother usually ate.

"Yes, miss. Mr. Fairfax is becoming quite set in his ways," Iverson noted with a touch of disapproval. Having been at the Hall since well before Isabelle's birth, the butler felt no compunction in offering his opinion. And because he had been something of a father figure to Isabelle during her unhappy childhood, she would never dream of correcting him. He was more family to her than servant.

Isabelle raised her brows. "Are you of the opinion that Alexander should dine at a different time?"

"Of course not." The butler's chest puffed out indignantly. "But it's high time Mister Alexander brought a wife home," he said, slipping into his old familiarity with the current master's name. "Not that you aren't a perfectly capable mistress, of course," he amended, "but he's turning himself into a confirmed bachelor!"

Isabelle smiled wryly. "I don't know about that," she said. "He's only thirty."

"Old enough to have a babe in the nursery and another on the way," Iverson countered.

Isabelle patted the old retainer fondly on the arm and went to her room to freshen up before supper.

Her room was much the same as it was when she'd left at eighteen to become Marshall's marchioness and then duchess. The bedspread was a dusty rose, as were the curtains and many of the accessories. Accents of light green and ivory completed the color scheme. During Isabelle's adolescence, she'd thought her room the loveliest she'd ever seen, like a private garden. Now, it struck her as tired and juvenile.

A small tortoiseshell cat emerged from beneath the bed and mewed. "Miss Bigglesworth!" she exclaimed, dropping to her knees to scoop the animal into her arms. The old cat butted her head against Isabelle's chin and purred contentedly.

When Isabelle was eight, she and Justin had rescued the kitten from a sack in the stream. The poor drenched thing was half-drowned and shivering with cold. Justin teased her for crying over it, but Isabelle brought the kitten home and nursed her back to health with the help of Cook's generous supply of cream.

At the time, she'd thought Miss Bigglesworth a very dignified name for her pet. Now it seemed childish, just like her room.

She took a turn around the room while she stroked the cat's graying fur.

"Wouldn't the bed look nice in something bolder?" she asked Miss Bigglesworth. "Sapphire and silver brocade, perhaps." She sighed and turned. "And the mantel," she tsked. It would be improved with the multitude of girlish knickknacks cleared away and replaced by a few beautiful, well-chosen pieces. "A crystal vase would be becoming against the dark wood," she murmured, touching the left end of the mantel. "A miniature or two in silver frames *here*, and perhaps a potted plant . . ."

Isabelle sucked in her breath; her fingers clutched at Miss Bigglesworth's fur. The cat yowled in protest before Isabelle relaxed her grip. *You ninny*, she chastised herself. She'd been mentally redecorating her room to look like the master bedchamber at Hamhurst, the one she had shared with Marshall.

Seeing him at the inn had done her no good. She'd been fine before he turned up in the dining room at the George. Now she kept remembering the stolen hour they'd spent together.

She'd awoken in the darkest, coldest part of the night, shivering and hungry for his touch. The flame he'd rekindled deep in her belly flared hotly every time she thought about it. It was distracting beyond all reckoning. Just a hint of kissing was dragging up other memories she would do well to forget, like the bed they'd shared as a married couple.

Miss Bigglesworth squirmed in her arms. "You're right," Isabelle muttered, bending at the waist to release her onto the carpet. "I am the most pathetic woman ever born."

Isabelle turned her attention to getting herself ready for supper. She had no lady's maid, and Alexander obviously hadn't thought of assigning one of the house maids to act as such, since her trunk still sat untouched at the foot of the bed where the footmen had deposited it.

She retrieved a lavender muslin frock that wasn't too badly wrinkled. Isabelle put it on and tied her hair back with a ribbon. It still wasn't time to go down to the parlor, so she spent the remaining time before supper hanging the few other simple dresses she'd brought along. The ice blue gown she'd repaired received special attention. That one, she hung with plenty of room around it so the skirt would not be crushed. Isabelle had no reason to suppose she'd need a fine gown again in the foreseeable future, but she couldn't bear to allow that dress to be ruined.

Satisfied with her work, she descended to the parlor. The door stood open to the room they'd always called the French Parlor. Their mother had decorated the room with furnishings from her own girlhood home in the Loire Valley so that it resembled the interior of a Provincial cottage more than an English parlor. The walls, Isabelle had always thought, were the exact shades of sunshine, an airy yellow striped with a richer, golden tone. A rustic, round table stood in front of a large window overlooking the back gardens, with an enameled milk jug serving as a centerpiece. A stout wooden chair, painted white with a cornflower blue cushion, stood near the fireplace. A low sofa in white and blue and two upholstered chairs completed the seating area.

On a low table between the chairs was a miniature of Isabelle's mother. She picked up the small portrait and touched her finger to the face of the woman she could scarcely remember. Her father said this was a good likeness, but Isabelle had almost no memory of her own of her mother's face.

"Hello, little sister."

Isabelle turned, hugging the miniature to her chest. Alexander stood at the threshold, his broad shoulders nearly filling the doorframe. At over six feet tall, he had always truly been Isabelle's big brother. Of everyone in her acquaintance, only Marshall matched him in stature. Looking into Alexander's face was like looking at an older, masculine version of herself. He had the same golden hair and green eyes. Their father sometimes said their mother must have sprouted them both all by herself, for all the contribution he made to their coloring.

"Hello, big brother," she said tentatively. His expression was unreadable. She still did not know whether he was welcoming her home or banishing her forever.

He took three strides to cross the room to where she stood.

For a moment, he only stood and looked down at her. Then he plucked the miniature from Isabelle's hands and turned it over in his own palms, looking down at the woman who had given them both life, and died along with their sibling. Isabelle folded her hands at her waist, waiting.

"You're the very image of her," he said quietly.

Unaccountably, a lump formed in Isabelle's throat. "Really?" she managed. She knew well enough that she had similar coloring, but no one had ever told her she looked like the beautiful woman in the painting.

Her brother nodded. "The portraits don't show the resemblance as well," he declared with a wave of his hand. "But your expressions, the way you hold yourself, it's extraordinarily similar."

"Thank you," Isabelle whispered, her throat tight with emotion.

Alexander returned the miniature to its place and guided her to the table.

The meal passed in companionable conversation. Alexander did a remarkable job, she noticed, of keeping their exchanges on polite matters: the weather, the state of the estate's tenants, how their neighbors fared.

When the meal ended, Isabelle started to rise, intending to allow her brother time to enjoy his after supper drink. Alexander waved her back down.

"Don't be silly, Isa," he said, smiling in his lopsided way. "I'm not going to send you off while I have a glass of port all by myself."

"I'll call for tea, then," she ventured.

"No." Alexander reached for the bottle the footman had placed on the table a short time ago. "Have a drink with me."

Isabelle blinked. "Oh. Certainly." She felt a little thrill as he poured a glass for her, as though she were partaking in some forbidden pagan sacrament, something beyond the province of her feminine world.

She took a sip of the beverage. As much as it looked like wine, it tasted very different. Her eyes widened at the unexpected strength of it, and then her tongue curled against the sweetness of the port. After a few sips, however, when the stress of the day's trials began to melt away, she understood why a man might want to take such a drink after supper.

A glass later, she and Alexander were laughing over stories from their childhoods. He told her about things that happened around the estate, stories of picnics with their parents, of being caught out at some mischief. Something inside Isabelle grasped onto the stories and cried out, *Yes, I was there*, although most of what Alexander related happened before she was born. The stories gave her a sense of connection to her past, yet also emphasized the emptiness she felt about her own family memories. She had none to speak of. By the time she was old enough to actively participate in family events, her mother was dead, her father despondent, and Alexander was away at school. Isabelle envied her brother the experiences he had with their parents.

Alexander refilled each of their glasses. "So," he said carefully, "what's this I hear about you cooking at an inn?"

Isabelle's eyes shot to his face. How had he found out? His mouth was set in a firm line. This was, she realized, the reason he'd brought her home.

Her stomach roiled sourly around the port. "Who told you?" she asked, sounding much like the guilty school girl she felt like.

"I had a letter from Monthwaite." Alexander leaned back in his chair and stretched his long legs out to the side, crossing them at the ankle.

"He gave me quite a nicely phrased dressing down."

Isabelle rotated her glass in circles, unable to meet her brother's eyes. How dare Marshall interject himself? Alexander probably thought she'd put him up to it.

"He was right, of course," Alexander said. "I shouldn't have cut you off. It was impulsive. I was angry."

Isabelle ventured a glance at him. He was staring at his own glass. "Why?"

He breathed a single, mirthless laugh. "I asked for a lady's hand and she rejected me."

She wrapped her arms around her middle, trying to quail the sinking feeling. Somehow, she had something to do with his rejection. She could tell it by his tone. "Why?" she whispered, fearing his answer.

Alexander looked at her and said gently, "On the grounds that no respectable woman wants a divorcée for a sister-in-law."

Was it possible for a person to feel any more wretched than Isabelle did at that moment? She buried her face in her hands. "I'm so sorry, Alex. If there was any way I could fix it—"

"There is."

She lifted her face.

"You have to marry again," Alexander said. He took a long pull at his drink.

Isabelle's eyes widened.

He raised a hand. "Not to put too fine a point on it, little sister, but you are frankly ruining my chances at making a good match for myself. The lady I courted was a baron's daughter, and she was not, I believe, without regard for me."

"Of course not," Isabelle said in a mollifying tone. "You're a wonderful man. Any woman with a bit of sense—"

"Would marry as best she can," Alexander interjected, his eyebrows raised. "A landowner of only modest means, with no title, a smallish estate, and a divorced sister does not exactly bowl the ladies over with awe."

"I see," Isabelle said miserably.

"There is little I can do," Alexander continued, "about my fortune, at present. I've made improvements to the estate that I hope will prove profitable, as well as some investments, but it may be a few years before I see a return." He put his hands behind his head and looked toward the ceiling. "There is nothing I can do about the fact that I have no title. The chances of the Crown bestowing a title upon a perfectly unremarkable farmer are nonexistent."

"That's true," Isabelle said, "but Alex—"

"The only thing within my control," Alexander said, lowering his gaze to regard her, his eyes hard, "is the fact that I have a divorced sister. I can either pack you off to a convent, Isa, or see you married."

"We aren't Catholic," she said petulantly.

"No, but Mama was."

"She converted!"

He waved a hand. "Don't drive the conversation off course. Mama's Catholicism doesn't signify."

"But you can't send me to a convent."

"You're tempting me." Alexander jabbed a finger at her glass of port. "Drink that," he ordered. "I don't like having this conversation with you quite so sober."

She gave him an exaggerated nod, then took a sip of her drink. "Forgive me for highlighting the logical flaws in your scheme to disown me," she said.

"I don't want to disown you, Isa," Alex said hotly. "What I want is to eradicate your divorced status. And the only way to accomplish that is for you to remarry." He pulled his legs in and leaned toward her, resting his elbow on the table. "Don't you want to marry?"

Of course she did. Well, not really. She exhaled loudly. Still, she wanted children, and to achieve that goal in a respectable fashion, she needed a husband.

Once again, she remembered herself in Marshall's arms at the George and squirmed uncomfortably against the heat that sprang to life. No matter how she'd like to share more of such intimacy with him, she was instead going to have to share it with someone else. The thought brought a bitter taste to her mouth. "Yes," she said in a flat tone, "I should like that very much."

"Good." Alexander nodded. "I'm glad we're in agreement." He cleared his throat. "Now, Isa, you know I'm not one to preach; however, you must realize that you cannot go on now as you have before."

She furrowed her brows. "What do you mean?"

He cut his eyes to the left and cleared his throat again. "The reason Monthwaite divorced you."

Hot shame shot through her. "Alex!" she cried. "Tell me you do not believe that! I have told you repeatedly, Justin and I did nothing wrong."

"I don't know what to believe." He sighed and raked a hand through his hair. The light from the candles on the nearby sideboard flickered across his features. "At this point, the truth doesn't matter."

"Of course it matters," Isabelle protested passionately, nearly quivering with her desire to be understood. "It matters very much to me that my brother thinks I'm an adulteress, when I'm not!"

"You were divorced for adultery, whether you committed it or not. To the world, you *are* an adulteress, Isa, and that's just the way of it."

It was true. Society had branded her with a stigma, and there was nothing she could do to rid herself of it. Denying impropriety had never gotten her anything for her trouble but a dry throat.

"You're not going to have scads of suitors," Alexander continued. "You'll be lucky to have any choice whatsoever."

Isabelle's tongue recoiled in her mouth at his words, as though being forced to swallow a particularly bitter medicine.

"I mean for you to find a husband this Season."

"*This* Season?" Isabelle asked, bewildered. "The Season is almost underway!"

"There is plenty of time for you to get to town and attend all the balls and routs you'd like."

Isabelle remembered the pitiful collection of clothing she'd brought home in her trunk. "Alex," she said, mortified to confess her lack of wardrobe, "I sold my good dresses when I moved to the cottage. I haven't had any new ones in years now."

His green eyes were piercingly clear in the light. "I cannot outfit you like Monthwaite did."

Her cheeks burned. "I never suggested you should!"

"You shall have new things, of course. I've already written to the Bachmans. You're to stay with them in town."

Isabelle's heart lightened at the prospect of spending the Season with Lily and her family, but something else bothered her. "Are you not coming?"

He nodded. "I'll be down in a few weeks to conduct some business, but there's no point in looking for a wife until I've made you respectable again."

"Oh," she said in a small voice. "I see. That makes sense." She remembered Iverson's despair at her brother's unmarried state. What would he say if he knew Isabelle was the reason Alexander couldn't find a good wife and start filling his nursery? She lifted her glass and threw the rest of her port back with one swallow. "I'm going to bed."

Alexander rose. "It's good to see you again, little sister." He kissed her on the cheek.

Hardly believing that, Isabelle smiled weakly and started to the door.

"One more thing."

Isabelle turned at his voice.

"You'll accept the first respectable man who offers for you, Isa. You might not get another chance."

Chapter Five

Marshall sat behind his desk in the study of his house on Grosvenor Square, going over the acquisition list sent to him by the captain of the *Adamanthea*, the ship he'd hired for his South American expedition. His plans were coming together more quickly and easily than he would have imagined. At the last meeting of the Royal Society, he'd announced his intention to get such an expedition underway. Several members offered financial backing, and others had given him the names of men who could make valuable contributions to such an endeavor: artists to sketch the plant life they encountered, guides, local contacts, and someone with a ship to let for just such a mission.

His mother swept through the study door after a quick knock, dressed in an elegant, rich brown court dress over a green petticoat. She wore a three-stranded necklace of diamonds and emeralds, each successive strand longer than the previous. The requisite plumes erupting from behind her coif gave her the appearance of a rather severe duck.

Marshall smothered the smile tugging at his mouth and smoothed a hand down his black waistcoat. He stepped out from behind his desk to press a kiss to her cheek. "You look lovely, Mother."

"Thank you, dear." Her lips curled up in a pinched smile. "But it will be a relief to change into something more comfortable for the ball."

Thinking of the elaborate pains women went to in preparation for a ball, Marshall could not imagine regarding a ball gown as more comfortable, but the stays and hoops involved in his mother's court dress looked downright torturous.

"Naomi is all in a dither about being presented," Caro said, "and her maid is as nervous as she. I should be helping her get ready. Why did you want to see me?"

Direct as ever, Marshall thought. Since returning from his tour of the estates, he'd been pondering how best to approach the subject of

Isabelle's accusation. At first, Marshall thought not to mention it at all. What good could come of implicating his own mother in the demise of his marriage? Then he remembered the point of Naomi's come out and the dozens of new gowns he'd bought for her first Season: marriage. He did not expect—nor even desire—his sister to select a husband her first year out, but it might happen. And in the event of such a scenario, he wanted to have this discussion with his mother in the open and out of the way. If there was anything Marshall could do to ensure his sister a happier fate in her own marriage, he would do it.

"I wanted to talk to you about something that happened while I was away last month," Marshall said. "Do you care to sit?" He gestured to the chair in front of his desk.

"In this monstrosity?" Caro swept her hands over her wide, hooped skirts. "You cannot be serious. The coach will be trial enough."

Marshall nodded. "As you say." He leaned on the edge of the desk and crossed his arms.

"Do not behave in that casual fashion," Caro scolded. "You'll make a mess of your coat."

Marshall straightened and tugged the cuffs of his black evening jacket while he tried to formulate the best tack to take. His mother had always held a tight rein on the family, brooking no argument against her judgment. While he'd attributed descriptors such as "self-assured" or "confident" to her in the past, he now glimpsed something darker in her motivations.

"What is this about, son?" Caro demanded impatiently. Her eyes darted to the clock on the mantelpiece before snapping back to him.

Marshall drew a deep breath. "I saw Isabelle."

At the name of his former wife, Caro's mouth curled into an expression of extreme distaste. "Oh?" She quirked a brow. "Shall I inquire after her health, or may we move on to a pleasanter topic of conversation?"

"She and I had a talk," Marshall said, ignoring Caro's jibe. "We never did talk too much back then, you know. We divorced with scarcely a word passing between us, after the unpleasantness at Hamhurst. Does it not strike you as odd?"

His mother's features cooled into a semblance of bland indifference.

"It strikes *me* as odd," he continued.

"She has the manners of a dock rat," Caro snapped. "I wouldn't expect better from a mushroom like her."

"Hmm." Marshall nodded. "That is certainly one perspective." He held up a finger. "But Isabelle suggests you manipulated events to force us apart."

Caro lifted her chin in a guarded expression. Her bejeweled fingers clasped together at her waist.

"In fact, after I agreed to the divorce, I recall you insisting I hasten to London at once. You did everything you could to part me from my wife."

"Your *estranged* wife, whom you were divorcing," Caro replied. "You had your father's business to conclude and Parliament to petition. I hardly think it signifies now."

"Why, Mother?" Marshall asked, his eyes wide, seeking. "Why did you deliberately keep us apart?"

Caro's lips pursed, then she let out a disgusted sound. "You were too soft-hearted about that girl by half. I didn't want her conniving her way back into your good graces."

Could Isabelle have convinced him to abandon the divorce? His mind once again returned to their undeniable attraction in the inn, and he had to admit she very well could have done such a thing.

"You wouldn't want to have given your name to another man's bastard, would you?" Caro asked. "A commoner's bastard, at that."

He shook his head. "Isabelle had no child."

"She would have, eventually," Caro said emphatically. "Yours or that Miller person's, and no one to say who the father was, and no choice for you but to claim it." Her chest heaved against the silky constraints of her gown. "I saved you from that, Marshall." She jabbed an index finger into the opposite palm. "I saved this *family* from having a nobody's bastard become heir to one of the oldest titles in the kingdom."

"You interfered," Marshall said without much heat. Under his breath, he cursed in frustration. *Both* women were right. Isabelle's suspicions were well founded, but so were his mother's reasons for her actions.

"Yes, I did," Caro said, "and I would do it again if I had to." She patted Marshall on the arm. "Come now, it's a new Season—balls to attend and ladies to woo, perhaps?" Her lips twisted into something he supposed she meant to resemble an encouraging smile.

He frowned. "You'll see me at the altar soon enough. Belaboring the issue won't get me there any faster."

Caro gave an injured sniff, but took his mild chiding with an air of satisfaction.

Marshall still had every intention of choosing a new wife, and soon. However, the Isabelle situation needed sorting out. It brought to the surface uncertainties regarding matrimony he'd thought long buried.

The notion of another disastrous union caused his gut to churn. Drawing a calming breath, he reminded himself that he had amended his expectations of wedlock. Realizing as he now did that he could presuppose neither physical nor emotional fidelity from a wife allowed him to go in with eyes wide open. If he expected nothing, he could not be hurt by anything.

An excited squeal, followed by the patter of slippered feet on the stairs, announced Naomi's imminent arrival.

Marshall woodenly offered Caro his arm and led her toward the entry hall to collect his sister for her presentation at Court. His mother glanced up at him and said carefully, "I've had it that Lucy Jamison has refused Lord Northouse. She has so had her hopes set on you, and I'd like to see the match. Elizabeth Ardwick is also amazingly still unattached. You'd do well to cast your attention to those quarters, if you take my advice."

"Thank you for the information, Mother," Marshall said coolly just as Naomi burst from the stairs in a snowy billow of lacy ruffles. His sister was trussed up in a fashion similar to their mother, but everything she wore was pure white, down to the feathers and pearls in her strawberry-tinged golden hair. "There you are, darling," he said, his thoughtful frown turning to a sincere smile at his sister's unrestrained enthusiasm. "Pretty as a picture and twice as dear. It's just as well Prinny already has two wives, otherwise he'd snatch you up for himself."

Naomi giggled behind a white-gloved hand. "Marshall, you are too much," she said, lightly swatting his arm with her fan.

"Indeed I am," Marshall said, bowing gallantly. "I have the pleasure of escorting the two loveliest ladies in England. How could I not be positively bloated with pride?"

As he handed first his mother, and then Naomi, into the carriage, Marshall thought about another lovely lady he knew and wondered whether his letter had had any effect, or if she was spending this brisk March evening in the hot kitchen of a Leicestershire inn.

* * *

A month into the Season, everyone who was anyone was now in town to see and be seen. The Peels' ball was an absolute crush. Marshall looked over the heads of the throng to the dance floor, where a young fellow named Henry something led Naomi through a set. It had become increasingly difficult to keep all of his sister's suitors straight in his mind. As he'd suspected, Naomi was a success and considered one of the Season's best catches.

Marshall feared one or two of the fellows were on the verge of offering for her. He dreaded the moment, as he would have to dash someone's hopes. He'd determined to refuse all offers for her this year. Naomi's debut had been delayed a year because of Marshall's own reluctance to see her sweet, open nature tossed to the society wolves to be torn apart and changed into something cynical and cold.

Naomi tossed her head back and laughed gaily at something her partner said. She looked lovely in her demure peach gown, which brought out the strawberry undertones in her hair.

She had her whole life to be someone's wife. This year, she would enjoy herself. She could set her cap after a husband next Season, if she liked, or the year after. He was in no hurry to push his beloved sister into matrimony.

"Rarely have I seen a man," said a male voice beside him, "so hawkishly observe his intended."

"Hmm?" Marshall turned to see Jordan Atherton, Viscount Freese beside him. The two men had been friends since their Eton days. Jordan had sown his wild oats rather more zealously than Marshall had in their youth, but that same unbridled lust for life had also led Jordan to volunteer for some of the fiercest campaigns in Spain.

One memorable incident had left them both scarred. While Jordan was about some clandestine business in a small village, French infantry attacked. Marshall and his men, along with a band of plucky Spanish peasants armed with farming implements, defended the village from French plundering.

During the action, Marshall was shot in his side. His parents fretted over losing their heir, and insisted he come home. So Marshall sold out and returned to England to recuperate.

When he saw Jordan many months later, his friend's handsome face had been changed forever. A long scar left by a French saber slashed through his right cheek.

Despite the prominent mark, the ladies returned Jordan's regard in equal measure. He was the only man Marshall knew who could turn such a visible disfigurement to an advantage, but somehow Jordan wore the scar so that it seemed a part of his ensemble as much as the diamond stickpin in his cravat. His hair was as dark as Marshall's, but where Marshall's was merely wavy, Jordan's curls were barely restrained by an abundance of pomade and threatened to sprout loose at the slightest provocation.

"I don't take your meaning," Marshall said.

Jordan's eyebrows waggled sinuously. He cut his blue eyes to the dance floor. "Were you not observing Lucy Jamison?"

"I was keeping an eye on Naomi," Marshall replied with a laugh.

He followed his friend's gaze away from his sibling to where the lady in question danced close to Naomi. Whereas his sister looked like a proper, unassuming young lady in her first Season, Lucy Jamison was sheathed in a daring, topaz-colored gown, which scarcely concealed her various attributes. The color suited her to perfection, flattering her sable hair and matching her eyes. She was considered a beauty, and Marshall couldn't argue the title; she was a fine specimen of anatomical achievement.

Lady Lucy had a fortune to go along with her pretty face, and a corresponding ample share of hopeful beaux. It was no secret that she'd set her sights high, upon the vacated position of Duchess of Monthwaite.

When he'd met her last year, Marshall had initially been put off by her calculated smiles, though they drove half the men in the *ton* to distraction. There was something to be said for persistence and ambition, however, and she seemed to possess the qualities he sought in his future duchess. If nothing else, Lady Lucy would relish the prestige that marrying Marshall would bring. He felt confident that, once attained, she would not do anything to jeopardize her social standing.

Quite unlike Isabelle, he thought. For that matter, Lucy Jamison was unlike his former wife in almost every way. If he wished to steer clear of another calamitous marriage, choosing a wife wholly dissimilar to his first seemed prudent.

As the dance ended, Lucy curtsied to her bowing partner, her neck bent in an elegant curve. When she rose, her eyes met Marshall's. Her lashes lowered demurely, though her lips turned up in a knowing smile.

"You're as scrupulous with Lady Naomi as a *duenna*," Jordan said. Together, they observed Lucy's slender form as she moved to the side of the ballroom to join a group of friends. Jordan clapped him on the shoulder. "Go take her for a twirl. I'll watch over Naomi, if it will make you feel better. No blackguard will spirit her away under my watch; I swear it." He clicked his heels together in a mocking salute.

Marshall turned from his friend and swept his gaze over the assembly to pick Lucy out of the throng. In the light of ten thousand candles, the Peel's ballroom teemed with color and life. The women with their coifs and gowns, slippers and scents, seemed to meld together in a single mass of femininity. The men wearing dark clothes, such as Marshall and Jordan, vanished behind the women, serving as a backdrop for their plumage. A few gentlemen stood out, mostly older men who still favored the gaudy satins of their own youth.

Marshall barked a laugh. "The thought of you keeping an eye on my sister is enough to send me to an early grave."

Bidding his friend adieu, he made his way around the perimeter of the crowded ballroom. He neared the group of acquaintances where he'd last seen Lucy, but she was no longer with them. Frowning, he looked to see if she was among the couples gathering on the floor for the supper waltz.

A rap on his forearm brought his attention to the beautiful female who'd materialized at his side.

"I declare, Monty," Lucy Jamison said, "you've quite neglected me this evening."

He arched a brow. "Have I?"

She nodded, sending ribbons of light dancing across her shining blue-black hair. "I began to despair of having a set with you, even though I promised you one at the park today." She pouted in flirtatious petulance.

"You have not lacked for partners," Marshall pointed out. "I was merely biding my time, hoping for a chance. Dare I hope my turn's come 'round?"

Lucy lowered her lashes in calculated demureness.

"Shall we?" Marshall asked, offering his arm.

The woman smiled like a cat with a saucerful of cream as she placed a hand on his arm. On the dance floor, the other couples swept them up into the waltz. Briefly, he looked over the head of his companion at the other ball goers, wondering where Naomi had gotten herself off to. He finally spotted her standing next to Caro, with a few of her friends and young men in the group.

Content with his charge's well-being, he let the music wash over him, soothing his tired mind. Despite being early into the Season, the social whirl already wore on him. He distracted himself by thinking about some cuttings he wanted to make at Bensbury, his house outside of town. Much to his chagrin, propagation had never been a personal strong suit of his, but there was a fern he would like to try the pinning method on . . .

"You certainly know how to make a lady feel the center of the universe," Lucy chastised.

Marshall accepted the rebuke with good grace. "I apologize. Chaperoning an eighteen-year old girl is more taxing than I'd imagined."

Lucy tilted her head sympathetically. "How unfortunate your father is not here to look after Lady Naomi's interests. Still, she is well launched—she's quite a success, Monty. I'm sure you'll have her off your hands before the Season's out."

"Thank you, but there's no hurry to get Naomi to the altar."

Lady Lucy's smile faltered under his glowering expression. "On the subject of spouses," she said abruptly, "I've had an interesting tidbit from my father."

Marshall had no interest in gossip, but he struggled to attend. "Oh?" he asked, his mind already drifting back to the ferns waiting for him in his greenhouse.

"Yes," she said. "He attended supper at the home of a political acquaintance of his in Commons, a Mr. Bachman."

Marshall nodded. "I'm acquainted with the family." Would copper pins be better than steel, he wondered. Or maybe twine? If he just held the fern to the soil with twine stretched across the stem, there would be no risk of injury to the developing roots beneath the surface . . .

"Their guest for the Season is the Duchess of Monthwaite," Lucy said in an impatient tone.

His eyes flew to her face. One side of her mouth turned up in a smug, satisfied smile at capturing his attention.

So, his letter to Alexander Fairfax had done its job.

"Isn't that interesting?" Lucy pressed. "No one has seen her in over a year, and suddenly she reappears in town. Why is she here, I wonder?"

"I do not make a habit of conjecturing as to the motivations of people with whom I am not personally involved." His words held a tone of scolding. It was badly done of him, he knew, but her aspersions against Isabelle, however vague, were despicable. If they were to wed, she would have to learn to hold her tongue on the matter of his previous marriage. It was none of her concern.

Lucy's mouth opened in a startled O. "I—" she began.

"Tell me, Lady Lucy," Marshall said abruptly, "do you cook?"

She laughed nervously. "Cook? Certainly not! Are you funning me, Monty?"

He shook his head. "I recently learned that a lady of my acquaintance is an excellent cook, a fact that had previously escaped my notice. It led me to wonder how many of our young ladies secretly harbor culinary ambitions."

Her brows furrowed. "I have all the proper accomplishments, of course," she said. "I speak French fluently. My drawing master was always pleased with my work. I've been told that my playing at the pianoforte is wonderful."

The waltz ended. Marshall patted her hand as he led her from the floor. "Don't trouble yourself, Lady Lucy. I'm sure you are perfectly adequate in every way."

Her mouth set in a hard line, but then she favored him with a sparkling smile. "Thank you, Monty," she said, as though he'd bestowed the highest compliment.

She'll do, Marshall thought. He gave her a small smile, satisfied at having so easily concluded his wife hunt. All that remained was an appropriate period of courtship and engagement. Neither Lucy's mind nor personality particularly captivated him, but they didn't have to. All he needed was a duchess and mother to his children. As to that, she was certainly attractive.

It was then Marshall realized he'd not paid the least bit of attention to her abundant physical charms so amply on display. And now that he did notice them, it was only to think that as becoming as Lucy looked in her fashionable gown, the only dress that had made an impression on him in recent months was woolen cook's garb with no pretension of shape and a splatter of grease on the sleeve. Its owner still made it look better than Lucy Jamison did her flimsy frock.

* * *

Naomi's hands swayed to the music as she watched her brother lead Lucy Jamison in the waltz. The swirling couples seemed to float on clouds, gliding in smooth circles, bobbing up and down ever so slightly. "Such a romantic dance," she commented to her friend Emily, who stood beside her on the outskirts of the ballroom. "Is it as marvelous to perform as it is to watch? Not that I'm in a hurry to try," Naomi hastily added. "The Lady Patronesses will grant me permission soon enough, I'm sure."

"I certainly hope so, for your sake," Emily stated. "The row Her Grace had with Lady Castlereagh was enough to get a lesser lady blackballed altogether."

Caro's tiff with the redoubtable *grande dame* had put the slightest damper on Naomi's Season. Lady Jersey granted Naomi her voucher to Almack's Assembly Rooms, but not even that formidable patroness could persuade Lady Castlereagh to allow Naomi the waltz.

"His Grace and Lady Lucy are a fine-looking couple," Emily observed, her attention turned to the dancers. "I suppose there will be an announcement quite soon."

Naomi's hands froze in midair and she wrinkled her nose. "An announcement?" She lowered her voice, careful to make sure no flapping ears overheard. "Surely you don't mean an engagement?"

Emily giggled. "What a funny thing you are! Of course I mean an engagement. What other sort of announcement could there be?"

Frowning, Naomi looked back at her eldest sibling and the elegant woman in his arms. "I wasn't trying to be funny. What makes you think they'll marry?" she inquired of her friend.

"Well," Emily said in a low, gossipy whisper. "Everyone knows they have an understanding."

"*I* don't know that," Naomi said. "No one has mentioned any such thing to me."

"Of course not; you're His Grace's sister." Emily shook her head and looked at Naomi as though she was the veriest goose. "Last year," the other young lady continued, "the duke only danced with hostesses and dowagers—never with eligible young ladies. But this year, he's danced with Lady Lucy at least once at every ball—sometimes twice, which *must* mean there's an understanding."

On the dance floor, Lucy said something to Marshall. Behind her cold smile, there was a hard glint in her eyes that Naomi could not care for. An uneasiness crept up her spine.

"Just because they've danced—" she began.

"The wedding will certainly be an elegant affair—the event of the year!" Emily looked toward the blazing chandelier and sighed dreamily. "You'll make sure I have an invitation, I hope?"

All this talk of weddings made Naomi decidedly uncomfortable. "Marshall is already married," she said flatly. Heat flushed her cheeks, as happened whenever she sidled up against the shameful topic of the divorce.

"But he has to marry again," Emily countered. "There must be an heir."

That had not occurred to Naomi; it was unexpectedly upsetting. Tears pricked the backs of her eyes. "The waltz is a wretched dance," she declared bitterly. "Spinning round and round in circles must be the stupidest, most tedious thing in the world, and would certainly make me dizzy."

At the final chords, the dancers all fell into bows and curtsies—Marshall and Lucy included. They came off the dance floor, headed right toward them.

"I believe I am sick, just from watching all that foolish spinning," she told Emily. Before her brother and his lovely companion reached her, Naomi whirled and ran to the withdrawing room as fast as her slippered feet could carry her.

Chapter Six

Isabelle couldn't contain her giddiness as she contemplated the pleasure of shopping for leisure. A mere two months ago, she would have waved away such frivolity as nonsense. Indeed, at that time, any purchase made out of anything other than dire necessity had been quite out of the question. Now, however, she could think of nothing she would rather do than walk down Bond Street with Lily, with no aim to her morning beyond procuring a new pair of kid gloves.

The sun burned off the morning's clouds, bringing in a lovely afternoon. A light breeze found its way through the London streets to tug at the tendrils of hair peeking out of Isabelle's fetching new bonnet, straw with silk flowers in a bunch at the brim, matching the lilac spencer she wore over her white muslin dress.

A gentleman Isabelle didn't recognize doffed his hat and bade them a good afternoon. She noticed the color in Lily's cheeks as the man continued down the street.

"Who is that?" Isabelle murmured.

"Mr. Reeves," Lily answered, a small smile spreading over her full lips.

They stepped into the shop while Lily's footman waited outside. Display tables were spaced at close intervals around the narrow space. Some showcased tempting kid slippers, but Isabelle headed right for her desired target.

She lifted a pair of oyster gloves from among a grouping of white and near-white ones. "What do you think of this pair?"

Lily wrinkled her nose. "Too cold a color for summer."

Intrigued by the mysterious Mr. Reeves, Isabelle cut a sideways glance at her friend as she returned the gloves to the table. "Has any particular gentleman captured your notice?" At Lily's wary expression, she continued, "We've not been here long, but with you new to town, you must be—"

"I'll have you know," Lily said in a querulous tone, "I've no intention of marrying just yet, and I'm under no pressure to do so. Father has decided to let me choose my husband this time—provided he has a title. I find myself not knowing very much about the opposite sex, and I intend to take my time in learning so I might make a sound choice." Her plum mouth twisted in a smirk.

Isabelle caught the bitter edge to Lily's last words. *Mister* Reeves didn't fit the one requirement Mr. Bachman had placed on Lily's marriage, then. She smiled sympathetically at the taller woman, but Lily just cleared her throat and returned to the task at hand.

"Do you like these?" Lily pointed to a pair made of pink lace.

"Pretty, but not practical for riding."

"Isabelle? Lord, is it really you?"

Isabelle swung around to see a lovely young lady wearing a fashionable sprig muslin frock, a breezy white pelisse, and a pale pink bonnet accented with white ribbons and daisies. There was something familiar about her face, but Isabelle couldn't quite place her. The gentleman standing at her elbow, glowering at Isabelle, she recognized at once: Grant Lockwood, Marshall's younger brother, which would make the young woman—

"Lady Naomi!" Isabelle forced a bright smile to her face. "What a delightful surprise," she lied.

The girl beamed as though they were the closest of friends; all the while, her brother's expression vacillated between a strong desire to flee and an equally strong desire to wring Isabelle's neck.

"It's been ever so long since I've seen you." The girl stepped forward and actually took Isabelle's hands in her own. "I wondered if you would remember me."

"Indeed," Isabelle said, her alarm increasing with every passing moment, "I scarcely recognized you. You've grown up since we last met. How very pretty you are looking."

Naomi's open countenance bespoke nothing but goodwill. Could it be that not the entire Lockwood family held Isabelle in the lowest possible esteem? Isabelle's nerves began to relax somewhat.

"Lady Naomi," Isabelle said, "please allow me to present my friend, Miss Bachman. Miss Bachman, Lady Naomi *Lockwood*." She did not miss the startled expression that flitted across Lily's face for an instant before her friend turned a sociable smile on Naomi.

Naomi introduced Lily to Grant, who bowed stiffly. He had a brusque greeting for Isabelle.

"This is just too delightful," Naomi gushed, looping her arm through Isabelle's. "Tell me, where are you staying?"

"With the Bachmans," Isabelle replied, inclining her head toward Lily.

"How marvelous," Naomi said. "I do hope I'll see you soon."

Isabelle's smile faltered. "That's kind of you, Lady Naomi, but I rather doubt it. I don't move in the same circles as you."

Behind Naomi, Grant cleared his throat meaningfully.

Naomi took Isabelle's hands in hers again and squeezed them. "It's been lovely to see you again, Isabelle." She nodded to them both then left the shop with Grant.

Isabelle stared after her, unnerved by the encounter.

"Well!" Lily exclaimed. "There's something we didn't expect when we left home this morning."

Isabelle gave her friend a wry smile and shook her head. "I'm surprised Lady Naomi even recognized me. I met her on several occasions, of course, but she was much younger, and it's been three years."

She returned her attention to selecting a new pair of gloves. Much of the delight she'd felt in the task had gone. Finally, she settled on a mauve pair to complement her new riding habit. "Still," she said after they'd stepped back into Bond Street, "it is gratifying to know Naomi has not been entirely poisoned against me."

"Not at all," Lily replied. "In fact, she seemed perfectly at ease. She greeted you like a long-lost friend, not as a woman who made a fool of her eldest brother. Lord Grant, however . . . ," her voice trailed away.

"He did look rather as though he'd swallowed a particularly sour lemon, didn't he?" Isabelle acknowledged.

* * *

The encounter had been so far outside the ordinary, by the next morning it had already begun to take on a dream-like quality. And so Isabelle was more than a little surprised when the butler walked into the parlor where the girls were working on their needlework to announce Lady Naomi Lockwood had come to call.

She and Lily set aside their hoops and stood just as Naomi entered wearing a guarded expression.

They exchanged greetings, and Lily invited Naomi to join them. Their guest nervously smoothed her light green skirts.

They were quiet as the maid arrived with tea and served it in china decorated with lavender and pink flowers blooming from sprigs of foliage.

"Her Grace did not accompany you?" Lily asked after the maid left the parlor.

Naomi shook her head. "My maid rode with me. Perhaps I ought not have come. I can see my arrival has distressed you."

"This is just unexpected," Isabelle explained. She exchanged looks with Lily.

"I understand," Naomi said. "However, I came personally because I wanted to issue an invitation for you. It's rather short notice, but I'm having a supper party on Friday, and I should like nothing more than having the both of you attend."

Isabelle paused with her teacup halfway to her mouth. "*You* are having a supper party?" she asked dubiously. It was a most unlikely suggestion.

"Well, I'm not hostessing, no," Naomi admitted.

Isabelle carefully set her teacup into her saucer. "I cannot imagine either your mother or your brother have consented to my attendance."

"Neither of them knows," Naomi blurted. A shocked silence followed her daring.

Naomi squared her shoulders and plowed on, "It's to be a small gathering of only thirty guests, both ladies and gentlemen. My Aunt Janine is acting as hostess, as Mama will be busy with the orphanage committee. Marshall has no plans to attend; he is not the least bit interested in the goings on of silly *débutantes*, as he calls us. The gentlemen will leave after supper. The ladies will spend the night, and we'll have a breakfast. That's all. I've already written to Aunt Janine, and she agrees there is no problem with your attending, should you so choose." Naomi brushed a strand of hair off her forehead and exhaled audibly.

Isabelle looked at Lily and barely shook her head.

"Your invitation is most gracious, Lady Naomi," Lily started. "Unfortunately, I cannot conceive how we can possibly accept."

"Miss Bachman," Naomi said, drawing herself up again, as though preparing to argue once more. Isabelle had to admire the girl's pluck. "Would you kindly excuse us for a few moments?"

Lily turned her brown eyes on Isabelle, questioningly. Isabelle nodded.

When Lily had gone, Naomi sprang from her seat and began pacing the room, wringing her hands.

"Lady Naomi," Isabelle said, concerned at the younger woman's vexation. "Is anything the matter?"

"No," Naomi said. "Rather, yes. Something is the matter." She stopped in front of Isabelle, who had to crane her neck back to look the girl in the eye. "Something is dreadfully wrong."

Isabelle's curiosity was piqued. She stood and took Naomi's cold hands. "You're trembling! What's happened?"

Naomi lifted her chin. "You called me Lady Naomi."

Isabelle blinked. "I beg your pardon?"

"You must not stand on ceremony with me, Isabelle. You are—were—my sister." Naomi spoke haltingly, a slight frown on her brow.

Isabelle bit her lip, which suddenly wanted to quiver at her former sister-in-law's kindness. "But I'm not any longer."

Naomi sank to the couch. Isabelle sat down beside her. "I can't wrap my mind around the notion," she said softly. "You became part of our family. How can you no longer be?" Her shoulders stooped slightly and lines creased her brow, as though the question weighed heavily on her mind. "You didn't do it," Naomi stated.

"No," Isabelle said with a shake of her head, "I didn't."

Naomi glanced at her hands in her lap. "I knew it. I never believed you'd done what they said you did."

Isabelle wanted to grab the girl into a hug for her quiet loyalty. Instead, she smiled sadly. "That doesn't change anything, Naomi. Marshall divorced me. In the eyes of society," she continued, "I'm an adulteress. It would be improper beyond all recall for you to have me as a guest at Marshall's home."

The younger girl's face drew together in thought. "It'll be at Bensbury, an hour outside town. No one minds so much in the country."

Isabelle opened her mouth to protest, but Naomi ran over her again.

"They took you away from me," she said, suddenly vehement. "When you married Marshall, you became a Lockwood, part of *my* family. You were the sister I never had. That dreadful Lady Lucy Jamison will never feel like family."

Isabelle drew back, thunderstruck by Naomi's words. Was Marshall betrothed? "It's kind of you to say such nice things about me, Naomi, but if your brother is to wed Lady Lucy, you must try to think charitably of her." The words felt like razors, slicing her up as she said them.

Naomi scowled. "Supposedly, there is an understanding, but I've heard nothing of it from Marshall. I pray he doesn't marry her. What a mistake that would be."

As flattering as it was to hear Naomi preferred her to Lady Lucy, it wasn't right to disparage the woman. She picked her words carefully before continuing. "Naomi, is this—" She gestured back and forth in the space between them. "You coming here, the invitation—is this about you not approving of Lady Lucy?"

The younger woman drew herself up. "Certainly not."

"Please think about what it is you're asking," Isabelle said. "Flouting propriety like this just isn't done. You cannot know—"

"I *do* know," Naomi interrupted, her blue eyes alight with fierce determination. "Everyone treats me like a Ming vase, ready to break at the slightest upset, only to be handled with the most delicate touch. You should see the way Marshall looms over me at balls, like my larger, uglier shadow. It is most provoking!"

Isabelle laughed against her fingers at the image of the unflappable Marshall closely guarding his darling sister.

"Mother treats me like the veriest goose. Just as she does Marshall and Grant, as if we lack possession of a sound mind between us, and only she can save us all from ourselves.

"I know I'm not supposed to pursue an acquaintance with you, or even acknowledge you. I wouldn't have, if Grant had his way yesterday. He was quite vexed with me for speaking to you, you know." Naomi gave her a look that universally bespoke the ridiculousness of the male sex.

"You mustn't alienate your family for my sake," Isabelle said.

Naomi waved her worry away with a hand. "As I said, Isabelle, I am not the ninny they'd like to take me for. I know the rules, and I know that rules are made to be broken. Sometimes," she amended, smiling wryly. "Perhaps, for the sake of appearances, we cannot see each other regularly, but we can correspond, and we can visit on occasion. Does this not strike you as reasonable?"

Naomi's words began to spread through Isabelle like the flame of revolution, igniting a heady change of perspective. All these years, Isabelle had punished herself, acting like the cast-off adulteress they all took her for. Though she'd not committed the unpardonable sin for which she was divorced, on some level she'd believed herself deserving of contempt.

For years, she blamed her friendship with Justin as the source of her woes. Had he not visited her at Hamhurst while her husband was away, the circumstances may have been different. Marshall had known about Justin from the start of their unlikely romance and had accepted their friendship without remark.

Since the divorce, she'd taken Justin's disappearance as evidence of some sort of guilt on his part and hers. But there had been no wrongdoing, other than the impropriety of inviting him without her husband's knowledge. At the age of eighteen, though, it had been as natural as breathing for Isabelle to call upon her longtime friend for company. She had been naïve, but she'd never been an adulteress. No matter what Caro said she'd witnessed in the woodcutter's cottage, what she'd seen had been Justin tending her injuries, not a tawdry liaison. The fact that Marshall persisted in his refusal to accept the truth did not *change* the truth.

She had been profoundly wronged, and nothing she did could change that. But she didn't have to think as society did, or act as they deemed appropriate for a woman in her circumstance. If Naomi Lockwood was intelligent enough to see the truth of the matter, and wished to remain on friendly terms, why shouldn't Isabelle do so? Naomi was old enough to choose her own acquaintances. It wasn't Isabelle's responsibility to dictate to her former sister-in-law who she could or could not visit— including herself!

She met Naomi's eyes with a steady gaze, grateful for the younger woman's courage.

"It would be my pleasure," she said, "to accept your kind invitation."

Naomi threw her arms around Isabelle's neck. "Thank you. I didn't think you would."

Isabelle returned her embrace and laughed. "You make a compelling argument."

Setting aside the neglected biscuit, Naomi rose. She wrapped her hands in the silk rope of her reticule. "I hate to impose, Isabelle, but I wonder if you could come early on Friday and help me see about all the arrangements. Aunt Janine is a dear soul, but she's an absolute bluestocking. She doesn't care a snap for social pursuits, and hasn't the foggiest how to go on as hostess. If Mama were there, I would leave it all to her."

"Of course," Isabelle said. She felt flattered that her former sister would not only seek out her company, but her assistance as well.

Naomi took her leave, and Isabelle went looking for Lily. Being needed by Naomi gave Isabelle a small feeling of pride she had not felt in a long time. It was a tiny step back toward acceptance—by herself, at least, and maybe, by society, too.

Chapter Seven

Friday morning dawned clear, promising a fine day for the party. Naomi took her chocolate in her bedchamber at Bensbury and was finishing her toilette when there was a knock at her door.

"It's Lord Grant," her maid announced.

Naomi checked her hair in the mirror. "He may enter."

Her brother strode into the room. He wore taupe breeches, tall black boots, a red striped waistcoat, and a ruffed shirt with no coat over his sleeves. A thundercloud obstructed his features.

A feeling of foreboding washed over her. "Good morning, Grant." She rose from her vanity. "I was on my way to breakfast. Will you join me?"

"I ate an hour ago," he snapped. "Tell me, Naomi, why did the butler just announce the arrival of Mrs. Lockwood and Miss Bachman?"

Naomi's stomach flipped. Although Aunt Janine thought inviting Isabelle was a grand idea, Naomi knew Grant wouldn't share her opinion, and so had kept the scheme from him. Rather than answer the question directly, she chose to prevaricate. "I didn't expect them quite so early, but it's good they've arrived. Aunt Janine suggested a Moroccan theme, which would be fine if we had weeks to gather the ingredients needed for such a supper, but with only a few hours' notice, I'm afraid it's not at all practical."

Grant's fist slammed into the wall. "Naomi!" he bellowed. "I will not have that woman in this house." A vein throbbed at his temple "I am disgusted by your disloyalty. How dare you bring her into Marshall's home?"

"They're *all* Marshall's homes, aren't they?" she retorted. "Which of his six estates is my home?" She crossed her arms under her bosom and thrust her chin obstinately. Because he was head of the family, as well as her guardian, Naomi had an obligation to obey Marshall. She owed no such deference to Grant. "In which house may I live as the grown woman I am and make decisions for myself?"

"You've been spending too much time in Aunt Janine's company," he said. "To answer your question, since you insist on being obtuse, none of Marshall's houses are your home. You get your own home when you marry, just like every other female in England."

"Oh, no!" Naomi raised a hand. "Then I'll live in my *husband's* home, and be subject to *his* whims."

"That's the way the world works." Grant impatiently tapped a foot. "Before long, there will be a new duchess here, and she won't appreciate the old one lurking about."

A vision of Lady Lucy as Bensbury's icy mistress made Naomi quail. It was too dreadful to contemplate, so she ignored the remark. "I suppose widows are the lucky ones." Naomi narrowed her eyes. "Or the ones who are cast aside, like Isabelle. Now, if you'll excuse me," she said, sweeping past him, "I will see to my guests."

Grant snatched her arm. "You'll do nothing of the sort. Because I'm a gentleman and because the person in question is ostensibly female, I shall refrain from forcibly ejecting that pox-ridden drab from this house."

Naomi's eyes widened and she gasped, appalled at his hateful epithet. Moments like this made her miss Papa. He never would have tolerated such hateful talk from one of his children. "How could you say such a vile thing?"

"However," Grant continued, bowling over her increasing agitation, "I expect you to do the proper thing."

"Oh, I will." Naomi's voice quivered with the force of her outrage.

Had Grant been a little less virulent in his protestations, she might have been cajoled into his way of thinking. As it was, his verbal assassination of Isabelle's character amounted to throwing a gauntlet at Naomi's feet.

"I will do exactly as I've been taught," she declared. Her hands knotted spasmodically into fists at her side. She closed the distance between them until she could feel the angry heat radiating from him. From this angle, his hard features took on a comical appearance. She had a clear view of his nostrils, which loomed large from her vantage point. She refused to cower before a man who needed to employ a handkerchief.

Grant pulled his head back to look down at her. "I sincerely hope so," he said.

"Oh, yes," she answered in a low voice. "I shall do right by my guests and ensure they are made comfortable." She hopped aside as he made to grab at her again.

"Do not defy me," Grant warned. "You will rue the day."

"You need either a new razor or a new valet," she said breezily. "Your shave is completely botched."

Grant slapped at his face and glowered when he found the missed patch of stubble.

She saucily waggled her fingers at him and strolled down the hall, head high and shoulders back. A thrill coursed up her spine at her own bravado. Not since taking her hair out of pigtails had Naomi ever spoken out against one of her brothers. She'd always behaved with comportment, in a manner befitting a member of the Duke of Monthwaite's household. Her rebellion against her family's abuse of her former sister-in-law was a rousing diversion.

She took deep breaths as she wended her way down the stairs, erasing from her face the evidence of her quarrel with Grant. A maid directed her to the front hallway, where Isabelle and Miss Bachman stood waiting. Isabelle wore a diaphanous muslin dress and looked as spooked as a deer cornered by hounds ready to bolt at a moment's notice. In counterpoint, the taller Lily Bachman wore a smart pelisse in the military fashion. She hovered protectively at her friend's side, a resolute soldier ready to take on any foe, one perfect brow arched over a rich brown eye.

Naomi tsked at the bad grace shown by both the servants and her brother. No matter how the rest of the house might regard Isabelle, she and Miss Bachman should have at least been shown to a parlor to await eviction.

"Isabelle, I'm so delighted you're here. Miss Bachman," she said, turning to Lily, "thank you so much for coming. Please," she gestured, "come with me."

* * *

Isabelle followed Naomi through the house without paying much attention to the beautiful décor. She'd never been to Bensbury while she was married to Marshall. She had the surreal thought that she should have been mistress here, but instead walked the halls a barely tolerated stranger. She kept her eyes on Naomi's back and let the house fade into the background.

They found the late duke's sister in the library, reading a thick tome beside the window. She looked up at their entrance. Isabelle had never met the woman before. Finally encountering her former aunt-in-law felt as unreal as having been mistress of this house she'd never set foot in. It was all like a dream, and if it weren't for the scandal of the divorce constantly hanging over her—and the memories of a man she could never quite put out of mind—Isabelle could convince herself her marriage never happened at all.

Lady Janine's face was comprised of intelligent, kind eyes, a strong jaw, and an overall air of alert watchfulness. Though she must have been well into her fifties, her eyes were a fresh, vivid blue, and her skin still retained a healthy glow, despite the creases touching the corners of her eyes and mouth. Her hair gave the impression of having been hurriedly shoved under the cap on her head. Isabelle could relate to the impatience—she had often done the same thing with her hair when she worked at the George. For all the harassed appearance, however, the lady looked every inch the noblewoman, and Isabelle felt a bolt of unease. What had ever possessed her to agree to this madness?

Lady Janine set her book aside, revealing a cotton dress, dark gray in color and absolutely devoid of adornment, which had never been fashionable, excepting perhaps in a convent somewhere in the French Alps.

"Good morning, Auntie," Naomi said, dropping a kiss onto the older woman's cheek. "I'd like to introduce you to—"

"John Dee," Lady Janine said in a clear voice.

Naomi gave Isabelle a nervous smile. "Pardon, Auntie? There is no Mr. Dee here. This is—"

"John Dee," Lady Janine repeated. She turned her piercing eyes on Isabelle. "What do you know of Doctor Dee, missy?"

Isabelle's mind hastily whirred through all the books she'd read from her father's library when nobody had bothered steering her toward appropriate material for a young lady. "He was employed by Queen Elizabeth," she finally recalled. "He was a natural scientist. A philosopher. He advised Her Majesty."

"Ha!" Lady Janine crowed. "Pretty good, my girl, pretty good." She nodded slowly, then quirked a graying brow at Naomi. "Better than you, with all your schooling from the best tutors money could buy." She snorted. "He was a conjurer. Did you know *that*?" She pointed a finger at Isabelle.

Isabelle sensed she'd walked onto a stage and she didn't know the script. "No, ma'am," she said carefully, "I did not."

"He was a magician. Said he could summon angels. Did you know *that*?" She jabbed her finger in the air again.

Isabelle cut a glance to Naomi, whose eyes rolled to the ceiling, as though praying for deliverance from her aunt's outlandish train of conversation.

Lily wore an openly baffled expression. She turned her widened eyes to Isabelle, silently asking what they'd gotten themselves into.

"No, ma'am," Isabelle repeated, stifling a grin, "I did not."

"Good Queen Bess relied on the advice of a man who said the angels gave him a new language. Now I ask you," Lady Janine's chin dropped to her chest, and she studied Isabelle and Lily as though over spectacles, although her glasses hung around her neck, apparently forgotten. "Was the man a complete charlatan, duping the most powerful monarch on earth, or did he have mystical powers?"

Isabelle blinked. In the silence that followed, Naomi covered her eyes with a hand. "Oh, Aunt Janine," she muttered.

"An interesting question," Isabelle mused. "I shall have to think it over before answering."

"Queen Elizabeth defeated the Spanish Armada," Lily ventured.

"Indeed she did," Aunt Janine said with an approving nod.

"She was the mother of the British Empire," Isabelle added. "She saved England from financial disaster and protected her throne from interlopers and would-be claimants."

"With a magician whispering in her ear all the while." Lady Janine wiggled her fingers in the air next to her left ear. She folded her hands in her lap and cocked her head to one side. "What do you make of that?"

Naomi's face burned red. Isabelle felt for the girl. Such a discussion, overheard by the wrong ears, could label a young lady a bluestocking. No respectable man wanted a bookish wife.

"I don't rightly know, my lady," Isabelle said. "I suppose it could be conjectured that Doctor Dee gave Her Majesty sound advice gleaned from his scientific inquiries or his probing into spiritualism. However," she ventured, "it could also be supposed that Queen Elizabeth kept the good doctor at her side precisely *because* she found his claims ridiculous."

"A court jester, you mean," Aunt Janine said.

"Yes, ma'am," Isabelle answered. "Humor relieves tensions, which is good for clarity of mind."

Aunt Janine threw her head back and let out great whoops of laughter. "Mercy, you're a saucy one," she finally said, dabbing at her eyes. "And Marshall got rid of you?"

Naomi's eyes went wide. Lily inhaled sharply. Isabelle merely raised an eyebrow. "Yes, my lady, he did."

Aunt Janine waved a hand. "That one always had more intelligence than sense."

"He is quite renowned for his good sense," Isabelle defended quickly. "Everyone says so."

"Do they?" Aunt Janine's eyes narrowed on Isabelle's face. "I'm not so sure."

Naomi gestured for Isabelle and Lily to sit. "We must get started on the menu," she said, "if that's all right with you, Auntie. Cook can whip up most anything, but we have to tell her what to make." She trailed off, her hands fluttering about her lap like butterflies.

Over the next hour, Isabelle suggested dishes, which Naomi wrote down in her neat hand. Lily had the idea to set up tables on the balcony and dine under the stars. Since it was such a fine, warm day, the evening would support such a supper.

Naomi squealed with delight at the notion. "May we, Auntie?" she asked, her face aglow. "My supper shall be all the talk next week if we do something so delightful."

Aunt Janine nodded her assent. Isabelle found her former sister-in-law's excitement contagious. Soon, she was looking forward to the evening's entertainment as much as Naomi. As noon approached, Naomi padded away to deliver the menu to the kitchen. Isabelle and Lily gazed out the picture window overlooking the front drive and chatted softly while Aunt Janine returned to her reading.

"You cannot imagine what he's done!" Naomi's voice wailed.

Isabelle and Lily turned at the same time Aunt Janine's book thumped closed. Naomi stopped in front of them, her carefully scribed menu crumpled in one fist and her bloodless face streaked with tears.

Isabelle rushed to the girl's side. "What's happened?"

"Grant," Naomi said, panic creeping into her voice, "has sent the entire kitchen staff away! I found only one maid in the scullery, washing the breakfast dishes." Her breaths started coming in rapid, shallow gasps. Isabelle guided her to a chair, afraid she would faint.

"Slow down," she instructed. Lady Janine crossed to the sideboard and poured a small measure of sherry into a glass.

Naomi took the drink and choked a little down. She closed her eyes and took several deep breaths. "Oh, Isabelle, I'm so sorry." She covered her mouth with her hand. Two identical tears leaked from her eyes and slid down her cheeks. She lowered her hand, revealing pink, swollen lips. "She said Grant told the kitchen staff they'd not cook for the likes of you. They could either take a free day today or leave for good. They're all gone."

Janine hissed and cursed. Her features twisted into a mask of dismay and anger.

This news washed over Isabelle like acid. Grant's hatred had no bounds, and now Naomi was being punished for the crime of being kind to her. Lily turned to her with sympathetic eyes.

Isabelle didn't want her sympathy. She was tired of being pitied. But the old self-hatred started to tug at her, threatening to pull her under. She knew she didn't belong here. A divorcée was wanted nowhere.

Just then, the butler stepped into the library to announce: "A party of your guests has arrived, Lady Naomi. Seven ladies and gentlemen await you in the garden."

A rock settled into Isabelle's middle as Naomi grabbed her hands and wailed, "Whatever will I do? It's all ruined! I shall have to send everyone home. I'll be a laughingstock."

Naomi's desperation was the lifeline Isabelle needed. She grabbed onto it, just as she grasped Naomi's hands in her own firm fingers.

An idea sprang to life—one that would save Naomi's name and show Grant how little his poor opinion of Isabelle mattered. Naomi would have her party. And if Grant didn't like it, he could jolly well take himself to the devil.

"No, you won't," she said, calm and determined. Lily regarded her with a questioning look. Isabelle met her expression with a conspiratorial smile. She turned back to Naomi. "Your party shall be a rousing success," she assured the younger woman. "You'll see."

Chapter Eight

Isabelle left an overwrought Naomi in Lily's capable care, while Lady Janine greeted the party guests beginning to trickle in. She made her way to the abandoned kitchen to survey her new domain. Grant could rail against her all he wanted, but Isabelle would be damned if she'd let his prejudice against her ruin his sister's Season. Isabelle knew only too well how one foible could set all the tongues a-wagging. The beau monde loved nothing more than news of a public mishap to devour alongside the canapés.

Down the cramped servant stairs to the basement level she went, passing the china pantry, the laundry, and the door to the wine cellar along her way. In the scullery, she found the same maid who had delivered the news of the kitchen staff's absence. She pulled the girl from dishwashing duty and brought her along to the spacious kitchen.

The kitchen contained all that she would expect to find: a large cast-iron oven and range, butcher block, pots, pans, and ample cutlery. In the pantry, she found a veritable catalog's worth of tinned spices. The meat larder contained a few hams, poultry, and cuts of beef, but nothing like what would be required for a proper supper for thirty.

Isabelle found an apron to tie around her waist then set about making a list for the scullery maid to take back to town.

By all that was holy, she could cook. And if her cooking could save Naomi from humiliation, then Isabelle would cook like her life depended on it.

While she waited for the maid to return with a dogcart full of meats and cheeses, she set about creating some desserts. Pastries had never been her strong suit, but Isabelle could do justice by a tart. For the under-the-stars evening Naomi envisioned, tarts filled with sweet summer fruits would be just the thing.

Two hours later, the tarts stood cooling on the counter. The scullery maid had returned, and Isabelle recruited a lad from the stables to help in the kitchen. The servants busied themselves cleaning up from Isabelle's baking, while she planned how to prepare the fifteen dishes she would need to do Naomi's supper justice. She would make a large batch of *Béchamel* sauce, she decided, and divide it in thirds, adapting it into a *crème*, a *mornay*, and a *soubise*. Each of these could feature with a vegetable course, cutting down the time she'd have to put into each one. She silently thanked her mother for bringing French cookbooks with her to England and the cook at Fairfax Hall for teaching Isabelle to use them.

* * *

Her friends appeared at about four o'clock and found Isabelle with her face over a steaming saucepan.

Naomi gasped, clasping her hands to her chest. "Look at these marvelous tarts!" Her eyes swept over the rows of strawberry, blueberry, and plum-filled desserts. "Did you really make them?"

"I did," Isabelle affirmed. Both Lily and Naomi had changed into stylish afternoon dresses. Their hair was neatly coiffed, and they smelled of lavender and powder.

For her own part, Isabelle still wore her white muslin, long since ruined with berry juice stains. Her hair was tied in a knot, but sweat-and steam-dampened strands had begun working their way loose. Isabelle's face flushed from leaning into the oven and over the stove, and she hadn't begun the soups or roasts yet. No, she would be much worse for wear before it was all over.

"I cannot believe this is true." Naomi pressed her hands to her cheeks. "You are an absolute wonder," she declared. "Grant is mad as fire at me for continuing with the party, but I don't care." Her eyes sparkled with devilment. "We're going to show him, aren't we?"

Isabelle gave her a crooked smile as she stirred her sweating onions. "Yes, we are."

Naomi's eyes crinkled with her answering smile. "When will you be up to join us?"

Isabelle looked at Naomi askance. Was the girl funning her? She had fifteen courses to prepare for thirty guests with only her own hands and those of two inexperienced servants at her disposal. "I won't be up. I'll be working all the way through supper, and by the time it's over, I shall be revolting to look at. I shan't even begin to comment upon how I will likely smell."

"But you must!" Naomi protested. "If you don't come, then it's all been for nothing."

Isabelle shook her head. "No, it hasn't been for nothing." It was true. Even though Isabelle would miss the supper herself, she could do this thing to repay Naomi's kindness. Besides, it felt good to be busy again. Her hands had been too idle since coming down for the Season.

"Do you need help?" Lily asked, already setting aside her shawl.

"Stay with Naomi. I'll be fine." Isabelle dipped a wooden spoon into one of her pots and ran a finger across the back of it. The creamy, white liquid stayed separated.

Lily shot her a questioning glance. "Are you sure? I'm only acquainted with a few of the guests in passing, so it would be no great thing for me to pitch in."

"I'll be fine," Isabelle insisted. She bundled her two friends out of the kitchen, scolding them for being in her way when she had so much to do.

With everything running smoothly for the time being, Isabelle selected two large baskets from a pile of them in the corner and went out to collect vegetables and herbs from the kitchen garden. One thing she could say for working in a botanist's kitchen, she thought after finding the expansive piece of land, there was no danger of running short of edible vegetation.

* * *

Marshall ran Grant to ground in the billiards room where his brother had ensconced himself with his foul mood and a bottle of whiskey. At this hour, Naomi's gentlemen guests would be mingling with the ladies in the garden. Grant was woefully neglecting his duties as host.

"What's this about?" Marshall held up Grant's hastily scrawled note.

Grant ignored Marshall for a long moment as he lined up a shot and sent a ball careening to a corner pocket.

"Grant," Marshall said testily, "You've pulled me away from business in Parliament, and I had to cancel this afternoon's ride with Lady Lucy. Tell me what this nonsense is about!"

"It's about," Grant said, looking up with bleary eyes, "our dear sister making a disgrace of herself by bringing that doxy here. To yer house, Marsh." He jabbed Marshall's chest with the tip of his stick.

Marshall swatted the stick away. Grant's note had begged him to come to Bensbury without delay to save them all from disaster. He'd expected to find the house on fire, or to discover Naomi had eloped with an enlisted man. Instead, his drunken sibling was playing billiards and rambling about doxies and disgraces.

"And by 'that doxy,' you mean who?" He gestured with the hand holding the letter, inviting Grant to fill in the rest.

"Isabelle," Grant sighed and slouched over, clinging to his queue like an old man to his walking stick. "She's here."

Marshall's senses heightened to full alert. His eyes darted to the sides, as though his former wife might pop out from behind a chair. How the devil had Isabelle come to be at Naomi's party?

Grant's eyes took on a glassy, faraway look. "Taken over th'whole house, Marsh," he slurred. "I tol' N'omi to make her go, but she din' do it." He shook his head sadly and rested his cheek on his hand.

Marshall's lips drew into a thin line. "I'll see about it." He shoved Grant's letter into his coat pocket.

"It was the wors' thing I ever heard, you know. Wha' she did." Sighing, Grant made a desolate swipe at the balls on the table and missed them entirely.

There was something both poignant and humorous about Grant's woeful state. "Me, too," Marshall said, leaving his brother to his whiskey.

He made his way to the garden, where the late afternoon sun brought richness to the green foliage and bright flowers. The young ladies and gentlemen wore light attire suitable for the occasion. Marshall, dressed in a dark suit for the meetings he'd left behind in London, stood out like an inkblot on white linen.

He spotted his sister a distance away, surrounded by a group of friends. Four young girls with their heads together, probably giggling over some poor devil's legs or some such nonsense.

A complete innocent, surrounded by other innocents. Isabelle had no place among this bevy of naïve virgins. Though not much older than the other ladies present, Isabelle's divorced status made her a wildly inappropriate companion for his sister and her friends.

He wondered where she was if not with Naomi. Perhaps she was providing one of Naomi's male guests with an afternoon diversion. Best not to look too closely behind the hedges, he thought grimly.

Suddenly, a female hand on his arm brought him to a halt, pulling him from his morose reverie.

"Monthwaite, a word." Lily Bachman stood before him, wearing a fetching marigold gown and bonnet.

"Miss Bachman," he said, inclining his head. "A pleasure to see you again. Just now, however, I must speak with Lady Naomi."

"About Isabelle?" she asked archly.

He was taken aback by her blunt manner. It was then he noticed the cross expression she wore.

"I'm not surprised to see you here," she continued. "I wondered how long it would be before that ogre you call a brother summoned reinforcements."

She had spirit, he had to hand it to her, as well as refreshing honesty in her approach. He would return the favor, he decided, with equal frankness.

"Miss Bachman, you exhibit admirable loyalty to your friend. Indeed, I wish Isabelle only happiness."

She smirked disbelievingly.

"But you must understand," he continued, "it is not acceptable for her to be here. You're welcome to stay and enjoy the party, of course, but arrangements will have to be made for your companion." As he spoke, her expression darkened. Best to be on his way. "I shall speak to my sister, and if you can point me in Isabelle's direction . . ."

Lily straightened. Her hands clenched into balls at her side. She was not a fashionably petite lady, and Marshall weighed the odds of her decking him. "Her direction?" Lily sneered. "Isabelle is in the *direction* of your bloody kitchen," she said through a clenched jaw, "cooking for this sodding lot, thanks to your misbegotten sibling."

Marshall drew back, thunderstruck. "She's cooking?" He stared at the seething woman in disbelief. "In *my* kitchen?"

Lily exhaled loudly through her nostrils. "I fail to comprehend why Isabelle continues to give this family the time of day. You've brought her nothing but misery. If she'd had any kind of normal family growing up, she would see in an instant how insane," Lily's eyes went wide with the word, "this one is."

She turned on her heel and left Marshall standing there to stare blankly into a flowerbed, considering her words.

"Those are lovely, Your Grace," said a young lady who'd happened by. "What are they?"

Marshall stared at her stupidly for a moment before he realized she was asking about the flowers.

"*Digitalis* . . . foxgloves," he said, the Latin escaping him for the first time in recent memory. "Excuse me." As he turned to go, he noticed Naomi glancing worriedly in his direction. No doubt, she realized she'd been found out and fretted about what he'd say or do to her. Somehow, though, Marshall thought as he traipsed back into the house, he was just as worried about what recriminating darts she might throw at him.

Isabelle . . . in his kitchen! He recalled her in that inn, wearing common servant's garb, toiling with her own hands to make supper for him, Hornsby, and dozens of villagers. He couldn't stand the thought of her laboring like that in his own house. What on earth had Grant done to bring this about? Marshall may well deserve Miss Bachman's derision when he found out.

Bensbury's basement level had not been constructed for large men. Twice he clipped his broad shoulder on the rounded corners in his haste to discover the full measure of his family's offense against his former wife.

At last, he reached the kitchen. He pushed the door open, prepared to shout to find her in the teeming morass of servants. He came to a halt just inside the door. The room was almost silent. Where there should have been a veritable army working on preparations for tonight's festivities, only Isabelle and one other liveried servant remained. The servant girl formed balls of dough on the counter next to the oven. Standing beside her, Isabelle chopped carrots.

Confusion tangled his thoughts. Where in the bloody hell were his servants?

He must have voiced his question out loud, for Isabelle set down her knife and looked up, her eyes bright with unshed tears. "They've gone." She wiped her hands down the front of her thighs. He followed the motion with his gaze, then flicked his eyes to her face.

His bewilderment only deepened. "Gone where?"

A stable boy popped up from a chair in the corner where he was scaling a bowl of fish. "Mutiny, Your Grace!" he exclaimed dramatically.

He toppled a bucket of fish scales in his enthusiasm. Flat, iridescent discs spilled out in a rainbow cascade.

"It's my fault," Isabelle said quietly. "Lord Grant found out I was here, and he sent the servants away, rather than permit them to cook for me." Her chin trembled, and Marshall felt a pang of tenderness at her obvious hurt. She sniffed and raised her head, her eyes flashing defiantly. "I won't let him punish Naomi for being kind to me," she said. "I will fix this, Marshall. She'll have a fine supper for her guests if I have to . . . cook it myself." She laughed humorlessly and returned to her carrots.

Marshall watched her work. Her slender wrist rose and fell as the knife rhythmically made short work of the root. She reached for another. He took in the whole of her appearance. Her usually silky hair was damp. Lank strands hung beside her face and onto her back. Her white muslin was a mess—red and blue splotches stained the bodice, and something crusty stiffened the fabric on her side below her left breast. The thin material clung to her in a way her woolen dress at the George hadn't, rendering the contours of her back clearly visible. She shivered slightly. He involuntarily pictured a bead of sweat running down her spine to the small of her back.

He had seen ladies in states of artfully composed dishabille. *This* was the effect all those women attempted to achieve, but at which they failed so miserably in comparison to Isabelle. The way her rumpled hair framed her flushed, glistening face, and the manner in which her dress clung to her curves like a second skin conspired to give her a delectably tousled appearance. He became acutely aware of his surging desire. This would not do.

He shook his head to free himself of her beguiling spell. He removed his coat and tossed it across a vacant stool. "All right, what can I do to help?"

Isabelle's knife paused above the carrot. Her green eyes, full of disbelief, found his. At the connection of their gazes, he again had to stomp down his insidious, wayward thoughts.

"Help?" she asked incredulously.

"Yes, of course." He removed his gold cuff links and neatly rolled the sleeves to his forearms. When he looked up, Isabelle was still staring at him as though he'd escaped from Bedlam. "I want to help," he insisted. "You can't prepare supper for thirty by yourself."

"Actually, I can." She picked up her knife and continued chopping. "If you'd be so good as to recall, I spent a period of time preparing supper for a whole inn full of patrons."

Marshall noted the curve of her mouth as she spoke. Amazingly, her time working at the inn seemed to be a pleasant memory. He crossed his arms. "I seem to recall," he said lightly, "waiting the better part of two hours for my supper because the kitchen was backed up with orders." He inclined his head pointedly and was rewarded with a delightful blush.

"Very well." The corners of her mouth twitched. She pointed with her knife to a pile of potatoes beside the cutting board. "You can peel these." Her eyebrow rose over a green eye in what he took for a challenge.

He sniffed. "Fine. I'll peel the potatoes."

He selected an able-looking implement from the cutlery rack, pulled a stool to the counter, took a tuber in hand, and set to work. Not a minute later, the blade raked across his knuckle. "Damn," he muttered and pressed his finger against his trousers. Beside him, Isabelle's shoulders shook with silent laughter. He glared at her blackly. He'd faced down a line of French infantry with only a pistol and a handful of Spanish peasants—he would *not* be bested by Isabelle and her vegetables. Marshall resolutely attacked the potato. Halfway through, he drew blood again. "For God's sake!" He slammed the knife to the counter.

Isabelle set down her knife and turned to face him, her hip resting against the counter, right at his eye level. "Anything amiss, Marshall?"

He pulled his gaze from her hip, raked it up her shapely torso, and settled on her face, which was full of knowing mirth. "Yes, as a matter of fact," he said gravely. "I seem to be at a loss as to how best go about my appointed task."

She smiled quickly then masked the expression by clearing her throat. Had he not been watching closely, he would have missed it altogether.

"Your technique is all wrong, if I may say so." She moved to stand behind him. "You shouldn't fling the blade around like that. You'll cut your arm off. Here." She handed him the paring knife and the partially denuded potato.

He prepared to give it another go and was startled by her hands lightly grazing down his arms; his muscles leapt at her touch. Isabelle wrapped her delicate fingers around his and began guiding him through the motions of peeling the potato. "If you hold your thumb firm, like this," her voice purred against his ear, her jaw brushing against his temple, "then you can control the knife better." Her soft warmth pressed against him and her breasts nuzzled into the nape of his neck.

"Like so, you mean?" he asked, deliberately holding his thumb at an awkward angle.

"No," she chided with a gentle rebuke. "Like this." She captured his wayward digit beneath hers. She smelled warm and comforting, like herbs, like home—and something else he couldn't name, something purely Isabelle. "Do you see?" she asked. A strand of her hair tickled his ear. He closed his eyes and inhaled deeply, breathing her in.

"Yes," he murmured. "I see."

Her hands stilled over his, and then they were gone. He turned and caught a glimpse of her face a second before her back was to him and she checked the roasts in the oven. While he had a fine view of her lovely backside, it was the look on her face that agitated him the most. Her eyelids were drooped, and her lips parted, and though she had turned away from him, he knew she'd felt the same stirrings he'd experienced.

Marshall resumed peeling potatoes, but in his mind's eye, his fingers were tangled in her hair and roving down her back and—

"Damn!" He pressed his freshly injured thumb against his pant leg.

Isabelle didn't even turn around. "Keep your thumb out of the way," she called, still occupied with her roasts.

All too soon, a battalion of liveried footmen lined up to receive platters of food to take to the diners on the balcony.

Isabelle had pulled off an incredible victory. Marshall watched as tray after tray of tantalizing dishes left the kitchen: turrets of cold crab bisque, asparagus in crème sauce, duck confit, venison roast accompanied by the carrots and potatoes he had prepared alongside Isabelle, and a dozen others.

She stood across the stream of servants from him, quiet pride lighting her face as she watched her supper pass. Even more incredibly, she had done all of this for his sister. In passing, he tried to picture Lucy going to such lengths for Naomi; he knew she would not. *You're not marrying a friend for your sibling. You're marrying a duchess.*

It wasn't as compelling an argument as it might have been that morning.

He toyed with the idea that this could have been an act of contrition on Isabelle's part, a small way of apologizing for what her adultery had done to his family. But as he regarded her beatific smile, it became increasingly difficult for Marshall to remember she had ever wronged him. In every other instance, she had always shown herself to be a woman of character. And tonight, she had gone above and beyond anything Marshall himself had ever done on behalf of a friend. Could it be that he was mistaken about her infidelity?

Isabelle caught him looking at her. "No beef stew?" he teased.

She grinned then—a wide, happy smile. "It's a little warm out for that," she replied.

Over the next few hours, Marshall oversaw dispensing the bottles from the wine cellar, while Isabelle and her two kitchen helpers kept trays mounded with food. Finally, the tarts and dessert wines went upstairs. It was over. After the sweet course, the guests would entertain themselves with cards and music until bed.

"That's that." Isabelle sighed happily. "Except for the dishes, of course."

Marshall wrinkled his nose. "Dishes? At this hour?" He extracted his watch from his pocket. "It's nearly midnight."

She playfully tossed a small towel at him. "Time and dishes wait for no man."

A noise from the hallway caught his attention. Marshall poked his head out the kitchen door to find his wayward kitchen staff returning from their forced day off, heading for the comfort of their beds in the servant quarters.

"Not so fast!" Marshall snapped.

Gasps and mutters of "Your Grace" swept around as curtsies and bows fell and rose again like ripples across a pond.

"Despite the abdication of your duties, there has been a supper here tonight, and now it must be cleaned up." He fixed the assembled servants in a glacial stare. The men and women wearing his livery fidgeted under their master's scrutiny. "Your day off is," he consulted his watch again, "officially over. Back to work."

He turned on a heel and strode back into the kitchen, where Isabelle was consolidating the leftover soup into a single tureen.

"Plates," he said. "We need plates."

"More plates?" Two shadows bruised the delicate skin under her eyes.

Marshall had not eaten since noon. When had Isabelle last eaten? Breakfast, likely. And then a long day of hard, physical work. She was exhausted.

"Who can still be hungry?" she asked wearily.

"I am," Marshall said. "And you are. Come, let's have our supper."

She gave him an amenable smile and nodded. A string of newly returned servants entered the kitchen, bustling around, shouting instructions to one another, and clattering pots and pans. Marshall and Isabelle worked together in a quiet little oasis to prepare their own supper tray. He went down the hall to the wine cellar and selected one of his favorites to accompany their meal. Then he carried the laden tray while Isabelle followed behind.

Neither of them was in any state to mingle with company. He led her out the servant's door and around the side of the house to the garden. Away from the balcony where the gentlemen lingered over their port and cigars, but dimly lit by the light spilling from the house, a small marble-topped table just right for two stood at the entrance to the rose garden.

He set down the tray and held a wrought iron chair for her. She took her seat and opened her napkin with a snap, as nicely as if they were sitting down to a state supper in the dining room.

He watched her eyes roam the shadowy garden with obvious delight. "This is lovely," she finally said. She turned her face to the velvety blue-black canopy overhead. "Look how pretty the stars are tonight, even with the house all alight."

He gave the heavens a cursory glimpse. "They're all the prettier for being reflected in your eyes."

Her smile faltered; her brow furrowed a fraction.

Marshall silently cursed himself. Why the hell had he said that? He sounded like some lovesick swain trying to woo a maiden, rather than the detached man he knew himself to be, sitting across the table from the woman he'd divorced. Lucy, the woman he was courting, by Jove, deserved his flattery, not Isabelle.

"I believe our efforts are telling on both of us," Isabelle said, smoothly disregarding his outlandish compliment. She retrieved the wine glasses from the tray and turned them upright. "Would you care to pour?"

They passed their supper in companionable conversation. The food Isabelle had prepared for Naomi's guests was delicious. Marshall regretted that their tray held only a few selections and not the full array of dishes. He would like to have tried each and every one of her creations.

He dabbed his mouth after a bite of the duck confit. "A transient art, is it not?"

Isabelle took a sip of wine. "What's that?"

He waved a hand, indicating the spread in front of them on the table. "Cuisine. It's your art form, but an impermanent one."

She tilted her head to the side. "I never considered what I do art. Everyone has to eat."

"True, but what you create goes well beyond survival."

Isabelle shrugged. "It is one of life's pleasures to survive in style."

Marshall laughed. He could not remember enjoying a woman's company so much since—since he'd been married to Isabelle, damn it all.

They ate until only two strawberry tarts remained on the tray. Isabelle put one on a small plate to pass to Marshall, but extended her arm too quickly. The tart slid from the plate and hit the garden walk in a splatter of crumbled crust and red fruit.

She bit her lip. "Oh dear."

"If you think I've grown thick around the middle," Marshall drawled, "you could have just said so. No sense dashing good food against the ground."

Her face relaxed, once again at ease.

"Still," he continued, "there's just the one tart remaining, and as you cast mine out for the birds, I feel it's only sporting of you to forfeit yours."

Calmly plating the last tart, she smiled impishly. "I imagine you do. You may be dismayed, then, to learn I have no intention of giving you my sweet." As if to reiterate the point, she forked a large bite, opened her plump lips wide, and made a rapturous noise as she tasted the tart. "One of my better crusts," she said around her mouthful. "Flaky, tender, and those berries." She swallowed. "Your Grace, I really must commend you. Your strawberries are divine."

His lips twitched. "I should like to try. Surely you could find it in your heart to split the tart with me."

She shook her head, eyes wide. "Oh, no. It's much too good to share. I'm afraid if you tasted any, you would want it all for yourself. And then what should I do?" she asked as though caught in a dire quandary.

He fought to keep a straight face. "You shall retain your girlish figure that much longer, my dear." He slowly reached across the table and made a grab for the fork, which she easily pulled out of his reach.

"I think not, Your Grace." Her brow quirked in the same challenging way she'd used in the kitchen. If she wanted to play, Marshall thought, he was game.

A lazy, wolfish grin spread across his lips. "You will stop 'Gracing' me, if you please. You and I are beyond formalities, Isabelle." He stood and leaned across the table again, this time swiping for her wrist.

She hopped up and grabbed the tart, plate and all. "As you wish, Marshall. You still shall not have my tart."

"You insolent little minx." He pushed his chair back and tossed his napkin to the table as he rose.

Isabelle squeaked and took several steps backward into the rose garden. He took two steps toward her and stopped to watch her again pierce the tart with the fork and eat another mouthful. Moonlight grazed the surface of the dessert, giving the glaze a liquid appearance. The night air was thick with the perfume of roses. Sensual temptation drew him. Isabelle and her ridiculous tart, the lush smell of the garden, the gentle breeze touching his face, were all enough to test the mettle of a stoic, which Marshall surely was not.

A promising delight tantalized him. Why not give chase?

A low growl escaped his throat. The cords in Isabelle's neck showed as she let out an excited squeal. She took a few more steps backward, glanced over her shoulder, turned, and started off. The chase was on.

Marshall stalked after, letting her gain distance on him. He had the advantage of familiarity with the garden. What Isabelle did not know was that the rose garden was actually a maze. It was a low one, and easy to see over the tops of the various rose plants. This only made it deceptive. Visitors were lured in for a stroll, thinking they were walking into an ordinary garden, when suddenly, they found themselves puzzling their way out again.

He watched in growing amusement as she rounded a corner. A dead end, he knew. Sure enough, Isabelle retraced her steps and reached the intersection just as he did. He lunged. She yelped and sidestepped, then took off like a deer.

Her herbal scent hung in the air behind her, mingling with the roses in a heady aroma. He caught sight of her frantically running up and down the aisles of flowers. She was trapped now, no getting out the way she'd come except past him.

He caught up to her in the center—the only secluded spot in the rose garden—where a tall wall of hedges encircled a graveled clearing. In the middle, a bed of roses surrounded a fountain. Isabelle sat on a stone bench, panting. They were cut off from the house lights here, and only a little moonlight filtered in. Her features took on an ethereal quality. He glimpsed only the outline of her face, a flicker of light reflected in her eyes, the gleam of her teeth through her parted lips.

"You, madam," Marshall said, lowering himself beside her, "are caught. I shall have my prize now."

He heard the smile in her voice as she spoke. "I still don't wish to share," she cajoled.

His voice rumbled in his throat. "Keep your dessert. I think I'd like something sweeter." He heard her intake of breath as he lowered his head.

Before reaching her mouth, he encountered a forkful of flaky pastry. He chuckled and allowed her to feed him the bite of tart. Juice flooded his mouth, and the buttery crust melted against his tongue.

"It's very good," he said sincerely. "You were right to keep it away from me. Now I must have more." He placed a hand at her waist and drew her to his side. Reaching down, he plucked the fork from her fingers, scooped up a morsel of pastry, and then returned the favor of feeding it to her.

Isabelle closed her lips around the offering. Marshall withdrew the fork and pressed the tines, still warm from her mouth, against his own lips.

He watched her jaw work and her throat move when she swallowed. Only highlights of her skin gleamed in the dim light, the rest was cast in shadow. The contrasting rises and falls of her contours invited his touch. He brushed a finger along her jaw, and before she could rebuff him, he bent his neck and pressed his lips to hers.

She stiffened and made as though to withdraw. Marshall kept a hand on her back, and ran the other down her arm in a soothing touch. When she calmed he took advantage, deepening the kiss.

He teased his lips back and forth. A hand slid up his shoulder and hooked around his neck, and then her lips parted, inviting him in. What was left of his rational mind melted away. She was warm and tasted like strawberries and wine. Heat stirred his blood, stoking the desire that he had been keeping at a dull roar ever since he'd clapped eyes on her in his kitchen.

His tongue plunged boldly into her mouth, exploring territory that had once been so dear and familiar. An aching sense of loss caught him off guard, and he crushed her to him, desperate to hold onto this woman who captivated him in a way no other had.

Would his body eventually come to crave Lucy the way it did Isabelle? He faltered for an instant and started to disengage.

A mewling sound escaped her throat and her arms snaked around his neck, driving Lucy from his thoughts. For the moment, at least, no other woman existed. His fingers twined into the tresses at her nape, pulling them free of their rumpled knot. Her hair was like a blanket over his hands, comfortable and soft against his skin.

He moved his hands to cradle her face. It felt so fragile under his palms, her cheeks cool in comparison to her hot mouth. But the fragility belied a strength he could not help but admire, and somehow contained this woman who had refused to wither away under the force of society's condemnation and his own. Instead, she made her own way and survived. He was startled by warm tears against his fingers. He trailed kisses up one cheek to capture a tear with his lips.

Her crying confused him. Had he scared her? She'd been willing enough to receive his kisses and had been flirting with him before. "Don't cry, sweetheart," he murmured against her temple. "What's wrong?"

She moved her face in his hands, shifting so his fingers once again entwined in her hair. Isabelle nuzzled under his chin, rubbing her cheek against his neck.

"It's been so long," she whispered. Then he understood. She'd felt everything he'd felt this evening, up to and including the overwhelming loneliness he'd experienced when they first came together. The realization was nearly his undoing.

With one smooth motion, he scooped her up into his lap. "Too long."

But she was here now, and so was he. And she was so achingly familiar. Her presence awakened memories held within his very bones. His body knew her, missed her. She touched his jaw, and the muscle vibrated beneath her palm. Her other hand rested on his shoulder. His skin burned at her touch; his thin shirt did nothing to muffle the heat, yet it was an unwelcome barrier.

Isabelle found his ear, and drew the lobe between her lips. A jolt of sensation shot through him. He heard himself groan her name, the word ripped from the very depths of his being.

It wasn't enough. He had to touch her; he needed to rediscover her.

Once again, her needs mirrored his own. Her lips fled back to his, and without breaking contact, she twisted to face him, drew a knee up and over, and resettled herself straddling his lap. His hands found her waist, and squeezed.

She rose up on her knees and arched against him. Marshall found himself in the erotic position of looking up into Isabelle's face. She controlled their kiss now. Her tongue set a throbbing pace.

She did that *thing* with his lip that only Isabelle had ever discovered to make him wild. His erection strained against his trousers, aching to join with her. Abruptly, her mouth was gone. She made a needy little whimper and guided his head downward. Isabelle arched her back, brazenly brushing her breasts against his lips.

Marshall chuckled low in his throat. Ah, but she had always been a sweet one. He happily obliged her unspoken request, and turned his attention there. His hands slid up to cup the firm mounds. She exhaled in relief against the top of his head.

Her dress was already a ruin, so he did not feel badly tugging the neckline and exposing her to his view. Through her thin chemise, he saw the darker circles of her nipples.

He dropped his head and pressed a kiss onto the top of one soft swell and then the other. Meanwhile, he captured both nipples between his thumbs and middle fingers and slowly began to roll the sensitive flesh from side to side. The nubs rose to erect points. He lightly grazed his teeth over one and suckled it through the gauzy fabric.

She gasped and thrust her pelvis against his middle. It was becoming more than Marshall could stand, more than *any* functioning male could stand. His hands found the hem of her dress hitched around her knees. He slipped his hands beneath and grasped her silk-clad thighs. Impatient, he quickly moved upward and squeezed the firm globes of her derrière. She responded with a delightful whimper. He pulled her down, bringing her into full contact with his arousal.

Rather than shy away, Isabelle rocked her hips over him. His body jumped, hardened further by the intimate contact. "Isabelle," he released her to unfasten his trousers, "I need—"

At the same moment, she said, "Marshall, we have to stop."

It was several seconds before her meaning sunk in. He only fully understood when she pulled her face away from his entirely.

He swallowed hard, willing his thundering pulse to slow. "Oh," he said lamely.

She shifted off him, stood with her back turned, and rearranged her clothing. The stoop of her shoulders, the way she hid from him as though she was ashamed, pricked his conscience.

He quickly set himself to rights and rose. When he placed a hand on her shoulder, she jerked.

"I'm sorry," he said. "I behaved abominably—"

"Don't." She looked at him over her shoulder. "Please don't, Marshall." She gave her dress a final tug and turned back to face him again. "You didn't do anything I didn't want you to."

Wrapping her arms across her middle, she turned her gaze to the nearby fountain. "It would have been improvident to go further. I'm tired, and the wine went to my head, and that is all years behind us." Her voice sounded wistful.

He reached out and took her hand. It trembled in his grasp.

Well done, he scolded himself. Isabelle had spent the entire day on her feet, working in the stifling hot kitchen. The poor woman was exhausted and probably ached all over, and he'd not only kept her away from bed, but also treated her most despicably, despite her denial.

"You're right, of course," he said. "Come now." He tucked her hand in his arm and escorted her through the maze and back to the house. He bade her goodnight and ordered baths be taken to both her bedchamber and his.

As he washed off his unprecedented day in the kitchen, he considered what had passed between himself and his former spouse. She was right; their behavior had been improvident. They should not have gotten themselves into such a situation. They both knew better. But she was dead wrong about one thing. It was obvious to Marshall that no matter what she said, it was not behind them now. Not by a long shot.

Chapter Nine

The sky was the middling gray between night and sunrise when Kelan dragged himself out of bed, dressed, and stumbled to the stables, still rubbing the sleep from his eyes. The morning fog clung to the ground; he amused himself by pretending his feet had disappeared, and that he was a ghost floating across the stable yard.

The lad entered the dark stable and was greeted by the familiar, clean smells of his trade: hay, dung, and oiled leather. A few soft wickers acknowledged his arrival.

Sometimes he resented that the horses ate their breakfast hours before Kelan got his, but then he reminded himself to be grateful. There were few jobs to be had in his native Midlands anymore, and the money Kelan sent home to his widowed mother and siblings helped keep food on the table and a roof over their heads. His Grace paid well, and the head groom was a fair man. Kelan reckoned if the Duke of Monthwaite wanted his horses kissed on the lips every day, he should be obliged to pucker up and thank his lucky stars for the chance.

He made his way down the row of stalls, doling out feed to His Grace's cattle.

Kelan approached Rosemary's stall. She was with foal, and so received a larger portion of feed than the others. He reached into the feed sack, not paying attention to his feet, and suddenly found himself sprawled on his back with the air knocked from him. Feed spilled across the clean dirt floor.

"Bollocks!" He had only been at Helmsdale a little over a month. He didn't want to foul up and give the head groom a reason to send him packing. He picked up the feed sack and turned on his knees to find the obstacle that had caused him to slip. It was a brown jar, half full of some sticky substance. Kelan stood, brushed the dust from his pants, and glanced into the stall. Rosemary was not waiting at the stall door for her morning feed like the other horses had been. She was usually more eager for her breakfast than the rest. He wrinkled his brow and leaned over the door.

The horse lay on her side on the stall floor. Kelan could see her stomach moving in and out, but she didn't look good. Slowly, he walked into the stall and crouched next to the mare's head, extending a trembling hand. She whinnied the instant he touched her. He snatched his hand back and wiped horse sweat onto his pants. Her breathing was hard and labored. She wasn't supposed to foal for another month, but if Kelan had to guess, that's what seemed to be happening. Fear gripped his heart. What if the horse died? Suddenly, the feed he'd spilled seemed a small thing.

"Hang in there, girl," he told the ailing animal. "Mister Roden won't let nothin' bad happen to you." He backed out of the stall and left at a dead run to fetch the head groom. He found the man at breakfast. Between panting gasps, he communicated to his superior that something was terribly wrong with Rosemary.

Together they went back to the stable. Roden had been head groom at Helmsdale for over twenty years, and regarded the horses almost like his own children. Kelan thought the older man might cry when he saw Rosemary's sorry state.

Roden made soft, shushing sounds to the horse, just like to a fretful babe. He pulled a rag from the waist of his pants and wiped the sweat from the mare's face. Kelan shifted nervously from foot to foot, wringing his hands as he watched, uncertain what, if anything, he should do. He didn't think he was making any noise, but Roden crossly told him to be quiet as he laid a hand on Rosemary's belly. The head groom closed his eyes for what seemed to be a very long time. After a while, he opened them again. "She's having contractions, but they're not strong. All we can do is keep her quiet and hope they stop. If she delivers now, the foal won't make it."

Kelan resumed his nervous stepping. The only thing worse than a dead horse would be a dead foal. His Grace would not be happy about that. He chewed anxiously at his thumbnail. Roden sighed and rose, leaning heavily on his knee and making the same grunting sound Kelan's grandfather made when he stood up.

The head groom patted Kelan's shoulder. "You did the right thing coming to get me, lad. We'll take care of her as well as we can and hope for the best. Go on with your duties now."

"Yessir." Kelan bent over to retrieve his feed sack.

Roden suddenly froze beside Kelan. "What's that?"

"What?" Kelan followed Roden's eyes to the floor, where the jar lay on the floor, forgotten. "It's a jar, but I don't know why it's here. It was sitting there when I came in this morning."

"Sitting where?" Roden asked, his weathered face grim.

"Right there," Kelan pointed to the spot where he'd fallen, "in front of the mare's stall."

The old groom snatched up the jar. He looked at it, cursed, and walked out into the stable yard. Kelan trailed after, blinking in the light of the newly risen sun.

Roden stopped just outside the door and peered into the jar, turning it so the weak, early light illuminated the contents. He scooped a dollop of the paste onto his finger, sniffed it, then lightly touched it to his tongue. He spat.

"God's blood," he muttered. "That misbegotten whoreson . . . " He rounded on Kelan. "Bring the steward. Run, lad. I don't care if you have to tear Helmsdale apart, you find the steward and bring him here fast as you can. He has to see this and send word south to His Grace." He cursed again and scraped his finger on the jar's mouth.

Kelan wondered what the fuss was about. It was just a jar with some kind of jam—

"Don't stand there with your jaw flapping in the breeze, boy," Roden snapped. "*Run!*"

Kelan jerked, frightened anew by the urgency in the head groom's voice.

He ran.

Chapter Ten

Isabelle enjoyed the pleasant sensation of slowly waking in a luxurious bed. After her bath last night, she'd fallen asleep before her head hit the pillow, and so had not noticed how extremely comfortable it was. The smooth sheets smelled faintly of powder, and if there were clouds for the cherubs in heaven, surely they could not be softer than this mattress.

At last, she opened her eyes. A tray with chocolate sat beside the bed. She lifted the bowl to her lips and sipped. Tepid. She furrowed her brow. What time was it? It was not her custom to sleep late.

She slid out from between the sheets and her bare toes curled into the thick nap of a fine carpet. Late morning sunlight streamed onto her face when she drew the heavy drapes. Turning, she spotted a clock on the mantle. Almost noon.

Not surprising, all considered. Yesterday *had* been a terribly long day. Her legs, feet and back still ached from standing so long. She had been up quite late . . .

Isabelle's face flushed as the memory of what she had been up late *doing* returned. She'd behaved like an absolute wanton, and only a happenstance reminder from her conscience that she should not, in fact, become intimately engaged with a man to whom she was not married had brought her kiss-addled brain back to its senses.

She was more than a little afraid of the way her heart skipped a beat as she thought about him. Developing an easy repartee with her former husband was one thing, but he'd already broken her heart once; Isabelle couldn't allow him to do it again.

She donned a light blue dress with green leaves embroidered on the sash. After styling her hair in a neat twist, she went looking for Lily. Her friend was not in her room. A maid told her Lily was having a late breakfast with Lady Naomi and her guests.

Isabelle started toward the dining room but stopped short when a number of feminine voices floated down the hallway. She suddenly felt very conspicuous and out of place. No doubt, Naomi would welcome her to the table, but how would she explain Isabelle's presence to the others?

Instead, she decided to find Marshall. He was an enormous help last night. She'd been overwhelmed and sinking fast; his arrival had bolstered her spirits, in addition to providing another pair of hands. It would be appropriate to thank him, if he hadn't already gone back to London this morning.

The butler informed her that, yes, the master was still at home and working in the greenhouse. Following the butler's directions, she took a path past the expansive vegetable garden she'd raided yesterday, into a more sheltered area. Tall trees mingled with the plantings, giving the garden the appearance of having just sprung into being, although Isabelle knew Marshall's hand had been at work here.

The intimate, raw beauty of this garden made her feel like a fairy tale princess wandering through the woods. She smiled, restraining the girlish temptation to skip along the stones.

At a curve in the path, the overhead canopy opened to a clearing, in the center of which stood Marshall's greenhouse. She gasped at the sight of it: a beautiful structure, all sparkling clean glass and white iron. The framework divided the glass into a neat grid. A row of pointed finials marched down the length of the roof. Boxwoods lined the sides, and roses and lavender mingled together in a bed near the entrance. The whole effect gave the greenhouse the appearance of a cozy cottage— albeit one made of glass.

Isabelle hesitated with her hand on the weathered bronze doorknob. Inside, Marshall stood at a worktable along the left wall. He wore buckskin breeches and soft brown boots. For a shirt, he wore a plain tunic suitable for a gardener, but it didn't look out of place on the Duke of Monthwaite. He elevated the status of the lowly garment, rather than look more common himself. Several containers and a scale stood on the table in front of him, and he was writing something on a sheaf of paper. He probably wouldn't appreciate the interruption.

Before she could repent her decision to seek him out, he looked up. Their eyes locked. A thrill coursed up her spine, and her skin suddenly tingled all over, just from the force of his glance. His lips turned in a lazy, half-smile. She swallowed, suddenly very sure coming here had been a bad idea. An instant later, he was at the door, opening it, beckoning her inside.

"Isabelle," he said warmly, nodding. "If I'd known you were coming, I'd have had a stove and saucepans brought from the house to make you feel at home."

All her anxieties melted away at his jest. It was better this way, she thought, stepping past him into the greenhouse's enveloping warmth. He knew her in a way no one else did; it was a good feeling to be on friendly terms with her former husband.

He closed the door behind her. "To what do I owe the pleasure?" His eyes were alight with mirth.

His tunic neck hung open in a vee, exposing his neck and a tantalizing bit of his upper chest. She raised her eyes and found him studying her closely. Heat flooded her cheeks at being caught examining him.

Isabelle cleared her throat. "I wanted to thank you," she explained, watching as his brows rose a fraction. The mildly surprised expression was so familiar and dear, she felt a pang in her chest. Pushing it aside, she forged ahead. "Your help yesterday was invaluable." She smiled, awaiting his gracious reply.

Instead, he watched her thoughtfully for a moment, then turned his head. He rotated a pot containing a violet. "I thought my bumbling must have been more trouble than it was worth." He smirked in a disarmingly charming way. A jolt of nerves shot through her.

She nodded, feeling once again that being here was a mistake. "I'm sorry for intruding. I'll be on my way. I only wanted to deliver my thanks." The ridiculous urge to drop a curtsy nearly overcame her. He'd thrown her off balance with a simple twitch of his lips. Time to go.

"Would you like to return the favor?" he asked.

She turned and gave him a questioning look.

"I could use some assistance." He gestured to his worktable with a toss of his head. "The gardener usually attends, but he's looking after his ailing wife."

Isabelle felt like a rabbit in a snare. She couldn't refuse him, not after he'd given her so much help last night. "Certainly," she replied at last. "I should be the most ungrateful woman alive if I didn't."

He nodded. "Good. This way, then."

Sunshine streamed through the glass ceiling, and the air was thick with the aromas of flowers and earth. Being inside the glass house was like walking through a dream, she thought drowsily. The light had a different feel than it did out of doors. Isabelle could only interpret the sensation as green and nourishing.

At the worktable in the back, Marshall handed Isabelle a smock. It was too large for her, and she felt silly in it, especially with Marshall looking so fine in his own work clothes.

"What are we doing here?" she asked as she buttoned the voluminous smock, nodding toward the bowls, bottles, and jars on the table.

"I'm mixing a formulation of plant food to give the tenant farmers at Helmsdale. We had good success with it last season at Hamhurst."

Isabelle cut her eyes at him. "Do your farmers know they are being experimented on?"

Marshall clicked his tongue. "I haven't couched it in those terms. Besides, I experiment on myself before giving formulations to my tenants. The garden here is the first to try my concoctions."

"The vegetable garden?" she asked.

He nodded.

Isabelle furrowed her brow. "Do you mean to say your dinner guests are on the receiving end of your unproven botanical research?" She recalled how liberally she had taken from the vegetable garden for the previous night's supper and hoped she hadn't inadvertently poisoned anyone.

Marshall winked. "It'll be our secret, all right?" He pressed a finger to her lips. Isabelle laughed, and put a hand on his wrist to push it away. When she touched him, her laughter died in her throat. Her heart hammered. She bit her lip.

His smile faltered. "On to work, then?"

For the next hour, she ignored her jangling nerves while she carefully measured various minerals into small bowls, which Marshall then weighed on his scale. He was an amiable partner, patiently explaining the purpose of each mineral and demonstrating the correct way to clean the spoon between minerals, so as not to contaminate the other vessels.

She watched Marshall tinker with a bowl of powdered calcium, his jaw set in concentration, and his eyes focused solely on what he was doing. His ability to become so engrossed in his work was admirable. So many aristocrats whiled away their lives, never achieving anything worthwhile.

"A bit like cooking, isn't it?"

"Hmm?" His eyes flicked away from the scales to give her a sidelong look.

"Putting these ingredients together just so." She gestured to the containers. "Get it wrong, and you've got a big mess on your hands. Get it right," she continued, "and you create something wonderful."

He looked at her for a moment, his face unreadable.

She shrugged awkwardly. "Or perhaps not."

He shook his head. "No, I think you're right. It is very much like cooking. I just hadn't thought of it that way." Carefully, he tipped the calcium powder into an enameled jug. With a nod, he straightened and wiped his hands together. "Now for the most delicate part of the whole operation. Please stand back."

Taking his grave tone to heart, she moved several steps away and held her breath while Marshall corked the jug. Then he lifted it, one hand on the bottom, the other around the neck, and shook vigorously. "Very scientific, you see," he said.

She smothered her laugh with a hand. Marshall grinned.

A servant knocked at the door, announcing lunch on the little patio outside the greenhouse.

"I'll leave you to your meal," Isabelle said when the servant had gone. They'd spent a pleasant hour together, but now that their task was completed, Isabelle's insides once more performed somersaults.

A tone of mock severity crept into his voice. "I beg your pardon? Did I or did I not give you an entire afternoon and evening yesterday?"

"You did," she conceded.

"You shall share my meal," Marshall continued, giving her an arch look, "and then resume your labors beside me. I shall be fully compensated for my efforts."

She took off her smock and hung it on a peg on the wall. They washed their hands at a basin in the corner before repairing to the patio. Bensbury's cook seemed to believe the duke in imminent danger of wasting away; though his tray had only been set for one, the quantity of food could have easily fed three.

They shared the spread of cold meats, bread, cheese, and wine. Isabelle felt as though they were in their own little secluded world. The trees and shrubberies surrounding the clearing shielded the greenhouse from view of the house.

She turned her face to the sky and closed her eyes, enjoying the cool breeze and the birdsong coming from the trees all around.

"Magical," she murmured. "A perfect day." She sighed contentedly and opened her eyes, to find Marshall looking at her with his steepled fingers pressed to his mouth and a bemused expression on his face.

"I'm being silly." Isabelle waved a hand. "Don't mind me."

"No, you're not. This is a rather lovely day." He swirled his wine and regarded her with a suddenly intent gaze. Isabelle feigned interest in the trees to keep herself from squirming under his scrutiny.

His casual demeanor unsettled her. Neither of them had raised the issue of what passed between them in the rose garden the previous night. It occurred to Isabelle that Marshall was likely appalled at her shocking behavior. Combined with his belief that she was an adulteress, it was nothing short of amazing that he tolerated her company at all. She shouldn't care about the opinion of this man who had so wrongly cast her aside, but she did. And his opinion was probably quite low. Silently, she cursed her own, treacherous heart for giving a damn about him.

"Shall we?" Marshall rose.

Isabelle nodded woodenly. As soon as she could, she would collect Lily and get as far away from Marshall—and this disastrous house party—as possible.

He led her behind the greenhouse to another worktable pushed up against the glass wall. Gloves and spades occupied a wooden box standing on one corner. Marshall retrieved a stack of pots from beneath the table.

At his instruction, Isabelle pulled on a pair of gloves and started filling the pots with soil from a bin at the end of the table. As she worked, the knots of tension in her shoulders relaxed. The breeze played across her face and neck; loose strands of hair tickled her skin. She tamped down on some soil, and glanced up at Marshall. He was watching her again, his eyes heavy-lidded and a small curve crinkling the corners of his mouth.

"Why are you smiling?" she asked.

"When we were married," he said in a low voice, "I never would have imagined mucking around in the dirt with you."

The sentiment provoked a small laugh. "And I couldn't have imagined spending a day in the kitchen with *you*."

"I didn't even know you cooked," Marshall protested. "I might have joined you for some," he waved a hand, "recreational culinary undertaking, had I known my wife could hold her own against the French chefs the *ton* dotes over."

Isabelle lowered her eyes. Hearing the word "wife" come from him was like a knife to the heart.

"It wasn't very long, was it?" His soft words were a caress, instantly soothing the hurt of his previous remark.

Isabelle looked up into his dark eyes. They smoldered like embers ready to flare up at the smallest breath of air or bit of tinder.

"No," she agreed, "it wasn't." She clamped her teeth onto her suddenly trembling lip.

Marshall did not look at her with the scorn she was accustomed to when the topic of her supposed infidelity arose. Rather, his expression was sympathetic and warm, and—it was probably just her jumbled emotions wishing for something that wasn't there at all, but his eyes seemed to convey wanting, as well.

"We had last night," he said in a husky voice. He ducked his head and lifted her chin with a finger, forcing her to meet his gaze. "And today, Isabelle."

He stroked her chin lightly with his thumb. Isabelle felt like she was falling into the depths of his mesmerizing eyes. He tipped her chin up a little more and lightly covered her mouth with his own, a tender greeting. Then his tongue traced across her bottom lip. Little sparks of pleasure shot up her spine.

Alarm bells clanged in her mind, urging her to run away from this man—but it was already too late, and she knew it. As she opened her mouth, willingly deepening the kiss, she felt her reckless heart likewise opening to let him inside once more. She was being foolish. He would hurt her again. But her own silent protests found themselves drowned out by her hammering heart and the blood rushing in her ears.

Without breaking the kiss, she pulled off her gloves and buried her fingers in the thick waves of his hair. Meanwhile, Marshall worked the buttons of her smock. He lifted his head and shot her a smoldering look. Isabelle returned his seductive glance, gratified to know she was not the only one so affected by their kiss.

Marshall turned to the worktable. "Take that off," he directed, kneeling to pull a folded canvas tarp from beneath the table.

Isabelle felt the slightest bit wicked as she pulled the smock from her arms, though she was still dressed in all her clothes.

"Come." Marshall's hand clamped possessively around hers as he led her a few yards to the edge of the clearing, where he spread the tarp in the shade of a towering elm. He rested his hands on her waist and squeezed. "What do you say, Isabelle? Do we have today?"

She dropped her forehead against his firm chest while she tried to pick through her tangled emotions. Isabelle knew she was dangerously, unwisely close to tumbling into love with him again. But here he was, wanting her like he used to. And that part of it felt so right.

He drew her into a close embrace, molding her soft curves against his unyielding, masculine body. "It was always so good between us," he murmured against her ear. She shivered at the feel of his rumbling voice. "We had a little taste of it last night. Don't you wonder?"

She nodded weakly, the thrumming desire already reducing her mental faculties to porridge. "I do."

He cupped his hands over her bottom and tugged her hard against his arousal. "Then let's satisfy our curiosity."

She felt a brief worry that this might be just a game to him, but then his hands slid up her sides and claimed her breasts, and the storm of sensation building inside her overwhelmed all her misgivings.

Last night, Isabelle had neither seen nor touched enough of Marshall to slake her thirst. Now, she slipped her hands under the hem of his tunic and ran her fingers up his bare back; his skin was like warm suede. She lightly pulled her nails back down his spine. He lifted his head and made a sound like a satisfied lion before pulling the tunic off and tossing it to the grass. Isabelle stepped back to admire him. Instantly, she was drawn to the scar on his right side where he'd been wounded in the war. Had things gone worse for him then, she never would have known him at all. Fierce protectiveness blazed against the unbearable thought.

Her eyes roved his muscled shoulders and chest, with its light covering of dark hair, down to his tapered waist. A trail of hair leading from his flat stomach disappeared inside his trousers. The thought of following that trail was deliciously erotic.

She laid a hand against his hard chest, then rested her cheek beside it and drank in his scent: clean earth and his own, natural maleness. The heady smell went straight to her brain like the strongest brandy. Her lips brushed his skin while her fingers roamed, finding his nipple and lightly raking it. He drew a sharp breath.

Knowing she aroused him fed Isabelle's own lust. Her breasts felt heavy, her nipples tender. Aching need built between her thighs.

Marshall pulled her closer and unfastened the buttons running down the back of her dress. With a little encouragement, it fell to the tarp in a soft heap. While she stepped free of it, he worked on the ribbon at the neck of her chemise.

"I have to see you," he said urgently, feathering kisses over her neck and shoulders between words. "All of you."

Isabelle could scarcely believe the effect she had on him. For years, being a woman had made the sin of her divorce all the more shameful—Marshall had not suffered for the very same divorce the way she had. Now, being a woman seemed the finest thing in the world. She felt a heady rush of her own feminine power as the solid, heavy evidence of Marshall's arousal strained against his trousers.

Soon, she'd been divested of her chemise. Her slippers and stockings

The sensation of being filled by him was just so delicious. His presence surrounded and permeated her. God, had anything ever felt so right? Her arms reached over her head along the cool tarp. Marshall caught her hands; their fingers twined together. Then he started to move inside her, slowly at first, a gentle rocking back and forth. Isabelle reveled in the weight of his large body pressed against hers.

Marshall propped up on his elbows—caging her in—and devoured her mouth with a ravenous kiss. "You're perfection," he breathed against her ear. "So damn good, Isabelle. I knew it would be. You've always made me feel . . . so . . . good."

Isabelle thought her heart would burst. She took his face in her hands. "Just like I remember . . . oh!" The pace of his thrusting increased. There were no more words for Isabelle, just the heat mounting again between her thighs.

She tightened the grip of her legs and arms around him, barely noticing the whimpers and soft cries she made. She met his demanding pace, lifting to meet every thrust. He was driving them both to the brink. And then she was over the edge and beyond, as a jolt of pure, brilliant sensation erupted inside her and shattered into a thousand shards of sunlight.

An instant later, a roar tore from Marshall's throat. She was flooded with his warmth, and in that instant, the love she'd felt for him as a young bride roared back to full life. With a final thrust, he shuddered and collapsed atop her, sated and panting.

Isabelle languidly stroked his damp back. He kissed her temple and rolled off, breaking their intimate joining. She protested with a whimper.

"Ah, sweet girl." Wrapping his arms around her, he drew her against his damp chest. "Let a man recover, won't you?"

She snuggled against him and pressed a kiss to his collarbone. His skin smelled musky. Her tongue darted out and tasted the slight tang of salt. Isabelle noticed every sensation, jealously hoarding them away in her memory. In the years that had passed since the last time they'd been together, she'd forgotten how amazing it was between them; she vowed not to forget again.

She wished she could cocoon herself in this moment forever. The warm sun washed over her and the comfortable weight of Marshall's arms kept her snug against him. Though a niggling voice in the back of her mind warned her to get up and be done with him, she burrowed deeper into his embrace and sighed contentedly, instead.

She must have dozed off then, for she returned to awareness with a soft tickle at her side.

"Sweetheart?" Marshall murmured. "Are you awake?"

Her eyelids fluttered. "I am now. Sorry."

He chuckled. "I didn't realize I'm so deadly dull as to bore you into insensibility."

At the warmth in his expression, Isabelle's heart kicked. "You did not *bore* me to sleep, Marshall."

"Darling, you're blushing. Don't tell me you've turned maidenly now, not after the luscious vixen I so recently encountered." He playfully pinched her bottom. She giggled, enjoying their banter. Maybe things would be different now, after all. Maybe their coupling had meant as much to Marshall as it had to her.

She turned onto her left side again and let her eyelids drift closed. Marshall idly ran a hand up her flank and chest. Isabelle relished the simple delight of his touch. Each pass of his fingers left a mark that scorched its way to her soul, more memories to cling to and examine later.

His hand paused below her right breast, his fingers pressed into the skin. She felt his whole body stiffen.

"What is this?"

"Hmm?" She opened her eyes again and rolled onto her back. Marshall's hand followed, probing harder against her side. His brows knit together, as though he was thinking very hard about what his fingers had discovered.

"Isabelle, what is this place on your side?" The gentle banter had vanished from his tone.

"Oh, the lump, you mean?" She'd lived with it for so long now, she scarcely thought about it. "That's where I broke my rib when I fell off of Davey Boy that day." At the dark expression that crossed his face, she hurried, "It doesn't hurt. The bone healed, just not evenly."

He laid his hand flat over the place where she'd been injured, then squeezed lightly. As his fingers again encountered the lump in her rib, Marshall grimaced. He suddenly looked so sad. Her heart lurched at his concern on her behalf.

Without thinking, she lifted her head and kissed him.

He pulled back as though startled, his expression growing more serious.

"Don't tell me *you're* turning maidenly," Isabelle ventured, hoping to regain their easiness.

Marshall shook his head. "Isabelle . . ." Something in his voice made her nervous.

He sat up and held a hand out for her. Her hopes faltered and crashed back to earth at the impersonal civility of the gesture. Whatever affection he'd expressed this afternoon must have only been his male urges talking. Now that they'd been satisfied, she already felt him receding from her. He gathered her clothes. She desperately searched his face for any remnant of emotion as he handed them to her. He met her gaze dispassionately.

Isabelle turned her back and dressed as best she could, while unshed tears burned her eyes. What a fool she was! She silently berated herself while she wrestled with her dress.

"Allow me." Marshall's voice held a modicum of tenderness, but he was a gentleman, after all, and undoubtedly did as much for any of his paramours. She stood ramrod straight while he fastened the buttons.

When he finished, Marshall gave her shoulders a little squeeze. Isabelle wrested away from his touch. She retrieved her slippers and stood on one foot to put one on and then the other, shaking so badly she nearly fell over. Marshall steadied her with a hand on her elbow.

"Isabelle?"

She looked up at him. Dressed once more in his gardening garb, he looked every bit as handsome and composed as he had a couple hours ago, before her heart had been turned inside out. He blinked and opened his mouth as if to speak, but closed it again.

She wanted to fling her arms around his neck and kiss him until the warmth returned. She wanted to drag him back to the tarp and spend the whole day making love. She wanted to pretend their divorce never happened. But he didn't. It had been nothing more than a diversion for him.

"I can't do this again." It was a small victory that her voice trembled only a little.

She shook her head, turned, and ran all the way back to the house. She couldn't let him destroy her again. Time to collect Lily, go back to London, and forget Marshall Lockwood existed.

Chapter Eleven

"The provisions, Your Grace?" Perkins said.

Marshall blinked. His secretary held the list toward him with an expectant look on his face.

"Oh, yes," Marshall said. "Thank you. Put it there." He gestured to a pile of papers on his desk. "I'll look over it later." He cast around and picked up a book sitting on the corner of the desk. "After I sign these things." He distractedly flipped through an atlas of South America.

"As you say, sir." Perkins cast him a dubious look before bowing out of the study.

Marshall sighed and closed the book. It wasn't any use trying to get work done. He hadn't been able to concentrate in the three days since he parted ways with Isabelle.

He struggled to put her out of mind. Things here demanded his attention, he thought, glowering at the express packet sitting in the middle of his desk. Anxiety gnawed at his middle. The hastily scrawled missive from his steward at Helmsdale had been waiting for him when he returned to town from Bensbury. It described the eerily familiar poisoning of one of his brood mares and the substance found in front of the horse's stall.

The message rang loud and clear: Thomas Gerald had returned to England, and he was angry. Not that Marshall could blame him—were the situation reversed, Marshall would hate the man who had robbed him of his youth. "Well done," he muttered. "You've created a criminal in truth."

He'd sent an express back to Helmsdale, summoning Roden, his longtime stable master, to come to London with the jar. There was no doubt in his mind that the sticky matter was the same formula involved in the accident with his father's mare all those years ago, but he needed both Roden and the poison here to present to an investigator. The

143

matter had become urgent. He could not allow a vindictive convict to run loose, killing his horses and plotting God only knew what other kind of revenge.

A rustle of silk and the flash of color in the hall caught his attention. "Naomi," he called. His sister stepped into the room, greeting him with her usual cheerful smile. He rose to meet her.

After a brief exchange of small talk, Naomi leveled a shrewd look on her brother. "What's on your mind, Marshall?" At his raised eyebrow she explained, "You've commented on the weather twice in the space of five minutes. Something has you distracted."

It was no good prevaricating; Marshall came right to the point, although he attempted to mask his interest in the subject by casually straightening his papers as he spoke. "Have you heard from Isabelle?"

Naomi shook her head. "Not since our return to town." She settled herself in an armchair in front of Marshall's desk. "I've wanted to speak with you about her." She cleared her throat and smoothed her skirt with both palms. He waited for her to continue. "I was afraid you were angry with me for inviting her to my party and, well, I suppose I didn't want to raise the issue." She blushed prettily and looked down at her hands.

Marshall sat with one thigh on the edge of the desk, and the other foot on the floor. "Why?" he asked, bewildered. "Afraid I'd lock you away in a tower? Am I really such an ogre?"

Naomi's wide eyes flew to his face. "Oh, no, nothing like that! It's just that I knew you wouldn't approve. It was wrong of me to do it behind your back and Mama's. I apologize."

He resisted the urge to ruffle her hair. Young ladies of eighteen didn't appreciate childish gestures. Instead, he nodded. "Thank you. It was, indeed, improper of you to invite her, but I accept your apology."

His sister breathed a sigh of relief. "Thank you. However, I do want to discuss Isabelle further." She drew her shoulders back and lifted her chin to look him squarely in the eye. "It was really too bad of Grant to treat her so abominably."

"I agree," Marshall conceded.

"And it was wrong of him to treat me so abominably, too. He tried to ruin my party."

Marshall nodded firmly. "I agree with that point, as well. I'll speak to him."

"Isabelle rescued me from humiliation. Did you try the menu she prepared, Marshall? Every bit as good as any chef in London."

"She is quite remarkable." A smile touched his lips as he recalled her furiously whipping dishes together. "Would you believe I never knew about her culinary talents until recently?"

Naomi's eyes narrowed appraisingly. "Yes," she said at last, "I would believe that. I think there is a great deal about Isabelle you either don't know or have misjudged."

Marshall blinked. He was not used to having his younger sister rebuke him. His throat tightened a fraction. "That's possible."

"In any event," Naomi said with a wave of her hand, "Isabelle did me a great service, and ultimately you, as well. It would not do for word to get 'round that the Duke of Monthwaite's guests were left to go hungry. Lady Lucy wouldn't like hearing that," she said pointedly.

Marshall shifted in his seat. Not long ago, he felt confident about pursuing Lucy Jamison. Then Isabelle came along and mucked up all his neat logic, just as she'd always done. Lucy was still the sensible choice, but he had increasing difficulty picturing a lifetime with her. "Isabelle saved us all from unkind gossip," Naomi continued. "I should like to do something to thank her, but I won't proceed without your permission."

"That's a reasonable request," he said, somewhat begrudgingly. Why did Isabelle have to reappear in their lives? "What did you have in mind?"

"Oh!" Naomi exclaimed. She blinked in surprise. "I haven't gotten that far! I didn't think you'd actually agree."

Marshall smiled wryly. "Well, I do. We owe Isabelle a debt of gratitude, and it would be remiss not to acknowledge her efforts on our behalf in some way. I'll see what I can think of, and you do the same, all right?"

Naomi nodded happily. She rose, kissed his cheek, and departed to go on a round of calls with their mother.

When she'd gone, Marshall exhaled loudly and dropped into the chair she'd vacated. He propped his elbows on the arms and rested his chin against his steepled fingers, his long legs stretched in front.

As much as Thomas Gerald concerned him, he'd given that matter only a fraction of the attention it deserved, because his mind kept wandering back to Isabelle.

I can't do this again, she'd said. What couldn't she do?

Marshall's thoughts were in a whirl and his stomach in such knots he could barely eat these last few days. When Isabelle showed up at his greenhouse, looking like some sort of woodland nymph stepping out of a storybook, he'd been utterly enchanted and as aroused at the sight of her as he'd been the night before in the rose garden. He'd played on her innate sense of fairness and roped her into assisting him, just to keep her with him for a little while.

Time at her side hadn't been good enough—he'd found himself completely obsessed with the idea of making love to her again. And when he saw her standing in front of him, her beautiful body as glorious in the little clearing as Eve in the Garden, and as sweet and tempting as a forbidden fruit, he'd been driven to his knees with lust.

Being with Isabelle again brought back more than the memories of their sweet nights of wedded bliss; he'd been reminded again how she'd held him utterly captivated, besotted, very nearly in love. And now, those same emotions all came rushing back.

But those feelings brought a friend with them this time: guilt. For there was something else Marshall had discovered during the course of their love play—Isabelle's broken rib.

She'd told the truth. The day his mother saw her in the Hamhurst cottage with Justin Miller, his wife had been injured, not in the throes of committing adultery. When Caro described seeing Isabelle in a shocking state of undress with Miller's arms around her, he had been wrapping her torso with strips torn from her petticoat, not tupping her.

At the time, he'd innately *known* that the truth was other than it seemed, but he didn't trust his own judgment. He was still reeling from his father's sudden death and overwhelmed by his new responsibilities as duke. Caro's letter denouncing Isabelle stunned him. When he returned to Hamhurst and learned Miller had been there with his wife, it was too easy to believe the worst. Isabelle was the scheming adventuress Caro had warned him about. The "broken rib" seemed like a paltry lie.

If only he had calmed down and listened when she tried to explain, mayhap they could have avoided this mess. If only he hadn't taken Mr. Miller's disappearance as proof of guilt. A thousand other if-onlys tumbled through his mind. He groaned and pressed a hand to his eyes.

He'd divorced his wife on false pretenses. He had ruined an innocent woman, just as he'd ruined the innocent Thomas Gerald. In both matters, his own lack of awareness had led to disastrous results, ones he wished with every fiber of his being he could undo. The pain cut deep.

He put his mind to what he could do to rectify the matter. The fact was that she drove him to distraction. Isabelle spelled nothing but trouble for Marshall. He was as physically attracted to her as he'd ever been—perhaps even more so. As long as she and he were both unwed, he didn't trust himself to keep away. She was a loose end in his mind, flailing about to catch him off guard time and again.

The answer had to lie in tying up that loose end. Like all other unwed females of marrying age, Isabelle must have come to London to find a husband. Successfully doing so would be no easy task for a divorced woman. Socially, she was so beyond the pale, she might as well be branded with an "A" as the Puritans were wont to do in the old days.

If he could help her, though . . . He frowned in intent concentration; his fingers tapped a rapid beat against the desk.

Helping Isabelle marry again would serve multiple purposes. First and foremost, seeing her well settled would alleviate his new and profound sense of guilt. Ending their marriage had robbed Isabelle of all the comfort and security to which she had been entitled as his wife. Restoring her to a similar situation would go a long way toward reparation.

Second—*but just as important,* he thought ruefully—an attached Isabelle would be unavailable. Having previously been the betrayed party (or so he'd thought), Marshall reviled the very notion of cuckolding a husband. Seeing Isabelle with another man's ring on her finger would effectively quench his sexual desire for her. If not, his own marriage to Lady Lucy should put the nail in that coffin. His potent contempt for infidelity ensured that he would never be unfaithful to his spouse, even if he had no illusions of receiving the same loyalty in return.

He imagined Isabelle with a new husband: building a life and a home, sharing a marriage bed, having children. He envisioned her round with another man's child. Panic clawed at his throat and he felt the mental equivalent to a horse kick in the sternum.

Marshall squeezed his eyes shut and drew several deep breaths. These were just feelings stirred by the unwise dalliance they'd indulged in, he assured himself. Once they were both safely married off to others, he would no longer feel a possessive compulsion to have her for himself.

Chapter Twelve

Isabelle had spent the week since Naomi's party in a numb haze. She and Lily attended several modest balls hosted by gentry or well-to-do professionals, although she had difficulty mustering enthusiasm for such affairs. A few gentlemen came to call upon Lily, and with Alex's wish that she marry never far from Isabelle's mind, she tried to pay attention to the men and catch someone's notice. Every moment was a conscious struggle not to think about Marshall and what had happened the last time they were together.

It would not do, she chided herself. She had to snap out of her melancholy and evict Marshall from her thoughts. Someday, she would marry again. She would have children. To achieve those goals, she had to get past her stupid infatuation with her former husband.

To make matters worse, Lily had been shamelessly prying at Isabelle about the time she'd spent alone with Marshall at the greenhouse. Isabelle couldn't bring herself to tell her the truth of the matter. While Lily knew about the whole, horrible debacle that had been Isabelle's marriage, she worried her friend would think less of her if she found out Isabelle had allowed herself to get so carried away with Marshall again. Her humiliation would be even deeper, given the fact that Marshall had an understanding with Lady Lucy Jamison—a fact Isabelle could not bear to dwell upon, but couldn't stop obsessing over.

This morning, she busied herself in her room writing a letter to Bessie about the upkeep of her small cottage. The house needed repairs, and figuring out the funds and suggesting workmen to complete the tasks proved to be a welcome preoccupation.

A joyful shriek sounded nearby, followed by a door slam, and feet pounding down the hall.

Isabelle dropped her pen. She pivoted in her seat as her door flew open and Lily burst into the room, breathing heavily, her face aglow.

"Lily!" Isabelle proclaimed, half-rising from her seat.

"You will never believe," Lily panted, "where we are going tonight." Her friend's expression bordered on beatific. Isabelle shook her head. "The theater, I thought. Has that changed?"

Lily nodded. "It has. Father's just told me we will be attending . . . ," she squealed.

Isabelle had never seen her friend so excited. She laughed at Lily's giddiness. "Out with it! Where are we going?"

Lily walked toward her as though in a trance, her hands extended before her. "We are going to the Liverpools' ball," she said, then clamped a hand over her mouth as though she couldn't believe she'd said it. Laughter bubbled forth, spilling from behind her hand as she jumped up and down like an excited child.

Isabelle gasped. "The Liverpools?" Lily nodded and grasped Isabelle's hands. "As in, the *Earl* of Liverpool? The prime minister?" Lily nodded again and another delighted squeal escaped her throat.

Isabelle exhaled a laugh. The Liverpools' ball would be teeming with the very *crème* of the *haut ton*—much grander than any event they had attended so far. "How can this be?" she asked, all agog.

"I don't know," Lily breathlessly replied. "I suppose because of Father's connections in government. He only said to 'make damned sure you wear your very finest.'" She furrowed her brows and rendered a passable imitation of her father's gruff voice.

"It's unbelievable." Isabelle turned in a circle and cast her eyes around the room, suddenly feeling like Cinderella with nothing to wear to the ball, and no hope of a fairy godmother to come to her aid. "Whatever shall we wear?"

Lily's eyes widened. "I don't know." She brought a hand to her cheek. "I wonder if I even own anything that'll pass muster in Lady Liverpool's ballroom."

Isabelle's mind whirled through a mental inventory of the dresses in her own wardrobe. None of them seemed good enough for what promised to be a glamorous affair. "Such short notice," she despaired. "Why couldn't we have received an invitation even yesterday?"

"Oh, bosh," Lily said, returning to her typical practicality. "That would have just been one day more to worry about it. Let's pick out something for you, and then you can help me decide."

The day passed in a flurry of activity as the girls, along with Mrs. Bachman, fussed and fretted, and lost themselves in preparations. Only Mr. Bachman retained his equanimity. He hid in his study from the frenzied women.

All too soon, the carriage pulled to the front of the house. Isabelle took one last appraising look in the mirror. She'd chosen a daring gown of violet satin that set off her green eyes to good effect. Her shoulders were bare, and the deep neckline showed rather more of her bosom than made her entirely comfortable. A small train swept elegantly behind her as she walked. While the dress was free of adornment, Lily said it was the picture of sophistication.

Around her neck hung her mother's amethysts, three modest, round stones surrounded by small diamonds and strung on a gold chain. The gems were nothing compared to the fortunes society's ladies draped themselves in, but they were priceless to Isabelle.

Lily's maid dressed her golden tresses in an elegant chignon, with a few curls teased loose to frame her face. She took one last look in the mirror and pressed her hands against her fluttering stomach. Then she took up her silver satin reticule with matching beading and went downstairs.

Lily and her parents waited in the entry hall. Isabelle's friend wore a dramatic red gown with jet beads in a floral pattern down the skirt. Isabelle could never carry off such a color, but it became Lily beautifully.

As they made their way to Lord Liverpool's home, Isabelle watched the dimly lit streetscape roll by. She listened with half an ear to the conversation in the carriage, but it didn't fully grab her attention until she heard Mr. Bachman say something, followed by a groan from Lily.

"What was that?" Isabelle turned her head.

Lily frowned. Her dark eyes regarded Isabelle with pity.

"I said," Mr. Bachman repeated, "when we arrive at the Liverpools', first thing after greeting the Earl and Countess, we must give our respect to Monthwaite. We owe our invitation to him."

Isabelle turned to look out the window again, so her kind host would not see her shock and dismay. How could she ever hope to put Marshall out of her mind when he wouldn't stop interfering in her life?

* * *

The Liverpools' ballroom was resplendent with the light of thousands of candles refracted in crystal chandeliers and reflected in dozens of mirrors. Swags of marigold and red cloth had been draped across the walls, and vases of exotic flowers lent their sultry perfume to the atmosphere. On the musician's balcony, two guitarists played a duet with a distinctive Spanish flair, barely audible over the noise of the crowd. When she commented upon the unusual theme, Mrs. Bachman told Isabelle that the whole affair was a benefit for the Peninsular army, which was in sore need of funds.

The Bachman group greeted the Earl and Countess of Liverpool, both of whom spoke graciously to Isabelle.

Their kindness, however, did little to mitigate her nerves. From the moment they were announced, Isabelle felt the eyes of the *haut ton* upon her. She noticed, too, that the Bachmans were sorely outclassed at this gathering. The lords and ladies dripped with as many titles as there were jewels on their necks and fingers. Mr. Bachman's considerable fortune meant little without an old name behind it. What on earth had Marshall been thinking, having them invited to such a gathering?

She spotted him a short distance away, talking with a small group of gentlemen. He laughed at something one of his companions said;

his boyish grin made her heart skip. Then his eyes found her, as though he'd felt her looking at him. He lifted his glass in silent greeting. Isabelle flushed, then nodded tersely. Mr. Bachman drew her away to introduce her to an old political crony, Lord Bantam.

The elderly gentleman held Isabelle's hand in a tight grip as he recounted the story of a bitter argument that had broken out in committee over dispensing tax revenues for a proposed hospital in Leeds. Isabelle fought to maintain a visage of interest.

"Ah," Lord Bantam said in his frail voice. His rheumy eyes wandered over Isabelle's shoulder. She turned to see Marshall standing just behind her. "Monthwaite! What do you make of this business with the Leeds hospital?"

Marshall schooled his face into a suitably thoughtful expression. "I've not formed an opinion yet, Bantam. Has it come back from committee?"

The old man once again launched into his florid complaint against the vile Whigs bleeding the country dry with their hospitals and the like. With her hand still trapped in Lord Bantam's vise-like grip, Isabelle cast a look of desperation at Marshall. He winked, with the faintest hint of a smile turning the corners of his mouth. Then he looked back to Lord Bantam, once again the picture of attentiveness.

When Lord Bantam's tale finally wound down in a fit of dry coughs, Isabelle escorted him to a couch and deposited him with two older ladies. The sound of his impassioned complaints against the young reformers in the Lords followed her back to the Bachman's group.

Mr. Bachman was shaking Marshall's hand, thanking him for procuring the invitation on their behalf.

"Please think nothing of it. With your permission," Marshall nodded to Mrs. Bachman to include her in his request, "I would like to introduce the ladies to some friends of mine."

Mrs. Bachman snapped her fan open and waved it furiously, stirring up a breeze that set her curls to wagging. "Certainly, Your Grace." She raised her eyebrows to her husband, clearly exuberant at the prospect of making an excellent match for Lily.

For her own part, Isabelle stared after Marshall when he'd gone to collect his gentlemen friends, feeling a little bewildered and stung. His motivation was obvious. She and the passionate afternoon they'd shared meant nothing. He'd just confirmed her fears; he wanted to foist her off on someone else.

Fine, she thought, lifting her chin. She'd known all along that their liaison had been a mistake made even more egregious by her knowledge of his understanding with Lady Lucy. Her whole purpose in being in London was to find a suitable husband. She might as well make the most of it. Marrying a nobleman would go a long way toward fully mending the breach between Alex and herself. No lady could complain about having Isabelle for a sister-in-law then.

Marshall returned with several gentlemen. Lord Freese was an exceedingly handsome man. With a quick smile accentuated by a scar on his cheek and his unruly, dark hair, he cut a rather dashing figure. He bowed over her hand and Lily's, and dropped a kiss onto the back of Mrs. Bachman's. The older lady blushed like a schoolgirl. Isabelle couldn't fault her response to the charming gentleman.

Where Marshall and Lord Freese were both dark complected, Viscount Woolsley was strikingly fair. He had hair so light, it was almost white. His silvery-blue eyes swept over Isabelle in a frank, appraising fashion. He was slender and much shorter than Marshall, but moved with a fluid grace that put her in mind of a serpent.

Finally, Lord Raimond shared none of those traits; rather, he was squat, portly, and balding. However, she saw right away why he was Marshall's friend. His outgoing, cheerful manner put her at ease. Soon he had them all laughing at a story about a hunt gone awry.

When the dancing began, Isabelle accepted Viscount Woolsley's invitation, while Lily paired with Lord Raimond. Lord Freese flirted outrageously with Mrs. Bachman and would hear nothing but that she *must* dance with him. Marshall, meanwhile, vanished into the crowd.

Shortly into the set, she spotted him dancing with an elegant, dark-haired beauty. Judging from the way her hand curled possessively around his shoulder, the woman could only be Lady Lucy. A sick feeling twisted Isabelle's middle; she suddenly shivered, despite the warm press of bodies all around.

"I do not quite have the measure of your relationship with Monthwaite," Viscount Woolsley said carefully, "but he seems to have you distracted." Isabelle's eyes snapped to his face. His hard eyes pierced right to the truth of the matter.

No good could come of being discovered mooning after the man who'd divorced her, or wounded by his attachment to another woman. She forced a cheerful laugh. "We have no relationship to speak of, my lord. It's true he caught my eye. I know almost no one else here."

"No great loss." The briefest of smiles flitted across his thin lips. His hand tightened at her waist as he led her through the steps of the dance. His movements were even more graceful than his normal stature suggested, every step neat and deliberate. He made Isabelle feel like a bumpkin, and she had always held dancing to be something at which she was reasonably accomplished.

When the set was over, he led her back to the Bachmans. "Enchanted, my dear." He bowed briefly, then left to find his next partner.

Isabelle watched him depart. She felt depleted, drained by his intensity. Even seeing Marshall deliver a cup of punch to Lady Lucy produced little more than a heartsick thud in her chest. She welcomed a few moments of standing quietly with Mrs. Bachman, greeting the wives of Mr. Bachman's political acquaintances. Then those moments stretched and multiplied. No other gentleman came to claim her hand for a dance. No lady sought her company.

More, she noticed the old, familiar whispers springing up again: women with their heads together in conversation, eyes cutting her way. Men regarded her more openly. Every guffaw she heard produced anxiety. Were they ridiculing her? She longed to see a friendly face among the *ton*, someone to show the others that she wasn't an infectious disease to be avoided and despised.

Lily had not yet returned. She and Lord Raimond stood near the bowl of champagne punch. Lily laughed at something he said. Isabelle turned, feeling conspicuously out of place. Through a clearing in the crowd, she saw Naomi.

The young woman held court among lady friends and gentlemen admirers. She spotted Isabelle and with a gesture invited her to join the group.

Crossing the distance between them proved more difficult than simply wading through the crowd. As the whispering around her grew louder, she realized her suspicions were correct. She caught snatches of phrases: "Poor Monthwaite," "made a fool of him," "light skirt," "an absolute nobody."

For all their petty bickering, backstabbing, and gossip, the *ton* behaved like a close-knit clan when it came to outsiders. Isabelle had cuckolded one of their own, one of their loftiest members. This was a very pointed reminder that she shouldn't have set foot in this ballroom. At present, she wished she were back at the George, back in her cozy cottage with Bessie—anywhere but here.

The room began to swim, and the voices all took on a far-away quality. She had to get out of here. It was beginning all over again—the laughter, the rumors, the hatred. She looked for a nearby exit. There wasn't one. She wanted to scream.

"Isabelle."

She blinked. Naomi stood just before her, offering Isabelle her hand. She reached for it like a drowning woman for a lifeline. The younger woman's grasp was warm and sure. Naomi nodded and drew Isabelle to her side, then turned to introduce Miss Fairfax to her group. Most of Naomi's friends were too young to have known Isabelle from her infamy as the temporary Duchess of Monthwaite. A smile flitted across the younger woman's lips as she met Isabelle's questioning look. Isabelle understood using her maiden name was Naomi's way of guarding her from speculation.

Soon, Isabelle relaxed with Naomi's friends. Despite her warm, easygoing manner, her former sister-in-law was the obvious leader of the group. Naomi flirted artlessly with the gentlemen. The young bucks nudged each other aside to stand closer to her. The girls all deferred to Naomi's opinions.

However, it wasn't long before older siblings and hawk-eyed mamas came to collect their younger charges, throwing dirty looks in Isabelle's direction, as though her mere proximity had sullied their hands.

"Well!" Naomi planted her fists on her hips as yet another friend was led away by her indignant mother.

Isabelle sighed. "I'm so sorry, Naomi. It was kind of you to try."

Behind Naomi, the crowd began to part to make way for Caro Lockwood. She was aimed straight for Isabelle and Naomi and looked like she'd enjoy nothing more than skinning Isabelle alive.

"What is it?" Naomi asked. "Your eyes are big as saucers."

"Your mother," Isabelle answered in a low voice. "Oh, God, I can't take this. Not now." She felt her own imminent demise approaching closer with each of Caro's steps. "Why did Marshall bring me here? Does he hate me so?"

"No." Naomi took Isabelle's hands in hers. "We wanted to thank you for your help at my party. We thought you'd enjoy the ball, Isabelle, that's all. It wasn't supposed to be this way!"

Isabelle gaped at the girl. Were they all mad? How could it have been any other way? Other than her sullied reputation as a divorcée, Isabelle was mostly unremarkable among the gentry. But in this crowd, she was a walking target for gossip and vitriol. Maybe Isabelle was the mad one, to think she could ever be forgiven or accepted.

Caro halted just behind her daughter. "Naomi!"

Isabelle became acutely aware of the circle of space around them, as onlookers lapped up the scene.

"Mama!" Naomi turned with a smile on her face, as though nothing in the world was amiss. "Isn't this the loveliest party? Lord Liverpool is usually so dull, but this turned out to be quite a success, don't you think? We must congratulate Lady Liverpool."

"Young lady," Caro hissed, "do not be glib with me, not when I find you fraternizing with this . . . creature." Her hard eyes turned on Isabelle.

Isabelle's feet turned to ice. She swallowed, trying ineffectually to think of something to say to counter her former mother-in-law's *hauteur*.

"I beg your pardon, Your Grace." The eyes of all three women went to the man who'd appeared beside them. Viscount Woolsley bowed to Caro and then greeted Naomi. "Forgive my intrusion, but I wondered if the duchess could be persuaded away for the dinner waltz?" His face betrayed no pretense, but Isabelle could have kissed the man for swooping to her rescue.

"Certainly, my lord," she said.

The dowager visibly seethed, but said nothing as Lord Woolsley led Isabelle to the waltz.

This dance with the viscount came more easily, as Isabelle was familiar with his own particular gait and matched hers to his.

She leaned her head closer to her rescuer. He inclined his as well, the barest hint of humor touching his eyes. "I suppose it comes as no surprise to hear you saved me from a most unpleasant encounter, my lord."

"Really?" His pale eyes glinted. "And here I thought I was stealing you away from something of a family reunion. Your former mother-in-law's regard for you is legendary."

Isabelle flushed at his jibe.

He squeezed her waist. "I'm afraid I've caused you a new problem, however."

"What do you mean?"

"This is our second dance," he said gravely. "People will talk."

At that, Isabelle could not help but throw her head back and laugh. "My lord," she said when she'd recovered herself, "if people did *not* talk about me, I should be forced to conclude I'd died and gone to heaven. Being the object of gossip is nothing new. If the worst people can comment upon is two sets with a gentleman, I shall consider myself lucky."

Viscount Woolsley's eyes widened slightly. "You do not mind being the object of salacious gossip?"

Isabelle scoffed. "Of course I mind! But what's to be done? The *ton* ripped me to shreds years ago. If they want to work themselves up over the scraps of my reputation now, there is little I can do."

Viscount Woolsley's eyes softened at the corners and his lips turned up at one side. "What a remarkably refreshing attitude. Might I come to call tomorrow?"

* * *

"Viscount Woolsley?" Alexander had finally arrived in town after being detained by some difficulties at Fairfax Hall. He accepted a glass of sherry from the Bachmans' butler and waited for the man to shut the parlor door. Then a wide grin spread across his face. "That's wonderful, Isa! We couldn't ask for better. No duke, to be sure, but still, a viscount is nothing to sniff at." He clapped Isabelle on the shoulder as though she were one of his male friends. "Are you sure?" he asked. "Shall I be expecting a visit from him?"

Isabelle plastered on a bright smile for her brother's benefit. "Let's not get ahead of ourselves, but I believe he is not without regard. He's been to call twice in the last week, and this afternoon he's taking me for a ride."

"Ha!" Pride beamed from his eyes. "Well done, little sister." He tossed back the rest of his drink and relaxed into the sofa cushions. "You don't know how relieved I am to hear this. I don't mind saying now that I was becoming nervous, with you still unattached."

Isabelle flinched. Her brother's thoughtless words reminded her how undesirable she was to society. She should be as thrilled as Alex that she'd managed to interest someone like Lord Woolsley.

But she wasn't.

The things Woolsley could provide for her—a good name, children, a home of her own—were enticing. The man himself, however, did little for her. Something about him unsettled her, and not in the happy way she remembered from her courtship with Marshall.

"Why are you frowning?"

Isabelle looked up to see Alexander studying her intently. "Was I?" Her smile clicked back into place.

"Isa . . . " Her own name became a word of warning. "Don't muck this up. You'll continue to encourage Lord Woolsley's attentions, and you will accept him when he offers for you, which could very well be at Montwaite's musicale this Saturday."

She looked down at her hands and nodded. "I know, Alex," she said softly.

Chapter Thirteen

The musicale at Marshall's Grosvenor Square house began well enough—it was the end that became the talk of high society for days afterward.

Isabelle descended from the stuffy confines of the carriage and patted her upswept hair, making sure it had not come loose as a result of the unusual bout of heat and humidity. A footman escorted Alexander and Isabelle to a salon at the rear of the house, where fifty guests mingled around the perimeter of the room. Rows of padded chairs occupied the room's middle, and a large, dark pianoforte stood front and center.

Instinctively she sought out Marshall. She spotted him across the room at the same time as Alex. Her brother steered her toward their host.

Marshall shook Alex's hand and bowed over Isabelle's. By now she expected the near-palpations his touch induced, but enduring the sensation never became easier.

He released her slowly, their fingertips lingering in whisper-light contact. "You look well this evening, Isabelle."

"As do you, Your Grace." The understatement of the century.

In his evening attire, he was a vision of sophisticated masculinity. The fine cut of his black coat emphasized his broad shoulders, while the gold buttons marching down his waistcoat invited her gaze to follow them to his close-fitting trousers. Her mouth went dry at the briefest glimpse of his lean, muscled thighs clad in black. She jerked her eyes back to his before he caught her gawking at his physique.

When he inclined his head to look down at her, his jaw brushed against the standing collar of his waistcoat. Isabelle fought the urge to lay her hand on that beloved face. Instead, she twisted her fingers into her skirt.

"Monty," said a female voice, "aren't you going to introduce me?"

The corners of his eyes tightened and his lips firmed. He stepped back from Isabelle and turned to the speaker.

Seeing her from a distance in a crowded ballroom did nothing to prepare Isabelle for the shock of meeting Lady Lucy face to face. The beauty at Marshall's side took Isabelle's breath away. She had lustrous sable hair, high cheekbones, and eyes of the most interesting aqua color. Her gown of midnight blue satin was adorned with shimmering gold embroidery across the bodice and down the skirt.

In comparison, Isabelle felt hopelessly frumpy in her diaphanous white muslin and coffee-colored sash.

"Lady Lucy Jamison," Marshall said, "Mrs. Lockwood."

Isabelle cringed inwardly. She hated hearing Marshall call her Mrs. Lockwood. It was his family name, divested of meaning. It simply labeled her as his castoff and was only mildly preferable to him calling her Duchess. Had she no name, no identity of her own?

Shame engulfed her from head to toe. Being presented to the woman who would take her place as Marshall's duchess was nearly beyond enduring. Yet, if she were to marry Lord Woolsley, Isabelle would move in the same circles as they. She must adapt to seeing them together. Somehow, she summoned the strength to acknowledge the introduction.

Lady Lucy raised her chin and turned her lips in a satisfied smirk. She laid her hand on Marshall's forearm.

Isabelle's first impulse was to swat those bejeweled fingers off his arm. It was no surprise Naomi deplored a potential union between her brother and the calculating Lucy Jamison. The woman seemed cold. Yet, no one could deny she also possessed every quality Marshall's wife should have. She came from a noble family, if one of only middling fortune and influence; it was still far greater status than the Fairfaxes could claim. Lucy had been groomed from girlhood to marry high. The duties of a society hostess would come easily to her. Marshall deserved a duchess from his world, one who wouldn't be a constant source of embarrassment. So, while Isabelle sympathized with Naomi's plight, she could see no way to justifiably interfere.

Besides, she thought glumly, she was here to convince Lord Woolsley to offer for her, not to pine after her former husband.

"Ah." Marshall gestured to a man passing by. "Herr Kaufman, a moment. He will be playing for us tonight," Marshall explained. "We're most fortunate he's agreed to join us."

The man inclined his head to acknowledge the compliment. "I am always delighted to share the work of my compatriot." His English was quite good, but carried a heavy German accent.

"Who is your compatriot, sir?" Alexander asked.

Kaufman spread his hands. "Herr Beethoven, of course."

A cool hand touched Isabelle's elbow. She turned to see Viscount Woolsley just behind her. She hadn't noticed his approach at all; her senses had been tuned to Marshall.

"What selection will you play, sir?" Woolsley asked. His pale eyes found Isabelle's, and a faint smile touched his lips.

She smiled brightly in return, clamping down on the panic rising in her middle.

The pianist warmed to his subject, and his face became more animated as he spoke. "The twenty-sixth sonata for pianoforte, *Les Adieux*. It is a newer piece, published but two years ago."

"I've not heard it." Isabelle remarked as she surreptitiously pulled her arm out of Woolsley's grasp. "I look forward to your performance."

She glanced at Marshall. He stood stock still with Lady Lucy's fingers curving over his arm, but he maintained a polite distance between them. Though his face was schooled into a placid expression, the unrest in his eyes was palpable.

Isabelle hid her frown as she contemplated that look. What could one of the most powerful men in England have to be displeased about? He had a beautiful woman on his arm, the crème of society in his home, and his botanical studies to occupy his mind. With everything a man could possibly want, why did he look as though someone was twisting a knife in his gut?

With a gentle tug at her elbow, Lord Woolsley drew her away. She lifted her chin and told herself not to pity Marshall Lockwood. He didn't need it.

Soon, the assembled guests found their seats. Marshall sat in the front row, with Lady Lucy on his left. Isabelle sat several rows back with her brother and Woolsley. A hush fell over the audience as Herr Kaufman lowered himself to the plush bench at his instrument. He raised his hands; his fingers hovered a breath's width above the ivory keys. As the movement progressed, Herr Kaufman persuaded his instrument to convey sounds of pained longing and guarded happiness through passages that were by turn heart wrenching and exhilarating.

Her eyes settled on Marshall's back. Lady Lucy leaned against him to whisper in his ear. Isabelle's chest tightened at the intimate gesture. But then—hope! Marshall waved her away like an annoying fly, just as the movement ended with two strong chords. Isabelle exhaled a sigh of relief.

The second movement was more poignant even than the first. Discordant notes interjected throughout the sweeter passages struck to the very core of her own rather precarious situation. No matter how she tried to arrange her life in a semblance of ordered civility, she was tripped by new, unhappy hurdles: her divorce, her exile in the cottage, her impending marriage to a man she did not love. It was as though Herr Kaufman—and Beethoven before him—put her woes to music for all the world to hear.

At the end of the frenzied third movement, less than twenty minutes after his fingers first touched the keys, Herr Kaufman stood to receive his applause. Isabelle joined with the rest of Marshall's guests in enthusiastic appreciation of the man's virtuosity.

The guests began to migrate into other rooms for refreshments and cards. She startled at the cool breath that ghosted over the back of her neck.

"You're pale, my dear," Woolsley's brow creased in concern. Maybe being married to him wouldn't be so bad after all, she thought dejectedly.

"I'm all right." Isabelle waved a dismissive hand. "Just a touch lightheaded. It's quite warm."

Woolsley led her through the French doors at the back of the room and out onto the balcony. Still dazed from the overwhelming musical experience, Isabelle accompanied him to the far end, beyond the light spilling from the music room. The air outside was only marginally cooler than inside, but at least a faint breeze stirred the tepid atmosphere.

They stood in silence for a short time. Isabelle's mind replayed bits of the music over and over. "It was a lovely performance, don't you think, my lord?"

"Nyle," he replied.

She furrowed her brow. "What does the sonata have to do with Egypt?"

"My given name is Nyle."

The next instant his hands were on her waist and he was pulling her close. Isabelle's heart beat against her ribs like a bird trying to escape its cage.

"May I call you Isabelle, Duchess?"

She detected a mocking note in his voice, but nodded and made a sound of agreement. He pressed cool lips to her cheek then grazed her jaw. She closed her eyes and tipped her head back to accept his kiss.

The mechanics of the kiss were similar to those she'd shared with Marshall. But it *felt* completely different. There was no warmth in her blood at Woolsley's touch, no fire in her belly—only a cold fist slowly closing around her heart.

When he broke away from their embrace, however, Lord Woolsley—Nyle, she reminded herself—gave a lazy grin. He traced her collarbone with a gloved finger. "You're exceedingly lovely, Isabelle."

"Thank you. Nyle," she added.

"We suit admirably," he said in a low voice, while his hand slid down to splay across her bottom.

She nodded quickly. "Oh, yes. Admirably."

He cupped her face with his free hand and bent to kiss her neck.

This time, she could not contain the shudder that coursed up her spine. Could she really endure his touch for the rest of her days? It was unthinkable. She suddenly envisioned herself with chronic headaches springing up just after dinner every night until she died. Or he died. Or they both died of fatal unhappiness.

"A shiver of delight?" His voice grated against her throat. "It pleases me to see you so affected." He straightened and fixed his concentrated gaze on her. "I believe there is something we should discuss."

This was it. She drew her shoulders back, steeling herself to accept his proposal.

Woolsley, however, resumed his onslaught of caresses. His pelvis rocked provocatively against her hip.

His touch made her skin crawl. "If you wish to talk, Nyle," she said, "perhaps you should release me. It's difficult to attend your words with you behaving so . . ." She would have liked to say "abominably," but bit her tongue just before offending her would-be fiancé.

"Passionately, darling?" He kneaded his fingers into the back of her neck. "I'm having trouble concentrating, too. You heat my blood."

She had trouble believing that. The glints of moonlight reflecting on his eyes looked like ice.

"I am most gratified to know you feel the same." His teeth nipped painfully into her neck.

Isabelle gasped. She disengaged herself from his arms and took a couple steps back. "Talk, my lord, you wanted to talk."

Behind Isabelle, someone on the other side of the balcony coughed loudly. She turned her head at the sound, but her attention immediately returned to the viscount when he snatched her hands.

Lord Woolsley chuckled. "I see I've alarmed you, m'dear. Or are you feigning modesty?" He squeezed her hands a little too firmly to be reassuring. "Let us be frank. You're an experienced woman. Monthwaite undoubtedly taught you well."

Heat rose in her cheeks. She was glad for the shadows concealing her discomfiture. Though her familiarity with the matter was limited, this was the strangest prelude to a marriage proposal Isabelle had ever heard of. "I confess I find myself at a loss for words, sir. Nyle."

"It's not Sir Nyle." He furrowed his brow and pressed his middle finger to his forehead. "My point is," his voice once again clipped and precise, "you, my love, are no fresh virgin on the marriage mart. Neither are you a widow with a fortune to attract a new husband."

Her tongue recoiled from the metallic taste of mortification. She swallowed hard and spoke through tight lips. "That does seem to be the situation in which I find myself."

"However," he said in a gentler tone, "you're a beautiful female. T'would be a crime to let your youth pass by unappreciated." He raised her fingers to his mouth and kissed the tip of each, then pressed her hands against his chest, pinning them beneath his own. "Isabelle." He spoke her name gravely; his eyes bored into her like twin ice picks.

She drew a breath and held it.

"I would like to offer you my protection."

His protection? She continued holding her breath. Wasn't there supposed to be more to a proposal? Making him the happiest of men, doing him the honor, he'd talk to her brother as soon as possible? But the viscount stood there impassively, seemingly at the end of his speech. She exhaled.

"Your protection?" She frowned in confusion. "What do you mean, your pro—" As the words left her lips, his meaning hit her like a bolt of lightning. She gasped; her hand flew to her gaping mouth. Isabelle staggered back, the full import of his suggestion settling upon her. "I cannot believe this," she finally stammered.

"Believe it, darling." Lord Woolsley stalked toward her. "There will be a house for you to live in while our arrangement holds. A generous quarterly allowance. An outpouring of gifts if you please me." The moonlight gleamed against his wolfish grin. "All I ask of you is an open door and a warm bed."

For a fraction of a moment, Isabelle's shocked mind desperately wondered whether Alex would want her to accept Woolsley's offer. He wanted her off his hands, but never this way.

"My lord!" She drew herself up, shaking off the shock with a toss of her head. "You misunderstand me. I am overcome with disbelief, but not in the way you think. I will not be your mistress." She lifted her chin. "I'm a divorced woman, not a whore."

Lord Woolsley breathed a laugh. "There's not much difference, my dear. Think it over. When you come to your senses, let me know."

His words were delivered with such cool, indifferent disdain; they poured over her like icy water. He reached inside his coat and withdrew a cigar case, selected one, and returned the case to his inner pocket. Viscount Woolsley lit his cigar, took a few puffs, then kissed her hand and walked away.

She didn't turn to watch him go. She couldn't move. She felt rooted to the very spot on which she stood, the location of her lowest humiliation to date. Isabelle had endured many things the last several years, but never had anyone vocalized such a low estimation of her morality to her face.

She stared blankly at the balustrade, wondering what on earth she was going to tell Alex.

The sound of shouting snapped her out of her reverie. A woman screamed. She took a few steps and rounded the corner of the house. The sight that greeted her was like another icy dunk.

Viscount Woolsley was flat on his back on the balcony. Marshall knelt over him, delivering blow after punishing blow and shouting obscenities. Lord Woolsley attempted to fend off Marshall's fists, but the larger man had the advantage and it was clear Woolsley might not be conscious much longer. A group of ladies stood a short distance behind, ogling the scene in wide-eyed interest. A crowd was quickly gathering at the French doors.

"Marshall, stop!" Isabelle cried, lifting her skirts and sprinting to the site of the brawl. Grabbing his arm proved to be as effective as swatting at a rolling boulder. She rounded to his left side, where that hand was holding the hapless viscount against the stone. Woolsley's cigar smoldered a couple feet away; its earthy-sweet smoke reached diaphanous fingers into the air. Isabelle knelt beside the raging man, and laid a trembling hand on his shoulder.

"Marshall," she pleaded, "please stop."

Amazingly, he paused with his fist drawn back by his ear. He turned to look at her, his eyes wild with fury. "I heard him." Marshall's jaw jutted out defensively. "I heard what he said." He drew a ragged breath. "He can't say that about you. I won't allow it!"

With a sneer of disgust, he looked down at Lord Woolsley. "You hear that, you miserable bit of excrement?" His voice went frighteningly quiet. "You will not speak that way ever again, even if I have to rip the tongue out of your skull to make sure of it." For a final time, his fist connected with Woolsley's nose with a sickening crunch of bone and cartilage.

Woolsley groaned as blood oozed from his nostrils. Then his pale eyes rolled back in his head an instant before his eyelids fell closed.

Isabelle blanched at the sight of the man's pummeled face, already swelling and bruising in places. Marshall sat down heavily on his defeated opponent and turned to her, his face contorted with wrath. Instinctively, she fell on her bottom and scooted backward, putting distance between herself and that solid mass of unrestrained vengeance. When her back touched the brick wall, she drew her knees against her chest.

Marshall rose and stalked toward her; the heels of his impeccably polished boots tapped softly against the flagstones. Without a word, he reached out. Isabelle eyed his hand warily before tentatively placing her own upon it. He pulled her to her feet and searched her face. His temper was cooling, she was relieved to see. The lines creasing his brow softened, although the set of his jaw remained firm.

"Come with me." The steely edge to his voice brooked no argument. Isabelle nodded once, still mute with shock.

His eyes flicked to the door and leveled a hard gaze on the assembled onlookers. "Out," Marshall growled. The group drew back and cast nervous glances at one another. "Out!" he yelled. Several dozen aristocrats scattered like a flock of pigeons to summon their servants and carriages.

A liveried footman stood just inside the music room with a tray of champagne, doing a passable imitation of statuary. Marshall called him and nudged the unconscious viscount with his foot. "See Lord Woolsley to his carriage." The servant hopped to action, setting the tray of drinks on a stand before scurrying off.

With his hand still clamped around hers, Marshall led her back into the house. Isabelle's frayed nerves wreaked havoc on her stomach while she wondered what he intended.

They plowed through the crowd of evicted guests loitering in the entrance hall. Tonnish men and women tripped over themselves to move out of his way. Isabelle found herself on the receiving end of openly speculative stares. She grimaced and kept her eyes downcast. As they passed, murmurs sprang up in their wake. Undoubtedly, this spectacularly ruined evening would be all the talk for the foreseeable future.

Alexander fell into step on Isabelle's other side. "Monthwaite," he said in a low voice, "what the devil—"

Marshall cut him off. "Not now." They came upon Caro, Grant, and Naomi; Marshall gathered them up with a jerk of his chin. The youngest

Lockwood sibling turned her startled eyes on Isabelle and raised her brows. Isabelle shook her head—she had no better idea than Naomi what was happening. Caro paused to whisper at Lady Lucy before joining them. Lucy shot a murderous glare at Isabelle.

The group moved away from the crowd of guests and their baffled clamor. Marshall halted at the library and opened the door. "Inside, please."

Isabelle searched his face, but found no clues in his features, once again perfectly composed and unreadable. Only a tightness at the corners of his eyes betrayed any emotion whatsoever. With a deep breath and a sense of impending unpleasantness, she filed into the library with the others.

Chapter Fourteen

Marshall poured himself a brandy from the decanter in the library. He took a sip of the amber liquor, savoring the clean burn as it went down. He drew a deep breath and exhaled slowly.

He hadn't gotten into a brawl since he and Grant were in the schoolroom at Helmsdale Hall. *It wasn't a brawl*, he reminded himself. He'd attacked Woolsley, who never saw it coming—and Marshall had relished every moment of it, much to his chagrin.

But he deserved it. It had been bad enough to stand just around the corner from them, knowing another man was touching Isabelle, kissing her. Marshall felt himself getting irate again when he thought about how, after pressing his affections upon her, Woolsley had debased Isabelle with his tawdry offer. He flexed his right hand and winced at the throbbing pain in his knuckles.

One thing that crystallized in his mind with absolute certainty was that his life had been irrevocably changed out there on the balcony. Doubts and hesitations, the things he'd tried to convince himself he wanted, had all been swept away in that terrible moment.

He took another fortifying swallow of his drink. Then he turned around.

Five faces registering varying degrees of shock watched him.

Isabelle sat between her brother and Naomi on the sofa. Her beautiful green eyes were wide, and she looked ready to bolt for the door. Tight bands constricted around Marshall's chest when he saw her alarm. He wanted to toss the rest of them out on their collective ear, carry Isabelle to bed, and begin making up for lost time.

Caro perched in an armchair facing the sofa, but her seething face was turned away from the Fairfaxes, refusing to acknowledge their presence. Grant stood behind their mother's chair with his hands thrust into his pockets, his shoulders hunched forward, tense.

Alexander Fairfax's jaw moved side to side, banked fury evident in every taut muscle.

Oddly, of the entire group, only Naomi seemed perfectly at ease, as though the situation did not surprise or unsettle her in the least. *Poor thing.* She had no idea what all the hullabaloo was about.

It seemed everyone could use a drink. He poured brandies for the men and wine for the ladies.

Alexander caught his eye when Marshall handed him a glass. "I don't suppose you'd like to tell us what this is about, Monthwaite."

With a dull thud, Caro's fist slammed against the upholstered arm of her chair. "You will not address your superior so familiarly."

"Sod off, Your Grace," Alexander retorted with a sneer.

The dowager duchess' mouth fell open.

Alexander jerked his chin toward Marshall. "Were it not for your damned son's lunatic behavior, we would all be enjoying a pleasant evening right now."

"Now see here, Fairfax," Grant interjected. "Mind your tongue around my mother before I mind it for you."

A shouting match between the three erupted, with Fairfax accusing the Lockwoods of all manner of duplicity and dishonor. At one point, he called Caro a snake in the grass.

Showing true Lockwood spirit, Caro and Grant railed against the collective immorality of the Fairfax family, referring to them as peasants and gold-digging opportunists.

Marshall and Isabelle's gazes met. She rolled her eyes. He gave her a wry smile and walked behind the couch to lean between her and his sister.

"Naomi, you should go now."

His sister smoothed the skirt of her salmon gown. "No." She shook her head. "I don't believe I should." She sipped her wine and smiled her sweet, sisterly smile. Two feet away, Alex Fairfax leapt to his feet, pointed at the dowager duchess, and called her a hateful old hag.

Marshall ground his teeth. "This is getting out of hand. It's no place for you."

Naomi raised her face and breathed deeply, as though drinking in fresh country air, oblivious to the animosity flying over their heads. "To the contrary. Here I am with my mother," she gestured serenely to the irate Caro, "my brothers," she nodded to Grant, whose face had long since gone red with the force of his yelling, "my sister." She patted Isabelle on the leg. "Oh!" She covered her mouth in false embarrassment. "My *former* sister. And her beloved brother. Where should I be," she concluded, "if not in the bosom of my loving family?" She sipped her wine again, as calmly as if it were her afternoon tea.

Isabelle exhaled a small laugh. "Let her stay."

He opened his mouth to argue. Isabelle cut him off with a hand and leveled her gaze on him. "She's not a child." She arched a brow in a manner that drove home the resemblance between her and her brother. "Don't treat her as one."

Taking Isabelle's words to heart, he looked at his sister, and really saw her, perhaps for the first time in years. She not only had all the beauty and dewy youth that had kept him hovering protectively over her all Season, but also sharp intelligence behind her blue eyes. A little girl no more—his sister would soon be a formidable woman in her own right.

He nodded, granting Naomi permission to remain. Isabelle needed all the allies in this room Marshall could give her, after all. Then he straightened and raised a hand for silence. The feuding parties ignored him.

"Enough!" His voice cracked like a bullwhip. The warring parties fell silent, turning the combined force of their angry glares upon him. He met their stares head on; it was his turn.

"Why are we here?" Alex demanded again.

"What was the meaning of that shameful display? You'll be lucky if Woolsley doesn't bring charges against you." Strands of Caro's silver hair had fallen loose from her coif. Her lips were tight, and her eyes puffy. He was struck by how age was rapidly catching up with her. "And you'll be fortunate if Lady Lucy will still have you, after that unbecoming scene."

He answered calmly, "Whether or not Lady Lucy will have me is no longer of any import."

Caro's mouth fell open and she made a stricken sound.

"There were no promises made," he said. "I regret disappointing Lucy's hopes, but that is as it must be. I've come to the realization that the divorce was a terrible mistake."

Isabelle's startled eyes captured his. He could drown in those eyes; he wanted to. A lump of emotion formed in his throat and he drew a shuddering breath.

When he spoke, his voice was husky. "Isabelle, I stand here in front of you and our families to beg your forgiveness."

She eyed him warily.

"What are you doing?" Caro said in a rush. "I saw—"

He frowned, annoyed at the interruption. "I know what you think you saw, but you're wrong. What you witnessed that day was not infidelity."

His attention returned to Isabelle. "You were injured, just as you said. And I injured you further with the divorce." That awful word burned his tongue like acid. He threw back the remainder of his drink.

Isabelle opened her mouth as though to speak and then pressed her lips together again. He could tell she was not convinced.

"Marsh, are you sure you know what you're about?" Grant pointed an accusing finger at Isabelle. "She was in another man's arms. Mother saw them! How can you doubt it?" His brow furrowed in confusion.

Though it would make convincing the others easier, Marshall wouldn't compromise Isabelle by revealing the discovery of her unevenly healed rib. He shrugged. "I'm asking you to trust me, Grant."

"She knows the truth."

Marshall turned. Isabelle's gaze was fixed on Caro, whose face blanched to resemble thin parchment. "She was there at Hamhurst when I was still in the bed with my ribs wrapped. She talked to the doctor, even, but still accused Justin and me of carrying on."

Caro's eyes narrowed and she fidgeted in her seat.

Isabelle's voice raised in anger. "She didn't tell you that, did she, because she didn't want you to believe I'd been hurt!" Her fists were white-knuckled balls in her lap. "She preferred the public spectacle of a divorce to our marriage," she concluded with a bitter laugh.

Marshall started to ask Caro for confirmation, but the truth was written all over her features. At least she had the sense to keep her eyes downcast. Cold anger at his own mother's evil betrayal wrapped around his spine.

His hand tapped against his thigh as his mother squirmed under his intense glare. How could she? This treachery was even worse than he'd feared. It was bad enough thinking she'd misjudged what she saw, but she'd known the truth and twisted it into a vile falsehood. The edges of his vision went red.

"I will deal with you later," he swore through clenched teeth. Caro swallowed, her eyes wide.

With a considerable force of will, Marshall pushed his anger aside and set his glass on an end table. Tonight was for Isabelle, he reminded himself. All else must wait. He crouched in front of her and took her hands. Although they were cold and trembling against his palms, her face was remarkably calm. A fresh wave of admiration for her courage washed over him. This Season had been difficult for her, yet she'd thrown herself into the maelstrom of society with grace and dignity.

"I wish it had never happened," he murmured. "I need you to forgive me, Isabelle. It was all a horrible, wretched mistake."

Her green eyes softened. The corners of her mouth turned upward just the slightest bit.

"Apologies are well and good," Alex snapped.

Isabelle's face went flat, and Marshall saw the minutiae of ground he'd gained slip away.

"But, I don't believe you understand the full import of what this divorce has meant to my family." Alexander's words bristled with frustration bordering on anger.

Marshall found himself in the awkward position of looking up at his former brother-in-law. He cleared his throat and stood then gestured for Fairfax to continue.

Alex propped his elbow on the arm of the sofa and rested his jaw against his fist. "Because of your divorce, my sister was finally forced into anonymous exile, no longer fit for polite company. As you know," he continued, inclining his fair head, "she was reduced to employment in an inn to support herself."

Behind Marshall, Caro made a sound of disgust.

"Only because you cut her off," Marshall retorted. "What kind of a brother—"

"I would never have done so," Alex returned, his voice rising in intensity, "had you not been so bloody precise in your accusations. I read all about my sister's immoral conduct in the news sheets, Monthwaite. How d'you suppose that felt? What was I to believe? After a few years of everyone telling me Isabelle was a shameless adulteress, what would you expect?"

Marshall's eyes flicked guiltily to Naomi sitting steadfast at Isabelle's side. He would never do such a thing to her. Would he?

"Additionally," Alex said, "my sister's divorce has been an impediment in my own life. Believe it or not, Monthwaite, even lowly commoners such as myself aspire to marriage and children, but no decent woman will have me because of the scandal hanging over us like a pall." He made a popping sound with his lips. "I'm sure you can see my predicament." He gestured with both his hands. "Your words are like so much piffle, for all the good they do us. My sister came to London this Season to procure a respectable husband and ease the strain on our family." He lifted an ironic brow. "That worked out well, didn't it? You've seen for yourself how the world treats us. And you're *sorry?*"

Anger, guilt, and frustration ate away at Marshall. Hot breath whooshed from his nostrils. He looked from Alex's furious face to Isabelle's heartbreakingly resigned one. Alex was right. Marshall's ugly divorce had made a muck of their lives. It hadn't been enough to try to surreptitiously help Isabelle find a husband—though it had nearly been the death of him to see her with another man. He wished he could have another go at Woolsley's face for what he'd done, but it proved Alex's point that society would not accept the Fairfaxes.

He had to do more.

"I'll apologize publicly," he said.

Behind him, Caro gasped. "You'll do no such thing! Think of the scandal! Son, I forbid you to pursue such a reckless course—"

He rounded on her, his face a cold mask. "I'm the head of this family. You will not and cannot forbid me anything."

She startled as though he'd struck her; her eyes immediately filled with tears. Pressing a fist to her lips, she turned her face away. A pang shot through him, but he couldn't afford to capitulate to Caro's desires in the matter. Doing so in the past was one of the causes of all this grief.

Caro inhaled to compose herself and opened her mouth.

"No more." Marshall slowly shook his head. "You've done quite enough."

She bared her teeth in a snarl. "All I have ever done," she clamped onto the arms of her chair with a talon-like grip, her voice rising in fervor, "has been for the good of this family. But you refuse to see it. Understanding fails me when it comes to your unfathomable infatuation with this half-French nobody! No fortune, no name, no breeding, no connections, and more deficiencies than I can count."

"Out!" Marshall roared, rage pounding in his ears. His breath came in hot, labored pants. "And if you so much as think another maligning word against Isabelle, so help me—"

He forced his lips back together before he said something unforgivable.

Caro stood and twitched her black skirts behind her. "Come, Naomi," she said, her narrowed eyes on Marshall. "You and I shall remove to the dower house. This one is beginning to reek of the unwashed."

She exited the room only slightly faster than her normal, stately pace. Naomi gave Marshall a questioning look. He nodded. "It's your decision. This is still your home."

Naomi smiled gratefully. She squeezed Isabelle's hand and then followed her mother, leaving Marshall and Grant with the Fairfax siblings.

Marshall took several deep breaths until his blood pressure returned to something approaching normal.

"Grant, would you excuse us?"

"Actually," Isabelle said, rising from the sofa, "I'd like to go now. Please take me home, Alex."

No! She couldn't leave now—not after he'd just done battle on her behalf. "There are things we must discuss."

She shook her head. "Everyone's said quite enough tonight. I accept your apology." The smile she gave him was strained. "I can't tell you how long I've waited to hear it. But now that I have . . ." One slender shoulder shrugged.

Alex offered his arm.

She pinned Marshall with a weary look. "Please don't issue me any more invitations. They aren't good for either of us."

Marshall bit back a growl of frustration. Why was she suddenly so *blasé*? If he could just get her alone, he could talk some sense into her— or kiss some sense into her, should talking fail.

As they reached the door, Marshall called, "Fairfax! Please, a word." Alex murmured something to Isabelle. She nodded and continued down the hall, while Alex remained in the library.

"Grant." Marshall jerked his chin to the door. His brother's jaw tightened, but he nodded and left the two men alone.

Alex stood in the middle of the room, hands deep in his pockets. "Monthwaite?"

"With your permission, I'd like to call on Isabelle." Alex raised an eyebrow, but otherwise gave no response. Both men knew such a request was as good as a declaration of courtship. Marshall couldn't hold back a short, bitter laugh at the irony of having to request to court the woman to whom he'd already been married.

"Considering what Isabelle just said," Alex finally replied, "I don't think that would be wise." He pulled a hand from his pocket and rubbed the flat of his palm against his jaw.

Marshall grimaced at the knowledge that Isabelle's brother found him unworthy of her. "I understand." But he didn't. Being found lacking by others was a new experience. He despised it. Yes, he'd done wrong, but he would fix everything.

Fairfax turned to leave again.

"I meant what I said—I'm going to apologize," Marshall stated. The other man slowly pivoted to face him. "If that's not enough, if Isabelle still won't see me, I want to make amends. Her settlement, from our marriage contract," he touched his fingertips to his chest "I want her to have it."

Fairfax's jaw slackened. "The money, you mean?"

Marshall nodded.

"A quarter million pounds, if memory serves?"

Marshall nodded again.

Alex's eyes narrowed suspiciously. "Why not write a draft for it now?"

"Ah." Marshall smiled briefly. "I'd like to have the chance to give it to her properly."

Fairfax's brow shot up. "You mean to marry her, then?"

The thought of marriage still made him skittish; but marry he must, and it might as well be to the only woman he'd ever thought of as his wife. "We were off to a good start. And it seems like the right thing to do, after all the trouble I've caused."

"I don't know if she'll have you," Alex answered. "And I won't make her."

"Of course not." Marshall shook his head. "But I'd like to try."

Alex rocked back on his heels. "All right, then. All the money in the world won't make us respectable if people still believe she's an adulteress. Clear her name, Monthwaite, and then we'll talk about rides in the park."

Marshall extended his hand, hope sparking within him. "Fair enough."

Chapter Fifteen

Isabelle grimaced at her reflection in the mirror. She looked like a half-dead rat the cat dragged in. Dark circles hung under her eyes like carpetbags, and her lids were puffy. Despite having slept hours later than normal, she felt like she hadn't slept in a week.

She picked up her brush from the vanity and made a half-hearted attempt at working through her bedraggled tresses. Encountering a tangle, she struggled against it until tiny beads of sweat popped out on her forehead; she slammed the brush down with a curse. Would it really bankrupt Alex to hire her a maid? Lily had made her own available to Isabelle, but she hated to take advantage of her friend's generosity.

Giving up her hair and complexion for a lost cause, she rather unenthusiastically set about selecting her attire. Not caring a whit whom she did or did not impress, she chose the most unfashionable, utilitarian garment in the closet, a bilious morning dress. It didn't become her at all. If anything, she looked faintly jaundiced.

Good, she thought petulantly. It suited her mood to look as bad as she felt.

Having completed what would have to pass for her morning *toilette*, Isabelle went searching for her brother. They needed to have a very serious talk.

She found Lily first, curled up with a book in a chair in her father's study.

"Have you seen Alex?" she asked without preamble.

Her friend looked up from her book. "I saw him at breakfast, but he's gone out now. He mentioned a farm equipment exposition."

Isabelle sighed. "Did he say when he'd be back?"

"No." Lily straightened in her chair and closed her book. "What's the matter, Isa? You look dreadful, if you don't mind my saying. Are you ill?"

Isabelle shook her head. "No. I just have a headache." She squeezed her lids closed. A dull throbbing beat steadily behind her eyes. Maybe it had been a bad idea to drag herself out of bed at all.

"Sit down." Lily gestured to another chair, a worried frown on her face. "Have you eaten? I'll call for tea."

"Please don't." Isabelle waved away Lily's concern. She licked her dry lips. "Well, maybe just some tea. I don't think I could eat, though."

Lily rang for the maid and requested tea. She glanced sideways at Isabelle. "With heavy refreshments," she added.

When the servant had gone, Lily returned to her seat. "Whatever's the matter?" She scrutinized Isabelle's appearance with a questioning look. "Something worse than a headache is bothering you. Did Viscount Woolsley propose last night?" Her brown eyes lit up.

Isabelle laughed humorlessly. She dropped the strand of hair she'd been twirling around a finger. "He did, but not like you'd think."

She recounted the previous evening's conversation with Lord Woolsley.

With every passing sentence, Lily's expression darkened. When Isabelle repeated what he'd said about there not being much difference between a divorcée and a whore, Lily gasped in shocked outrage. "He never did! Why, that blackguard," she seethed. "How dare he insult you so? Did Alex call him out?"

Isabelle shook her head. Just then, tea arrived. The pastries and slices of cold ham on the platter looked a little tempting, after all. Isabelle helped herself to some.

"That's not the worst of it."

Lily set her teacup firmly in the saucer. "Tell me that vile man didn't open his mouth again."

Isabelle worked a piece of scone loose. "Oh, no." She shook her head, her heart pounding as she recalled every vivid detail of the previous night. "Marshall made sure of that." At Lily's questioning look she explained, "He thumped Lord Woolsley insensible."

Rather than the shock she expected to see on her friend's face, Lily grinned. "Did he really? How marvelously romantic."

"It wasn't romantic," Isabelle protested. "It was violent and foolish and . . ." She made an exasperated sound.

"Romantic?" Lily offered. She sipped her tea, smiling into her cup. "So, after Monthwaite jumped to defend your honor, what happened?"

Isabelle scoffed. "You won't believe me if tell you. This is where things really took a turn for the fantastic."

Lily quirked a skeptical brow. Isabelle proceeded to relate the rest of the story: the crowd he'd attracted and subsequently booted from the house, the arguing in the library, Marshall's empty apologies and promises.

"Ho, now," Lily interjected. "What makes you so sure he doesn't mean what he says?"

"Because he never means what he says when it comes to me," Isabelle snapped. "Not when it matters, anyway. He said his wedding vows, but he didn't mean those, did he?"

Lily shrugged. "But if he realizes the dreadful blunder he made, surely you can allow that possibility?"

Isabelle picked at a bit of lint on the chair's arm. "Why are you taking his part?"

"I'm not," Lily said. "Not necessarily. My primary complaint against Monthwaite was how he treated you so shabbily and believed horrid things about you." She set her plate on the tea tray. "If he's seen the error of his ways, I might be persuaded to think better of him. Lord knows," she said with a sideways smile at Isabelle, "he's handsome enough to make up for most other shortcomings."

"He *is* handsome." Isabelle's mind involuntarily took her back to that magical afternoon at the greenhouse.

"You're blushing, dear," Lily observed. "Is there something you need to tell me?"

"Certainly not!"

Lily made a tsking sound. "I may be unwed, but I'm not pea-brained. I'm sure it can't have been easy for you all these years to go from being married," she said meaningfully, "to," she worked her fingers through the air, looking for the word, "not." She ducked her head, her face reddening.

Isabelle giggled. "I should never accuse you of being pea-brained, but there are some conversations you aren't quite prepared for."

Lily cleared her throat. "In any event, all I mean is, I understand the added . . . strain this must be for you. Oh, bother!" She covered her face with her hand and collapsed to the sofa in a fit of laughter.

Her friend's mirth was contagious, and Isabelle felt the corners of her lips tugging upward. One breathy laugh burst from her chest and then another. A louder, more mirthful sound followed. She had to laugh at the situation; otherwise, she'd go deranged from the strain. Soon, she was laughing so hard she could scarcely breathe.

When they calmed, wiping tears from their cheeks, Lily's expression sobered. "What is it you want?"

The simple question struck something deep inside Isabelle. She smoothed her palms down her unattractive yellow skirt. "I want to go home. London isn't for me." Isabelle stood and restlessly paced the room. "You've seen how it is—the glances, the whispers, women holding their skirts out of the way so they don't brush against mine. That's what I want to talk to Alex about. I know he'll be angry, but I just can't bear it anymore."

* * *

Alexander didn't return until the sky had already darkened. By the time he arrived, Isabelle had worked herself into a nervous wreck imagining how furious he'd be with her for spoiling both their futures.

He strolled into the sitting room where she'd been pacing the floor the past hour, with an evening paper tucked under his arm.

Now that he was here, Isabelle was nearly overcome with trepidation. *He'll disown me for good this time.*

Alex's green eyes took in his sister's disheveled appearance at a glance. "I was told you wished to see me. You look ready to crumble to pieces, Isa. What is it?"

"Oh, Alex!" She clamped her left arm across her middle and pressed her right hand to her cheek. "I'm so sorry, dear, but I need to go home. Coming to London was a dreadful mistake."

He raised a hand. "A moment."

"Please let me finish." Tears burned her eyes. If she stopped now, she'd never have the courage to start again.

Alex sat in a chair, seemingly unperturbed—amused, even—at Isabelle's distress. He stretched out his legs and crossed them at the ankle, his folded newspaper lying across his thighs. "Go on."

Isabelle took several steps to the window. She saw nothing in the inky night but the lights from a few street lamps. All manner of city clamor was audible through the glass, however: horse hooves clattering against the cobbled streets, a door slamming somewhere, and very nearby raucous, inebriated singing. She covered her ears. Too much noise. Too much playing the merry divorcée. Too many balls and routs among people who would never accept her, no matter how she tried to ingratiate herself. Too many nights spent longing for the one man she would never have.

She leaned her forehead against the cool glass. "Oh, Marshall," she whispered. Why did he have to affect her so? How much easier her life would be if she could just put him out of mind. But he kept popping up in her life, kind to her one minute and accusing the next. Holding her close and then pushing her away. Foisting her off onto a man who wanted to make her his mistress and then jumping to her defense. It was too much. Her heart felt sick from the turmoil. She had to get away from him. And since he was in London, she needed to be anywhere else.

"I know you spent a fortune on my dresses. I'll find a way to pay you back, Alex, I swear. But I want to go home. There isn't anyone for me here. You've seen for yourself. If you want me to marry, I'll marry someone in the village at home. Anyone. You can choose. Only," she raised a hand, "not an old man. Someone who can . . . ," she paused, a delicate flush climbing her cheeks. "I'd like to have children. Other than that, I don't care. And then I won't be divorced anymore, and you can marry a nice woman, and I'll repay you, Alex."

"Hush about the money, Isa." Alex sighed dispassionately. "You won't make me any more respectable if you just take yourself off to toil in another kitchen somewhere. Besides," he said, inclining his head, "no gentleman would allow his wife to work like that."

His cool logic deflated her somewhat. "A villager wouldn't mind," she grumbled.

Alex stood, setting the newspaper on the table next to his chair. "Are you quite over your pout? You're not going home to marry a blacksmith or whatever cork-brained fancy it is you've taken."

His unexpected calm about this whole thing only made her uneasy. She touched his arm, the dark wool of his jacket soft against her trembling fingers. "I know this Season has cost money you can ill-afford. It's not your fault no one will have me."

He stuffed his hands in his trouser pockets. "Perhaps that will change. Monthwaite said he'd apologize."

Isabelle stared sadly at her brother. Poor, deluded Alex. He'd stood so strongly against Marshall last night. She didn't know what the two men had spoken of after Alex sent her ahead to the carriage. What empty, pretty words had her former husband filled his head with?

"That's highly improbable," she said gently. Isabelle returned to the window. A lone figure passed through a pool of golden lamplight. "I believe Marshall realizes his error in judgment," she allowed. "I even believe he is truly sorry for the divorce. However," she placed her hands on the window sill, "I do *not* believe he will do anything more. A public apology would be humiliating for his family. His mother won't have it, and he never crosses her. At most, he might tell a few of his friends that he might have been mistaken, when they're in their cups and not likely to remember. But that'll be the end of it."

Behind her, Alex's steps across the carpet were heavy and measured. There was a rustle of paper. "Then you might want to see this."

Isabelle turned. Alex held the evening paper so that the front page faced her. She gasped. Boldly inked in letters two inches high was the headline: DUKE DIVORCED IN ERROR.

She snatched the paper from her brother's hands. Beneath the headline were the words: *Dk. Monthwaite says former wife innocent of all charges.*

Isabelle sank to her knees in the middle of the floor to read the story.

"In an unprecedented interview," she read aloud, "His Grace the Duke of Monthwaite spoke with this humble journalist concerning the delicate matter of his divorce, the scandal of which several years past gripped the attention of the nation.

"According to the Duke of Monthwaite, facts have recently surfaced which absolve his former wife, the Duchess of Monthwaite, *née* Fairfax, of all wrongdoing.

"As the astute reader will recall, Her Grace was brought to trial on charges of the most serious nature. In light of the knowledge he now possesses, the duke regrets having ever subjected the lady to the public scrutiny and humiliation of the divorce trial.

"Said His Grace: 'It is my desire that the public hold the duchess blameless for past events. I know her to be of the highest moral integrity and unimpeachable character. I cannot adequately express my profound regret for the divorce, which stripped the lady of her peerage and reputation. If I could give her a message, I should like the duchess to know that if there is anything I can do to ease the suffering she has endured as a result of my actions, she need only . . . '"

Isabelle's voice failed as a she fought back the lump forming in her throat. A turmoil of emotions tumbled through her. Mostly, she was overwhelmed by the magnitude of Marshall's gesture. He had issued his apology in the most public venue—a newspaper that would be read throughout England and around the world, in every corner of the empire.

Alex offered her a hand. She took it and rose, clutching the newspaper to her chest.

His eyes glinted with amusement. "Well?"

She cleared her throat. "It would seem," she said in a small voice, "he kept his promise, after all."

Alex's face, so like her own, softened as he smiled. "I suppose you could say that, little sister," he chucked her lightly on the shoulder, "if understatement is your aim."

She exhaled a laugh. Did this really change anything? Marshall had made good on his word, but she didn't know if she could trust him not to hurt her again. "Oh, Alex, what now?"

"That, my dear," Alex said with the barest shake of his head, "is entirely between you and Monthwaite."

Chapter Sixteen

The ride to Bensbury should have taken only an hour, but a heavy downpour slowed Marshall, Naomi, and Aunt Janine's progress to a crawl, nearly doubling the time they were cooped up in the coach.

Aunt Janine passed the time with a disjointed ramble about various scholarly works she'd read on Egyptology, her latest passion. She intoned about long-dead pharaohs and their tombs until her voice began to crack. When she paused, Marshall exhaled in relief.

Naomi asked Aunt Janine a question about the Book of the Dead. "The Book of the Dead," Aunt Janine croaked. "Fascinating topic!" The old lady fished a flask out of her voluminous black reticule, took a long pull, and then launched into another lecture.

Marshall shot his sister a withering look. She had the grace to shrug sheepishly.

Fortunately, he was soon able to tune out Aunt Janine and think about the reason for leaving London. The printed apology was bound to ignite a frenzy of gossip and speculation. There was no possibility of meeting with Isabelle in town without it being reported in the *on dits*. If there was any chance of their relationship progressing, he had to get her out from under the scrutiny of the *ton*.

To that end, he sent her a note this morning, informing her of his intention to leave town and inviting her and Fairfax to join him if she desired to talk everything over. He had no idea whether she would come. The uncertainty gnawed between his shoulder blades, tensing the muscles in his upper back until he thought he'd crack.

When they finally arrived at Bensbury, Marshall made a hasty escape to his study. A short time later, there was a soft knock on the door. Naomi had changed out of her traveling costume into a pale pink dress with short sleeves and a high, ruffed neck. She crossed to the window, laid her hands on the sill, and looked out at the noontime sky darkened by roiling clouds. "It looks more like a chilly winter day, doesn't it?"

Marshall watched his sister for a long moment. She was still so young, and he was loathe to drag her into his personal affairs, but it seemed he would need a few enforcements to ensure he did right by Isabelle this time. He poured himself a drink, swallowed his pride, and prepared himself to beg his eighteen-year-old sister for help.

"Do you know why we're here?" he asked.

Naomi didn't look at him, but he watched her expression become thoughtful as she gazed out across the rain-drenched park. "An interesting question. The most important one, really. Why are we here? What purpose do our lives serve?"

Marshall groaned. "I wasn't speaking so esoterically."

She flashed him a mischievous smile. Gad, she had a disarming mind. He still couldn't get used to thinking of his baby sister as a grown woman, much less one with the intelligence to cross wits with her eldest brother, and to do it with such ease.

"*Touché.*" He inclined his head.

"You're here because of that apology, of course." Naomi took a brief turn around the room. She stopped in front of the *Athyrium filix-femina* in its pot atop a plant stand next to a bookshelf. "What's this one?"

"Lady-fern," he answered.

Naomi lightly ran a finger down a feathery green frond. "Do you love her?"

The simple question clapped him over the head like lightning out of the blue sky. Did he love Isabelle? He lusted for her, certainly, but he couldn't very well tell his sister that. And he was hideously remorseful for divorcing her and making a muck of her life. They were compatible. Marshall found he enjoyed her company, and it had surprised him to realize that such compatibility was important to him in choosing a wife, after all. He cared for her, and hoped she'd agree to marry him again—but that was just to make amends. Wasn't all of that enough?

He crossed his arms across his chest and cleared his throat.

"Oh, good," Naomi quipped. "You haven't gone to sleep. You stood there so long I was afraid you'd nodded off with your eyes open."

Naomi sat herself in the chair behind Marshall's desk. He started to object, but she gestured him to have a seat. He sighed and rolled his eyes, then plunked into the chair she'd indicated. Maybe she wasn't quite so grown up yet, after all.

She propped her arms on her elbows and pressed her lips against her steepled fingers in a spot-on imitation of Marshall's own gesture. "I've another question for you now," Naomi said in a serious tone.

He crossed his right ankle to the opposite knee and twiddled his thumbs. "I'm listening."

Naomi picked up a crimson enameled pen from the mahogany desktop and held it at each end, spinning it back and forth between her fingers. "Do you know why I invited Isabelle to my party?" Her blue eyes flicked to his face then back to the pen.

Marshall's fingers stilled. He'd forgotten to ever raise the issue with her. Finding Isabelle cooking in his kitchen had so thrown him off guard that the matter of precisely how it was she'd come to be there had flown from his mind. "No," he said. "I don't."

"I invited her because I wanted to show her that someone in this family did not think the worst of her. I wanted to show her that I wasn't afraid to be her friend."

They sat quietly for a moment, while Marshall considered the humbling implications of his sister's actions.

She tilted her head inquisitively. "So, I know why you're here, Marshall. But I'm still not sure why I'm here. Although," she said with a wry lift of her brow, "I think I have a good idea."

Marshall kicked back the remainder of his drink. "If your idea is that

I want to convince Isabelle to agree to marry me and that I don't think I can do it without your help, then you would be correct."

Naomi covered her mouth and made a squeaking sound.

Marshall glowered. "Are you laughing at me?"

She shook her head. "Oh no, of course not." She grinned widely. "I'm just very pleased to hear this. I must confess, Marshall, your apology in the paper was so dry," she said, wrinkling her nose, "I didn't know what you intended."

Marshall stared at his sister, stupefied. What did she expect? A public love letter, dripping with romantic pleas and pledges of undying devotion? "You've been reading too many novels again."

She scoffed then placed both palms flat on the desk and leaned forward. "*Do you love her?*" she asked again, stressing each word.

Heat flared up Marshall's neck. "You've an excess of ridiculous notions in your head," he said, jabbing a finger at his sibling. "To begin, whether or not I love Isabelle is not in the least bit your concern. Furthermore, it doesn't signify at all. I am fond of Isabelle. We suit well." His throat suddenly went dry as an image of her delectable breasts brushing against his lips flashed through his mind. He cleared his throat. "Very well, in fact." Just that bit of erotic thought had his blood thickening. He shifted; this would not do.

"Family," he said, "is of the utmost importance to Isabelle. She has spent all spring trying to find a husband, to please her brother. The actions she took at your party went above and beyond friendship. I know you're fond of her, as is Aunt Janine. She returns your regard, so I thought it might be beneficial to remind her that marrying me would restore her place in our family."

Naomi looked nonplussed. "But you don't love her?"

"Oh, for God's sake!" He stood and jammed his hands into his pockets. "Just forget it, Naomi. It was stupid of me to bring it up."

She rose and stepped out from behind the desk. "I'm sorry, Marshall, but I do love Isabelle. Like the sister she used to be." Her brows rose pointedly, and Marshall flinched under her recriminating words. Stopping in front of him, she planted her manicured hands on her hips. "I will be her friend whatever happens between you two. After all she's been through, she deserves every happiness—and if you can't give it to her, don't expect my help." So saying, she turned in a haughty swirl of silk and made her exit.

Damnation, but she did that every bit as well as their mother.

He exhaled and looked out the window. Through the rivulets streaming down the glass, he made out the distorted image of a coach approaching the house. Elation stole over him. She had come. Thank God.

If Naomi wouldn't help, he would go it alone. One way or another, Isabelle was going to be his wife. Again.

Chapter Seventeen

The next morning dawned clear, the rain having finally broken overnight. Isabelle had been tense around him since her arrival yesterday. There had been no opportunity to speak in private, but he intended to rectify that this morning. The cooperative weather inspired his plan.

When he went down to breakfast, Isabelle and Naomi sat with their heads together, talking softly. His former wife wore a long-sleeved dress, white with cherry stripes running the length of it. Alex Fairfax—or what Marshall could make out of him beyond the open newspaper shielding his face and torso—lounged with his chair turned at an angle, his long legs stretched out and crossed at the ankle.

"Good morning," Marshall said. The ladies returned the greeting. Alex bent down a corner of his newspaper and nodded, then returned to his reading.

Marshall selected a slice of ham and some thick toast from the buffet. He sat beside Isabelle, who continued her conversation with Naomi as though Marshall was of no more significance than a fly on the wall.

"I notice," he said while slathering his toast with the fresh, creamy butter, barreling over the ladies' voices, "the inclement weather has done us the favor of departing. Isabelle, would you care to join me in the greenhouse this morning for another session of—" He faked a cough and took a sip of coffee, immensely enjoying Isabelle's wild-eyed discomfiture.

"Mixing plant food?" he finished. He raised a brow.

Her face turned a charming shade of pink. She glanced toward Alex, who remained hidden behind the newspaper. "Well, you see . . . ," she fumbled.

Still on edge, he saw. What had gotten into her? He'd have thought his apology would put her at ease, but the opposite had occurred. Marshall blandly sucked a bit of toast from a tooth, waiting to hear what ridiculous excuse she'd concoct to keep herself out of his company.

"Ordinarily," she began again, "you know I'd be happy to help you. But Naomi and I had just been discussing whether we'd like to—"

"Actually . . ." Alexander lowered the paper and looked over the top to his sibling. Marshall saw the unspoken death threats Isabelle sent her brother with her eyes. Alex didn't pay them any heed. "I hoped I could convince Lady Naomi to join me for a ride." Alex inclined his head to Naomi. "Accompanied by your aunt, of course," he added.

Marshall thought he detected the barest hint of a nod from Isabelle's brother. He returned the gesture. *Reinforcements*, he thought wryly. He never would have thought he'd have to enlist the entire household just to get a female alone for an hour.

Naomi brightened at the suggestion. "That sounds lovely."

"Excellent," Alex said. "I'll meet you at the stable in a quarter hour?"

"Best make it half an hour," Naomi replied. "I'll have to pry Auntie out of whichever book she's buried herself in."

"Very well." Alex folded the paper and tossed it to the table with a flick of his wrist. He stood, stretching himself to his full height.

Marshall saw Naomi glance at Fairfax and then quickly look away again. A light blush touched her cheeks. Alarms went off in Marshall's head.

"I'll go find Aunt Janine myself." He stood and straightened his gray waistcoat. "I must change, anyway."

A short time later, Marshall had bustled Aunt Janine out the door, instructing her in the strongest terms to properly chaperone Naomi, and not allow herself to become distracted by a bee hive, or anything of that sort. Then he made her empty her pockets and confiscated a little notebook in which she was working on her own translations of hieroglyphics.

It wasn't that Marshall didn't trust Alexander Fairfax. It wasn't that he didn't trust Naomi. But nature had a way of conspiring to overwhelm the good senses of otherwise rational people.

He should know.

Isabelle awaited him in the entrance hall. She'd donned a pelisse and a straw bonnet, from the bottom of which peeked a few wispy curls.

"Shall we?" He extended his arm, as politely as for a stroll in the park, though he'd changed into the old clothes he used for greenhouse work.

Isabelle took his arm. They didn't speak until they were almost to the glass and iron structure.

They rounded the bend and Marshall's heart lightened at the sight of it. Though he had greenhouses or conservatories at each of his properties, this particular greenhouse was his pride and joy, and the heart of his botanical work. He came here as often as he could to conduct his experiments.

It was nice to be able to share his work with Isabelle. He glanced down at the petite woman on his arm.

"It was treasonous, the way they gave me up." Her eyes flashed defiantly.

"You're beautiful when you're irate," he replied.

She scoffed.

He leaned down and rumbled into her ear, "Almost as beautiful as when you're aroused." She didn't answer, but red crept up her face all the way to her hairline. Marshall whistled a jaunty tune.

He held the door and inhaled deeply when he stepped in behind her, relishing the warm, nourishing atmosphere. A quick glance around the space told him Bensbury's head gardener had taken good care of Marshall's various projects in his absence.

"Look at these!" Isabelle walked to a long table where several potted violets were in full bloom. "They're beautiful," she said, glancing at Marshall.

"That's a variety I developed myself."

Isabelle looked quizzically at him. "How do you do that?"

"It's a matter of finding different species willing to cross-pollinate."
His eye caught another row of plants several tables over. "Here, come
have a look at these."

The pots were larger than the violet containers. Each held a tender
vine growing up a wooden stake embedded in the soil.

She wrinkled her nose. "Peas?"

"That's right," Marshall said. "But a new kind."

Isabelle cocked her head to the side. "Why do we need new peas?"

Marshall's mind kicked into gear, churning with excitement for his
studies. "Our English peas grow lovely, large pods and are quite delicious.
However, the plant is prone to a condition called wilt, which destroys
entire crops." He reached over the pea plants and retrieved another
specimen from the back of the table. This plant was shorter than the
others and sickly in appearance. "You see how the leaves are curled in?"
He pointed out the damaged foliage. "And this—" He twisted one of
the slender tendrils. It snapped off in his hand. "Whereas, the healthy
plants . . . Here, you try."

He gestured toward one of the pots. Isabelle twisted a shoot. "It
doesn't break," she said. "It's pliable."

He nodded. "As it should be. The problem," Marshall explained, "is
that it's not enough to get rid of plants with the wilt. The entire field—
the earth itself—becomes diseased, and any pea plant grown in that
same soil will become sick."

For a moment, Isabelle looked thoughtfully at the peas. "What about
your plant food? Will that help?"

Marshall smiled and shook his head ruefully. "Don't I wish? No,
there doesn't seem to be a nutritive cure. However," he said, guiding
her down the table to another plant, "this is a French pea plant. It is
completely resistant to wilt."

"You mean it doesn't get sick?" Isabelle rubbed a leaf between her
thumb and forefinger.

"Yes."

"Then why don't farmers grow these, instead?"

Marshall tapped the tip of her nose. "Clever girl. That would seem ideal, but see the fruit?" He reached into the plant and picked a pod, then held it against one of the English peas.

"It's much smaller," Isabelle observed.

"A farmer would have to grow many more plants to produce the same yield," Marshall said. "So, what I'm doing," he placed a hand on her back and gestured to yet another set of pots, "is breeding together the English peas with the French."

"Why?"

"I'm hoping the offspring will have the best traits of both varieties—the size of the English peas and the wilt resistance of the French." He crossed his left arm across his body, rested his right elbow on it, and tapped a fingernail against his teeth.

Isabelle wore a look of frank admiration. "I truly have no words." Her eyes ran over his plants, the results of his studies and collaboration with colleagues. "This is marvelous." She turned to him. "Just think of all the farmers you'll help!" She took his hand and squeezed. "It's a wonderful thing you're doing and a very worthy endeavor."

Marshall drew her forward and ran a finger down the side of her face. "Thank you." He scanned the interior of the greenhouse. "This is only a small portion of the botanical work I hope to do, but it is satisfying."

Isabelle's arms wound around his waist. She rested her cheek against his chest.

Marshall's heart constricted at her sweet gesture. His arms wrapped around her in return. He pressed a kiss to the top of her head, then he moved his hands to her shoulders and pushed her back a little.

"Why have you been trying to avoid me?" he asked softly. Isabelle set her mouth, and her eyes slid past him. "No." He squeezed her shoulders more firmly. "Look at me." She did. "In case the fact escaped your notice, I intend to marry you."

Isabelle inhaled sharply. Then she shrugged free of his hands and turned, strolling down the row of pea plants. She rounded the table and started up the other side. Opposite him, she stopped and touched a diseased plant. "Not a very eloquent proposal," she said lightly. He detected something else in her voice.

"Why are you afraid?" He blurted the question before the thought even finished coagulating in his mind.

Isabelle's eyes flew to his face. She took a step back and wrapped her arms around herself.

"It isn't society, is it? Not the gossip or the unkind remarks." As he spoke, something clarified. "It's me. You're afraid of me." His eyelids slid closed as the bitter truth fell over him like a pall. "Why?" When he opened his eyes again, Isabelle was covering her mouth with her hand. She squeezed her eyes shut and shook her head. "Tell me," he pressed.

"All right!" Her arms jerked downward and her hands balled into fists at her sides. She quivered like a leaf in the breeze.

He wanted to put his arms around her again and soothe her worries, but he couldn't with a table full of peas between them. A few strides and he was around the table. She stepped backwards.

"Don't," She stopped and raised her hands in front of her, palms out, holding him at bay with her defiant stance. "I'm afraid," she said, "because I . . ." she clamped her mouth closed. The cords in her neck stood out as she choked on words unuttered.

She seemed on the verge of panic. Marshall was baffled by her behavior. "Because . . ." he said, gesturing with a hand.

"Because I loved you!" she cried. She whirled away.

Her words struck him as odd. "Because you love—*loved*—me?" He quirked a brow and started toward her again. "You don't anymore?"

"Yes," she said. "I mean, no, I don't. That is . . . Damn!" She bit down on a fist.

He closed the distance between them and gently pried her hand away from her mouth. Isabelle's eyes shone with incipient tears.

"I loved you when we were married," she said in a quiet, dignified tone. "The divorce was humiliating, Marshall. You made a pariah of me. But more than that—worse than that—you broke my heart."

A fresh pang of remorse shot through his gut.

She raised her chin and smiled weakly. "I stayed in town for two years afterward, hoping you'd come back even though I was shunned by your peers. I loved you even then, after being hurt so badly. God knows, I still can't stay away from you. But I'm afraid, Marshall, afraid you'll do it again."

His heart began a funny, lopsided beat. "Divorce you? My dear, I should be laughed out of the House of Lords if I so much as breathed the idea."

She shook her head and whispered, "Your apology was truly magnanimous, but I'm afraid you'll break my heart again. You didn't love me when we were married. You don't love me now. And there are many ways for a husband to leave his wife."

Of course I love you.

The words formed in his mouth, and only a tightening of his lips kept him from uttering them. The jolt he felt was similar to when he suddenly understood a botanical concept. It burned in his mind, bright and true.

Well, damnation. He was in love.

Marshall blinked and looked down at her through new eyes. She was his Isabelle, and he loved her. He *loved* her! He snatched her to him in a fierce hug.

She had to know. He needed to tell her. How best to do so? His mind started to churn.

He dropped kisses on her hair. Cupping her cheeks, he turned her face up. He rained more kisses across her forehead and the lids that covered those intoxicating emerald eyes. "Darling," he murmured. "My sweet girl, don't be afraid. Look at me, Isa."

Her eyelids fluttered open. A speck of hope seemed to shine in those green depths.

"I'm so sorry I hurt you," he said, his voice tender as a caress. "But you never have to worry about my leaving you ever again. I couldn't, sweetheart. You see—"

"Your Grace," called a voice.

Marshall startled. Isabelle jerked out of his arms as they turned to the intruder.

It was one of his footmen, his face ashen.

A growing unease stole over Marshall. "What is it?" he asked.

"It's Lady Naomi," the footman said. "She's been kidnapped."

Chapter Eighteen

Isabelle had never seen a house erupt into pandemonium such as what she witnessed in the hour following the discovery of Naomi's abduction.

Isabelle observed how Marshall, however, took the time to speak to and calm each man or woman in his employ. In turn, the servants responded favorably to their master. The worry lines eased on the housekeeper's face as Marshall spoke to her in even, reassuring tones.

If Isabelle had not seen firsthand how distraught and shaken Marshall was by Naomi's disappearance, she never would have believed it. He had pulled himself together and was now the unflappable leader his household needed him to be. Isabelle took her lead from him and tried to put on a brave face to mask her own dismay.

In Marshall's study, Aunt Janine sat in a chair holding a saucer and teacup, which rattled in her trembling hands. A groom stood near the desk, gripping his cap in tight fists. Alexander sat slumped over on a sofa, clutching a bloodied wad of cloth to the back of his head.

Isabelle startled at the sight of her wounded brother. "Alex!"

He lifted his head and gave her a wan smile, his face devoid of color. "Hello, little sister," he replied weakly.

She took the rag from his grasp to examine him. Behind his right ear, his light hair was stained red. She sucked air through her teeth at the sight of it but gingerly parted the matted hair. A gash in his scalp bled freely.

She glanced at Marshall. "He needs a doctor."

"Aunt Janine, please see about that," he told the elderly lady. "Also, write to Grant and Mama; tell them to come at once. Mr. Turner, my investigator, as well."

Aunt Janine looked like she'd aged twenty years since Isabelle had seen her earlier that morning. Her distant eyes blinked. Then she nodded and rose to carry out Marshall's requests.

"Fairfax," Marshall clipped, "what happened?"

Alex sat upright; he grimaced fiercely. "It's hard to say for sure."

Isabelle daubed at the blood seeping through his hair. Alex groaned. "Sorry," Isabelle muttered.

"Please," Marshall said, "whatever you can tell me."

"Get him a drink," Isabelle instructed a footman.

"We had our ride," Alex began. "Lady Naomi showed me a hedge she likes to jump, and a stream she thinks is picturesque." He smiled ruefully at Marshall as if to say, *Women. You know how it is.* "Lady Janine was stung by a bee—"

"Good God!" Marshall threw his hands up. "The one thing I specifically told her to do was to stay away from bee hives." He made a disgusted sound.

"In her defense," Alexander said, "she was admiring a flower, and when she touched the bloom, a bee flew out and stung her hand."

Marshall pressed his hands to his face.

"In any event, she rode back ahead of us to have the sting tended to. Lady Naomi and I were already coming back ourselves, but she wanted to show me—" He sucked in his breath and groaned.

"Alex!" Isabelle crouched beside him and squeezed his hand. Fear clutched at her throat. Alexander was her only remaining family. If anything should happen to him . . .

He waved her away with an irritated gesture. "I can't recollect where she wanted to go. We returned to the stable. I don't remember anything after I handed the reins to a groom."

"Weren't no groom!" piped up the liveried stable hand hovering nearby. "Begging your pardon, Yer Grace." He ducked his head. The servant was a tall, gawky man, with a thin face and protruding Adam's apple.

"What do you mean?" Marshall asked.

"A few o' the lads took sick after breakfast this morning," the man said. "Cramps and—" His protruding eyes cut to Isabelle. "Indisposition," he finished carefully. "Musta been somethin' bad in the eggs. Anyway, then this fellow shows up like a miracle, just when all the other lads were ailing and begging off work for the day. He wanted to know if there was an opening in the stable. Said his name was Jerry."

"Gerald," Marshall snarled.

The name meant nothing to Isabelle. "Who?"

"Thomas Gerald was a groom in my father's employ," Marshall quickly explained. "He was arrested and transported for poisoning a pregnant brood mare."

Isabelle made a stricken sound. "God above! But why—"

"Revenge." Marshall said grimly.

"He seemed nice enough," the groom continued, "and he had a good way with the horses. So the stable master told him he could work for the day, and then *he had* to beg off on account of his own indisposition. So it was just this new fellow and me minding the horses, and the Harper lad in the tack. When the ladies and Mr. Fairfax went to ride, was me and Jerry got the horses for them. When Lady Janine returned alone, Jerry helped me wipe the mare down—gave her a nice long feed, too. He said the mare was hitching her step a bit, and would I take her for an easy walk, since she knew me better. Like I said, this Jerry knew what he was about with the horses. So I said I would. And when I come back, there was Mr. Fairfax," he said, nodding toward Alex, "laid out on the floor. But his horse, and Lady Naomi and her horse, weren't nowhere to be seen." He pursed his lips and moved his chin from side to side. "And that's all I know about it, milord."

Marshall exhaled slowly. Then he walked to the window and braced his hands on either side of it. Isabelle longed to wrap her arms around him. She thought of poor Naomi in the hands of that monster and clamped an arm across her middle at a sudden wave of nausea.

"All right." Marshall turned from the window. He shoved his hands into his pockets. "He has Naomi and two horses. It's clear this was a planned attack. He gained admission to the stable under false pretenses to get close to her. The question is: where is he going, and what does he plan to do with Naomi?"

"Ransom, perhaps," Alex ventured. "Unless he means to do her ill."

Isabelle's head swam at the implications. She cast a tortured expression to Marshall. He stood stock still, staring at Alexander. Only the twitching muscle at his jaw betrayed the slightest hint of his unease, but Isabelle knew he was as horrified, if not more so, as she.

Marshall's eyes narrowed a fraction. "We cannot wait for a ransom note that may never come." His voice was cold and hard as steel. "The search begins immediately. If a ransom demand comes, so be it. In the meantime, I'll not allow my sister to be mistreated. I couldn't live with myself if something happened to her, and I hadn't done anything to prevent it." He opened the study door and called for the butler. The servant materialized so quickly, Isabelle wondered if he hadn't been standing near the door, eavesdropping.

In less than fifteen minutes, sixteen men had left their various posts around the house and grounds and assembled in the entry hall. Marshall divided them into three groups of six.

Marshall's group would ride back toward London. Naomi would not be cooperative, Marshall reasoned, and so Gerald would be forced to take a slower route off the main roads so as not to draw attention. They would have the advantage and cut him off before he reached town, if he meant to take her to a hideout in one of the capital's criminal sanctuaries.

The second group would take the road in the other direction, alerting the neighboring farms and estates and searching abandoned structures. Meanwhile, the third group would delve into Bensbury's hundreds of wooded acres in case Thomas Gerald had not yet removed Naomi from the property. A man from each group would return to the house every hour to see if the other groups had made any progress.

As the groups readied to leave, Isabelle grabbed Marshall's sleeve. "I want to come with you. I can't sit by and do nothing."

Marshall touched her face with a warm, firm hand. "I'll bring Naomi home safe and sound, I swear to you. But you will stay here."

Isabelle started to protest.

Marshall raised a hand. "You have your brother to look after. My mother and Grant will be here soon, too, and you must see to them."

The thought of keeping company with the two people in Marshall's family who despised Isabelle more than anything was not the plum assignment she'd hoped for.

"Isabelle," Marshall said in a warning tone. "I see that look in your eye. Please. If you care anything for me at all, do as I ask and stay put. It will be a comfort to me to know you're safe."

Isabelle sighed. When he put it like that, what choice did she have?

He pressed a brief kiss to her lips, and then he was gone. A few minutes later, the thundering of hooves filled the air as Bensbury's stable was emptied to carry the search parties on their missions.

An hour after they left, the first three men from the search parties returned. They gathered in the study to exchange information. There was none. Their reports represented just the first few minutes of the search, Isabelle knew. Something would come up soon.

In the next intervening hour, Mr. Turner arrived from town, then rushed to join the search after Isabelle brought him up to speed. His departure was followed almost at once by Caro and Grant's appearance.

Caro looked a fright. Lines creased her forehead and the corners of her eyes, and she had obviously dressed quickly and without care. Several buttons on the back of her dress were misaligned with the buttonholes, as though she hadn't been able to wait for the maid to do them properly. She gave Isabelle an anguished look.

Grant stoically asked for the latest news. Isabelle passed along the meager report. Caro pressed a handkerchief to her lips, visibly fighting to restrain tears. Unexpected pity for the woman who had tormented her for so long washed over Isabelle. She couldn't imagine how helpless a mother must feel in such a situation. She laid a hand on her arm before Grant gently led her to a sitting room.

Isabelle ordered tea for them then went to Alexander's room where the surgeon was attending him. She waited in the hall while he stitched up the wound in Alex's scalp.

After the surgeon spoke to her and departed, she went in to see Alex. A bandage wound around his head and he lay perfectly still. Isabelle's eyes widened in alarm, but she reminded herself he'd had laudanum.

She remained at her brother's bedside for several minutes. Too anxious about Naomi to maintain a vigil, Isabelle sent for a footman to sit with Alex and instructed the servant to alert her as soon as he was awake.

Isabelle's imagination concocted every sort of evil scenario into which her loyal friend may have been tossed. She closed her eyes against the distressing thoughts and hissed.

A bustle of activity from the entrance hall alerted her to the return of the search parties' representatives.

She rushed over to find two of the three men speaking with Grant. Marshall's brother dropped his face into his hands. Isabelle's heart skipped a beat.

"Has something—" she started, too afraid of the possibilities to finish the question.

"No," Grant said. "No news."

Isabelle exhaled. She nodded weakly. No news was preferable to bad news, but it was still a blow.

A few minutes later, the third searcher returned from Marshall's group. He shook his head. "Nothing." Then he turned and strode back out to his waiting horse. The other two followed close on his heels.

Isabelle stood for a moment, staring blankly at the heavy wooden door after it closed behind the men.

"There's no need for you to stay, you know."

Isabelle slowly turned to face Grant. Though his coloring was lighter than Marshall's, the lines of his face resembled his older brother. His gray eyes were like cold gunmetal.

"I beg your pardon?"

"This is a family affair." Grant's lips pressed together in a hard line. "It would be best if you go now."

She drew back. Even now, Marshall's family still had the energy to act so spitefully toward her? "What have I ever done to you?" she asked, her quiet voice full of hurt and bewilderment.

Grant turned his head. "You didn't see him after he found out about you and your friend. He lived in a bottle for a month. We were all afraid he was going to do himself harm, so I stayed with him until he snapped out of it." He raised his brows. "Did you know that, Fairfax?" he asked, pointedly refusing her his family name, "Your infidelity nearly killed Marshall."

Isabelle rubbed her tired eyes. She started to argue with him, but what was the point? Nothing she said or did would ever convince Grant or Caro that Isabelle was not the scheming adulteress they so wanted her to be.

"I'm sorry to hear that," she finally said. "And his divorce nearly killed me. But he and I have a chance to get past that now. I hope you will, as well. Either way, Marshall asked me to be here. You don't have to like it, and you don't have to like me, but I'm not going anywhere."

Grant's jaw tightened. Isabelle raised her nose a fraction of an inch and walked down the hall in even, gliding steps.

She found Marshall's Aunt Janine in the library. The older lady was sitting in the same chair by the window where she'd been when Isabelle first met her. She held a book loosely in her hands. Isabelle noticed it was upside down. "Do you mind if I join you?"

Aunt Janine lifted her left hand. Near the base of her thumb, Isabelle saw a small red welt. "Look at that," she said mournfully. "Nothing.

Nothing at all. I ought not have left her. My father died of a bee sting, and I've been afraid ever since. But I shouldn't have abandoned her."

Isabelle gently laid the book in Lady Janine's lap and took her hands. "No, my lady. Please don't. If you'd stayed, you might have been attacked as well. Don't blame yourself, Lady Janine."

She sniffed loudly, her chin all aquiver. "That's *Aunt* Janine to you, missy," she declared in a wounded tone. "Don't make me tell you again."

Isabelle smiled and nodded.

"If you don't mind, dear," the older woman said, "I think I'd prefer to be alone. But you will come the instant there is news?"

"Of course, my lady."

Aunt Janine mumbled her thanks, then she lifted her book, still upside down, and gazed blankly at the pages.

The minutes passed in agonizing slowness. When the door opened, Isabelle sprinted to the front hall. Mr. Turner was among the three returning men this time. Neither he nor the others had found Naomi.

When he heard the reports, Grant shot a hard look at Isabelle and left without a word.

Fear gnawed at her middle. Isabelle ran her hands up her arms and turned to the investigator. "How much longer can this go on?"

His shoulders slumped at her question. "It could be hours. Days. Soon, though, every watchman in London and every magistrate throughout the country will be on the lookout. Lady Naomi will be recovered, miss."

The next several hours were maddeningly repetitive. No news. Never any news. The men saw nothing. They found nothing. No one they spoke to had seen or heard anything that could lead them to Naomi.

As evening approached, Isabelle thought the waiting would drive her mad. The last group of men looked peaked. The search parties were surely tired, hungry, and flagging in strength. Isabelle decided to fix baskets for the next round of searchers to take back to their groups.

The men needed to eat, and Isabelle needed something to occupy her time.

The kitchen level was not as abandoned as it had been last time Isabelle was there, but still quiet. A couple of maids worked in the scullery. In the kitchen proper, a lad on hands and knees scrubbed the flagstone floor with a stiff-bristled brush. An elderly liveried footman emerged from the pantry, holding a tin of spice. He gave Isabelle a baleful look.

"Where's the cook?" Isabelle asked the man.

He tipped his chin to the interior of the pantry. Isabelle peeked into the small, gloomy room. The cook sat on the floor, hugging her knees to her chest with her face pressed against them.

"Excuse me," Isabelle ventured. "I'd like to make baskets of food for the search parties. Would that be all right?"

The woman's head reared up, her round face blotchy and streaked with tears. "Who could think of food at a time like this?" she wailed. "Not when our young lady's been taken!" She bit her fist and choked out a sob.

Isabelle tried reasoning with the grief-stricken woman. "But the men must eat. How will they have the strength to keep up the search with empty stomachs? Wouldn't you like to help me?"

The cook only shook her head and cried harder.

Isabelle sighed. Fine. She would do it herself.

In the larder, she found a large ham. She brought it to the table and carved the meat into a pile of slices. She made short work of a wheel of hard cheese, and several loaves of bread. Then she set about assembling sandwiches, which she wrapped in napkins.

She packed them into the baskets, and carried them upstairs. When she reached the entry hall, the butler was closing the door.

"Did I miss them?" At the butler's affirmative reply, she stomped her foot in vexation. "No news, either, I suppose?" she grumbled.

"No, ma'am."

Frustrated tears pricked the backs of her eyes. She set her load of baskets on the floor. "All right," she said, wiping her nose with the back of her hand. "Here's food for the men. Make sure they get these if I'm not here next hour."

* * *

Fatigue slumped Marshall's shoulders. Beneath him, his mount plodded wearily. Marshall thought ruefully that Amadeus would have better endurance than the gelding he rode, but his favorite stallion had stayed behind in London. His search party had ridden hard and fast down the road to London, hoping to catch up to Thomas Gerald if he was taking his sister back into the city. They'd gone as far as Lambeth, but careful questioning of the villagers revealed that Gerald and Naomi had not passed that way. When the party had reconvened, the eyes of Marshall's grooms and footmen had turned to him for guidance. *What now,* their expressions all asked.

With despair and fear gnawing at his gut, Marshall adopted the same tone he'd used when addressing his company in Spain. "We've gathered," he said matter-of-factly, "that Lady Naomi is not being taken into the city—at least not by this road. Good, that's valuable intelligence." In truth, it was worthless. It was akin to lifting a single straw from the proverbial haystack, and upon discerning the absence of the needle announcing, "Not here!" That still left the entire blasted haystack to sift through—or in Marshall's case—every village, byway, and port in England. The more time passed, the larger the haystack became.

Still, his forthright attitude reassured his men, who nodded sagely at his words. "We shall fan out," he'd announced, "and explore every track and drive in the area. Having foregone the speed of the main road, we can assume Gerald prefers the solitude of the less-traveled paths. Break into two groups. You two," he swept his finger at the group, gathering a pair of men with his gesture, "backtrack toward Bensbury. Check the farms we saw earlier, off to the west. You two," he nodded to the others, "explore the woods to the east. If he's going to send a ransom demand, he might be headed for a house, a shack, something of that sort. Look for anything suspicious. I'll take the turn going back to Bensbury this time."

On the way out of Lambeth, Marshall encountered another member of his party, Henry, returning from meeting the other searchers at Bensbury. Henry met Marshall's questioning gaze and shook his head once. "Nothing, m'lord."

It was a punch to his middle with a cold fist, but Marshall just nodded grimly and continued on his way. As he prodded his tired horse into a trot, Marshall considered his course of action. A glance at the sky showed the sun quickly descending to the horizon. By the time he reached Bensbury, met with the others, and made his way back to the party, it would be fully dark. Should they to continue searching through the night?

He recalled his guileless sister as she'd been at breakfast that morning, pretty and young and fresh, sweetly conspiring to allow Marshall and Isabelle time alone, blushing as she admired Alexander Fairfax. That memory was followed by a vivid vision of that sweet innocence blighted by a cruel Thomas Gerald—the fear she must be feeling, the desperation—

His throat constricted around a growl. Marshall had to find her. He would not force his men and horses to expose themselves to the danger of riding through the night, but he would. There could be no rest for him until his sister was safely returned to her family.

Of a sudden, Marshall was afraid again for Isabelle. What if Gerald returned to Bensbury and took her, too? He could have associates working with him, a whole gang of miscreants absconding with those most dear to him. His heart skipped a beat at the thought. "I'm coming," he said as he dug his heels into the horse's sides. He wouldn't leave Bensbury until he'd seen Isabelle and reassured himself of her safety. Protecting her and recovering Naomi were all that mattered.

The poor beast beneath Marshall strained forward at his urging, but he noted a quiver in the horse's haunch. Lathered with sweat, the mount was as exhausted as the rider. He pulled back on the reins, slowing the animal to a brisk walk. Marshall cast around for a watering place. In the distance, down a side track, he spotted a turning water wheel; sunlight dappled on the liquid falling from the black wood. Approaching the mill, Marshall heard the rumble of the great stones turning inside the tall wooden building, grinding grain into flour.

As the horse drank, Marshall strolled along the bank, stretching his legs. Here, the stream was only about fifteen feet wide. On the opposite side, trees grew all the way to the bank. His eyes roamed over stream and trees; he was too distracted to focus long on any one thing, and soon he was impatient to be on his way.

Turning, his gaze caught on something at the tree line. He halted and narrowed his eyes, anxiety mounting in his chest. There, on the opposite bank, unmistakably, was a campsite. The remains of a fire—no, he realized, his breath catching in his throat. *That fire has not yet burned.* Twigs and other kindling stood in a neat pile, awaiting the kiss of a flame. Nearby, he spotted a burlap pack on the ground.

An out-of-the-way campsite within striking distance of Bensbury.

"Naomi," he gasped. Marshall plunged into the stream, wading through the cold, waist-deep water to reach the far side. He scrabbled up the bank, his fingers clawing into dank soil to wrap around exposed roots.

Hauling himself over the edge of the embankment, Marshall took in the little campsite with an appraising eye. The fire had been neatly built atop a circle of earth brushed clear of leaves and other debris.

The pack lying beside the fire contained a rolled blanket and sparse, dried provisions. Marshall frowned. It didn't look as though Gerald had prepared the camp to take care of a hostage. There was only enough food to keep one man fed for a few days, and on tight rations, at that. One blanket. One flask laying among the food in the pack.

He shuddered involuntarily as a wretched thought occurred to him. "What if he's killed her?" he whispered harshly, his eyes darting around his shadowed surroundings. "Naomi!" he bellowed; fear clawed at him, driving him out of the camp. A deer track led into the dark woods, and Marshall followed it, calling his sister's name. He rounded a bend and noticed a discarded pile of suitable firewood on the ground an instant before a man wielding a pistol stepped out from behind a tree.

His light brown hair hung to his shoulders, sweat-damp and snarled with bits of twig and leaf. Clothes that had once been respectable showed hard use. The familiar face had aged more than the passage of fifteen years would suggest, but Marshall supposed forced labor would do that to a man. His eyes, though, gleamed clear with vitality, cold and hard with barely concealed anger.

"The Duke of Monthwaite himself," Thomas Gerald snarled. "If that ain't Providence, I don't know what is. You're just the man I've been wanting to see."

* * *

Isabelle made her rounds of checking in on Alexander and Aunt Janine. Her brother still slept, and Aunt Janine had nodded off in her chair, as well. At the drawing room where Caro and Grant waited, Isabelle placed a hand on the doorknob, then withdrew it again. There was no sense subjecting them to her unwanted presence.

Instead, she returned to the kitchen. She had no idea whether the men planned to search through the night. If they did, then Isabelle would work in the kitchen all night long, keeping them supplied with food and drink.

What to make next? She had exhausted the bread, so there would be no more sandwiches. Too bad she couldn't make Marshall a pot of her stew.

Inspiration struck. She would make her stew, she decided, only with a thicker gravy than usual. Then she'd make a simple pastry dough, and bake the stew into pies. It would be a few hours before they were ready, but the sandwiches would tide the men over in the meantime. Besides, a lengthy project to occupy her sounded perfect.

She set about gathering her ingredients. There was a roast just right for stewing in the larder. A bin of onions in the corner gave her all of those she needed. But there were no carrots.

A short distance from the kitchen door, however, was Marshall's vegetable garden.

His voice rang in her mind, asking her to stay inside the house. She shrugged it off. For goodness' sake, Naomi had already been abducted— Thomas Gerald had his victim. Isabelle wasn't vain enough to suppose he was lurking around waiting to snatch her, too.

She selected a wide, shallow basket from the stack in the corner and opened the kitchen door. No nefarious convicts leapt upon her.

The sun sinking behind the tall trees cast long shadows across the vegetable garden. Squinting in the dim light, Isabelle strolled the length of the expansive garden until she spotted leafy green carrot tops.

She knelt on the dark, soft soil and pulled. A well-formed root emerged, but it was only a few inches long. Isabelle wrinkled her nose at the unimpressive vegetable. Marshall's plant food hadn't done much for these. It would take a couple dozen carrots of this size to give her the quantity she needed.

Happy for the work, she went about pulling carrots and wiping them clean with her apron.

A faint sound raised the hair on her arms. *What was that?* Isabelle looked up and slowly dropped a carrot into the basket. She peered into the shadowy trees.

Silence.

She shook her head; she was hearing things. Her nerves were stretched to the breaking point, and now her mind was playing tricks on her.

Reaching for another carrot, she heard the sound again, louder this time. Isabelle jerked her hand back and gasped at the unmistakable sound of a woman crying out.

"Naomi," she breathed. Isabelle stood and cast her gaze wildly about. The garden and grounds were deserted.

She opened her mouth and almost yelled for help but then clamped a hand across her lips. What if Naomi's captor heard her? What might he do in desperation?

Naomi's piteous cry sounded again, but was cut off. Isabelle sucked in her breath. There was no one else and there might not be any time to waste.

The sound had come from the direction of Marshall's greenhouse. Isabelle quickly untied her apron and tossed it back toward the house. She gathered the carrots in her hands and left the basket where it lay. Every few yards she dropped a carrot, leaving a trail to the greenhouse path. Anyone who followed it that far would know where to go.

If anyone even thought to look for her, she thought with a jolt. She'd told the butler she'd be in the kitchen, perhaps for hours. No one would think anything of it if she weren't seen for a long time.

She closed her eyes against the panic rising from her middle and clamping around her throat. She stood at the mouth of the greenhouse path. Beyond it, Naomi was in trouble. Isabelle had to do something. She wouldn't allow her fears to conquer her, leaving Naomi to her fate at the hands of an unhinged convict.

Isabelle opened her eyes and dragged in several steadying breaths. She jogged the length of the path and skidded to a halt just before the greenhouse came into view.

What was she doing? She didn't have a plan, or a weapon.

"Think," she muttered to herself, knocking her fist against her forehead. Nothing brilliant rattled loose.

A loud clatter from inside the greenhouse brought a quick end to her brainstorming session. No time for plans. Naomi needed her.

Isabelle stepped into the clearing. Two saddled horses grazed calmly on the wildflowers at the tree line. The last of the day's dying light filtered weakly through the trees. It glared off the greenhouse, rather than illuminating the interior.

"No plan, no idea what I'm getting into. Perfect." Suddenly, she was angry. Isabelle's lips pinched together. It was just like when she'd been blindsided by Alex cutting her off. She'd plowed through that and come out the other side just fine. She would do the same now.

With a lift of her chin, she strolled serenely toward the greenhouse. All the while, her mind was in a whirl, madly running through the few facts she knew about Thomas Gerald and the conclusions to which those facts led her.

She knocked on the greenhouse door, then tried the handle. It opened. She lifted her skirt and placed one slippered foot on the stone floor.

"Don't come no farther!" barked a voice.

In the center of the greenhouse, a man Isabelle assumed to be Thomas Gerald stood with his left arm hooked around Naomi's neck. In his right hand, he held a pistol leveled right at Isabelle.

He was a short man, of a height with Naomi. He wore rough spun work clothes, and a hat pulled low over his face. A few coppery wisps of hair lay over his ears. Isabelle only made out the shape of the eyes in the shadow of the brim, but the man's cheeks were surprisingly full and soft. This fact registered with confusion—she'd expected a man exposed to years of hard labor to look more weathered.

The dire situation did not allow her to contemplate this mystery; Naomi's wild gaze was riveted on Isabelle. From what Isabelle could judge by a quick once-over, her friend appeared unharmed.

"Mr. Gerald, I presume?" Isabelle said in a clear voice. She raised her hands in front of her chest and slowly took another step into the greenhouse.

He thrust the pistol toward her. "I tol' you don't come no farther." His voice had something of an alto pitch about it, not the depth of most adult males. This puzzled Isabelle further, but she kept her attention trained on the task at hand: freeing Naomi.

Isabelle stopped and plastered what she hoped was a reassuring smile on her face. "I assure you I mean no harm, sir. I am alone, as you see. And I have no weapon." She turned her hands over and back again.

"Then you made a damned fool mistake coming here," the gunman snarled.

She waved a hand nonchalantly. "La, you may be right." She laughed lightly. "Naomi, dear, are you quite all right?"

"Don't talk to her," Gerald snapped. He turned the gun on Naomi, pressing it through her hair to her temple. Naomi's eyes squeezed shut and a whimper escaped her. Isabelle's stomach flipped. She had to be very careful.

"Who are you?" Gerald demanded.

"My name is Isabelle Lockwood," she answered.

Gerald's grip on the gun slackened slightly as he frowned. "Lockwood? You married to one of the sons, then."

"No, I'm afraid not." She gave him a rueful smile. "Not anymore."

The shadowed eyes clouded in confusion. "'Ere, then, what's that mean?"

Finally, an idea took hold. If Isabelle could just keep him talking, an opportunity of some sort would present itself. Or, she argued with herself, he would get tired of talking and kill both her *and* Naomi. *Oh, well,* she supposed, *in for a penny, in for a pound*—and she was already in for a guinea, at least.

Isabelle shrugged and exhaled. She strolled down the row of violets and stopped to pick a dead leaf from a plant. Gerald followed her movement with his eyes.

"I used to be married to Marshall Lockwood," she explained. "We wed before he was the duke. He divorced me after his father died." She met the gaze of Naomi's captor and spoke carefully. "I've been angry at him, too. I understand how you feel. But you need to release Lady Naomi now. She's no part of your quarrel with His Grace."

The convict shook visibly. His hat came loose and toppled to the floor. Red tresses tumbled to just past the *woman's* shoulders. Isabelle gasped. "Like hell she ain't!" the incensed woman spat. "He took everything from me."

Isabelle shook her head, bewildered. "How can that be? Who are you?"

"Sally Palmer," she said proudly, "the woman who loves Mr. Thomas Gerald."

Naomi met Isabelle's startled gaze with a bewildered look of her own. Isabelle extended a hand. "I'm afraid I'm a trifle lost. If you'll just put down the gun, I'm sure we can reach an understanding."

"Oh, no I won't!" Sally Palmer bellowed. Naomi flinched away from the mouth near her ear. "This here high-falootin' la-a-ady," she mocked with a sneer, "is part of the family what ruined my Thomas. I know all about Lockwoods and Monthwaites, and that nothing but bad ever comes of 'em. The old duke sent my Thomas into exile, but all on the fault of the new duke."

"Miss Palmer," Isabelle spread her hands to reason with the woman, who was little more than a girl in truth, "Mr. Gerald served the sentence for his crime. And unless I'm mistaken, you met Mr. Gerald during his exile, so you cannot say nothing but bad came of it. Done is done, is it not? Why continue to harbor ill will against the Monthwaite family?"

Sally Palmer's lips drew into a thin line, and her face turned an angry purple. "He didn't do it!" she shrieked. Isabelle stepped back at the force of her tone. Naomi let out a piteous cry. "That vile man's the one killed that horse and foal!" Sally continued. "And the bloody coward let Thomas take the blame!"

"What?" Isabelle shook her head. The woman was crazed, she reminded herself. Otherwise, she wouldn't spout such nonsense and behave in this erratic manner.

"It's true!" Sally's voice took on a pleading tone. "Thomas told me all about it when I nursed him through the 'fluenza." She licked her lips. "As Thomas tells it, they was like friends. Not really, I know," she said derisively, "but he used to come to the stables and talk while my Thomas worked. Spoiled, do-nothing lordling," she spat as an aside. "He used to tell Thomas about plants and things they could do."

Isabelle blinked. That did sound like a young Marshall.

Sally Palmer dropped the gun to her side, but kept a firm grip on Naomi. Her riding hat was askew atop her head, and her hair hung in loose strands over her captor's arm.

"Then there was a brood mare, Priscilla, Thomas called her." Sally shook her head sadly. "He told me how 'e worried over her, with her foal not coming when it should, and her starting to get sick-like." The young woman's voice took on a pleading quality as she continued her tale. "Then one day the young lord comes in to check on Priscilla. Says he had an idea to help her start her foaling. He mixes up this and that, but he asks Thomas to give it to her. So he do. Then here's the mare and her foal dead, and Thomas blamed for it, neat as can be." Rage and anguish warred, contorting Sally's features.

Isabelle's face went cold. She stared at the frantic girl. Somehow, she recognized herself in Sally's words; recognized the same tone of desperation as she told her story of a man wrongfully accused, just as Isabelle had been, and had longed for someone to believe her innocent of adultery. Reason told her Sally was lying. But if she wasn't?

"My brother would never do that!" Naomi protested.

Sally yanked her head back by the hair. Naomi cried out in pain. "He would and he did," she said darkly, looming over her.

She was coming unhinged, Isabelle realized.

"I know how you feel," Isabelle blurted. There was no time to analyze the veracity of the woman's claims. Right now, she just had to keep her distracted from Naomi. "If there's anyone held higher in public scorn than a convict, it's a divorced woman." She raised her chin and laughed nervously, hoping she conveyed some sense of fraternity.

Calmly, as though strolling through the roses at a garden party, she began moving toward the armed woman and Naomi.

"Monthwaite did quite a number on me, too." She stopped to smell a blossom on Marshall's pea plants.

"Then you know exactly what I mean," Sally said. "You know why I've got to get back at him."

Isabelle nodded once, firmly. "Indeed I do, Miss Palmer. But consider: The Duke of Monthwaite is a ridiculously wealthy, powerful man. If you bring harm to his sister or property, you will hang. But a ransom," she said widening her eyes, "might be just the thing. He could give you and Mr. Gerald enough money to start over. You could go to Canada," she suggested. "What do you think?"

Sally's brow creased. "I don't think Thomas would like that. We passed a couple years in the islands, but he tol' me he was going to bring me to England, that we'd have a life here." She stared blankly out the glass wall; her arm around Naomi's neck slackened. Isabelle inched toward Marshall's workbench.

The greenhouse door flew open with a crack. "Release her, Miss Palmer," Marshall demanded, pointing his own pistol at the miscreant.

Isabelle's heart kicked at the sight of him. His wavy, dark hair was in windswept disarray, and the dust and mud splatters all over his finely tailored clothes bespoke his long day in the saddle.

In a flash, Sally's arm clamped around Naomi once again, and the gun pressed to her head.

Isabelle cursed. Marshall's eyes flew to her. Isabelle nodded once, answering his unspoken question. Yes, she was all right.

"So glad you've descended from on high to join us, Yer Grace," Sally mocked. "I'd begun to think I wouldn't have the pleasure of making your acquaintance, but now that you're here, there's something I'd like to discuss."

"And what would that be?" Marshall mused.

"Do not play stupid with me!" Spittle flew from Sally's lips. Her nostrils flared. "I'm going to make it real clear for you, Monthwaite. Drop your gun, or I kill your sister."

Isabelle heard the sickening sound of Sally's pistol cocking.

Marshall held his hands out and slowly bent his knees, placing the gun on the floor.

"Kick it," Sally demanded.

Marshall shoved the pistol with his foot. It spun away under a table, out of reach.

"And now," Sally said through tight lips, "we're going to have that discussion. Or, to be more precise, *you're* going to do some discussing. I'm going to listen and so are these ladies. And so help me God, don't you dare pretend you don't know what I mean."

Just then, another man burst into the greenhouse—lean and hard in appearance, his face had the rugged look of a man much used to working out-of-doors. Panting, he pressed one hand to his heaving chest and raised the other. "Sally," he gasped, "stop this madness!"

"Thomas!" Sally beamed at the newcomer. "I was going to come home to you again, my love, just as soon as it was all over."

"It's over now, Sally," the man proclaimed. "You made your point with the mare, though I wish to God you hadn't done—you know I wouldn't have wanted you to," he chided. "There's no need to harm anyone else. Put down the gun."

Sally shook her head; a strand of hair clung to her sweat-sheened cheek in a graceful curve incongruous with the mad gleam in her eyes. "I can't, Thomas. Don't you see? I'm doing this for you, dear heart, for us!" She nodded fervently, then returned her attention to Marshall. "Even better," she announced with a triumphant lift of her chin. "You can say it in front of these ladies *and* Thomas. Do it!"

Isabelle's eyes went back and forth between Sally and Marshall. At last, Marshall ducked his head in a gesture of capitulation.

When he lifted his head again, his dark eyes were filled with anguish. "I'm responsible for the death of the mare and her foal."

Isabelle inhaled sharply. That wasn't really true. He was just saying it to appease Sally, wasn't he?

"I cooked the herbal medicine," Marshall said. "I made a mistake, and it went wrong." He shook his head slowly. "I was scared and ashamed, and I let Mr. Gerald take the blame. For that, I am sincerely and utterly sorry."

A cold, hard weight settled in Isabelle's stomach. It was true, all of it.

Marshall held his hands out, palms up. "I understand why you are angry. But if you'd just listen—"

"You ruined his life!" Sally snapped. "When I met him, my Thomas was on a labor gang of criminals instead of practicing an honest trade. D'you know how hard it'll be, with that hanging over us?" A strangled sound came from her throat, and it took Isabelle a moment to realize the woman was holding back furious tears. "But I'll do it, Thomas," she swore passionately. "I'll stay by your side through thick and thin, just like a good woman should, no matter how this lyin' bastard has spoiled things for us."

"Sally, please put down the gun," Thomas begged. "You're not helping me none this way!"

Isabelle watched the young woman in horrified fascination. She shook visibly with the force of her anger and hurt, her countenance as terrible as an avenging angel.

"Will taking Lady Naomi's life somehow make it all better?" Marshall reasoned.

Sally sniffed. She wiped her cheek with the back of her hand holding the gun. She shook her head. "No," she said in a quieter, calmer tone. "But taking yours will." In one smooth motion, she raised her hand, then lowered her arm and pulled the trigger.

The gun's rapport slammed against Isabelle's eardrums. Marshall collapsed to the greenhouse floor.

Naomi screamed and Thomas bellowed.

Isabelle barely registered what had happened. She seized one of the heavy jugs Marshall used for mixing plant food from the workbench and ran. With the murderous shot still ringing in her ears, she brought the jug crashing down on the crown of Sally's head. The woman fell in a heavy heap with her arm still around Naomi, pulling her down to the floor, too.

Isabelle tossed aside the remnants of the jug and dragged Naomi free of Sally's grasp. She grabbed the gun then raced across the floor and knelt beside Marshall.

A trickle of blood seeped from beneath his prone body, spreading crimson fingers across the flagstones. "Help me roll him," Isabelle said. Together, the women and Thomas Gerald turned Marshall onto his back. Thomas then sprinted to assess Sally's condition.

Marshall's face was ashen; he groaned weakly.

A wound in his upper thigh bled freely. Isabelle clamped her hand on top of the bullet hole. Marshall's blood welled up between her fingers, hot and wet, and spilled down to join the rapidly growing puddle on the floor. In desperation, she hastily wadded her skirt and pressed it against the wound. She had to stanch the blood; a leg wound could easily prove fatal. "Get help!" she yelled.

Naomi blanched as she watched in wide-eyed alarm. She nodded quickly, scrambled to her feet, and ran from the greenhouse, screaming at the top of her lungs.

Isabelle pressed down on Marshall's leg with all her strength. His lips drained of color, and it seemed to her that his breathing was becoming shallow.

Her heart felt as though it were ripping in two. She cried out in anguish. "Don't you die," she wailed. "You cannot!"

The fabric of her skirt was soon sodden with his lifeblood. Marshall was slipping away beneath her fingers. A primal scream tore from her throat. She redoubled her efforts at compression, willing her own life to pass into Marshall.

He drew a shuddering breath and was still.

Chapter Nineteen

Pain.

He was on fire. Fire all over.

"He's waking."

"Keep him still! There's no room for error. If I slip, we'll lose him."

"Drink, Your Grace."

Something wet touched his lips. He drank deeply and greedily, trying to quench the fire.

A cool touch on his head, like a breath of air.

"Isabe—"

* * *

Pain.

Sharp and throbbing all at once, radiating from his thigh. His stomach felt weak. His very bones hurt.

"You awake, Marsh?"

He dragged his eyelids over hot, dry eyes.

Sunlight filtered around the heavy curtains covering his windows. He squinted. Grant sat in an armchair that'd been brought near the bed.

He opened his mouth to speak, but coughed. His tongue was dry and swollen. "Water," he croaked.

Grant poured a glass from the carafe on the bedside table and supported his head while he drank. "Now that you're awake, I suppose the danger has passed and I've missed my chance to become duke." He smiled wryly.

Marshall exhaled a raspy laugh. "Still could happen. Don't have a surplus of heirs at the moment."

He fell heavily against his pillow and stared at the plaster ceiling for several minutes. "How long've I been out?" he slurred.

"Almost two days."

Marshall nodded. His memory of the greenhouse was hazy. He remembered riding like hellfire after encountering Thomas Gerald. He'd gone looking for Isabelle when she wasn't in the kitchen, and followed her silly, ingenious carrot trail to the greenhouse. It was all murky after that. The raw fear at finding his sister and his beloved held by an armed kidnapper was all that remained.

"What happened?" he asked.

Grant ran a hand through his light brown hair. "Your former wife saved the Monthwaite line from near extinction, is what happened."

Marshall's eyes widened.

"Naomi told us how Isabelle cracked Sally Palmer over the head after she shot you. Then she ruined her dress keeping you alive until the surgeon took over." His eyes widened in frank admiration. "You should have seen her, Marsh. She was like a mother bear, snapping at anyone who came too close. When we carried you back here on a stretcher, she walked right alongside with her skirt hitched up to her hips to keep the pressure on your wound."

Marshall must have looked scandalized, for Grant waved a hand. "Her petticoat kept us from becoming better acquainted."

He pictured Isabelle as Grant described her, throwing propriety to the wind to save his life. A surge of overwhelming love and gratitude would have knocked him flat had he not already been prostrate. How had he ever not known he loved her?

One additional thought tugged at him. "Where's Gerald? And the woman?"

"The magistrate's got them," Grant said. "We were waiting to see what the charges would be." He suddenly became very interested in his hands.

"Waiting for me to die to charge her with murder?"

"Oh, for God's sake, Marsh. No one was waiting for you to die. But if you had, then yes, they would have been charged."

"Gerald didn't do anything. It was all the woman's scheme. In fact, the trail Mr. Turner followed was the one Gerald left chasing her all over the countryside, trying to stop her tour of vengeance. Have him released at once." Marshall scratched idly at his cheek. Long stubble dug under his nails. "I need a shave," he said. "And a bath. And then I'd like to speak with Isabelle." As eager as he was to see her, he wanted to be decent when he did. He should be presentable when he told her that he loved her.

Grant summoned Clayton to see to Marshall's needs. Before he left him to his bath and shave, Grant clapped Marshall on the shoulder. "I'm glad you're on the mend, Marsh." He shoved his hands into his pockets and clicked his tongue. "I'm starting to think perhaps I misjudged Isabelle." His mouth twisted to the side, abashed. "Mother's beginning to come around, too. She owes the lives of two of her children to your former wife. Hard to be angry after such heroism."

Marshall's eyebrows rose. "I'm glad to hear it."

A little more than an hour later, Marshall was shaved and reasonably clean. He was dressed in a fresh nightshirt and bed jacket, and propped against a small mountain of pillows when a soft knock sounded on the door. In answer, his heart thundered against his ribs.

Isabelle stepped into the room and carefully closed the door behind her. Her satin dress was the pinkish gold of perfectly burnished copper, tied with a light green sash. She looked furtively around the room, as though expecting to find another assassin waiting to assail them.

Her beauty made his breath catch in his throat. She was a vision of everything that was good in Marshall's life. He wanted nothing more than to take her in his arms and show her better than he could say just how much he loved her. "Isabelle." Voicing her name brought a smile to his lips.

Her eyes darted to him, then flitted away again.

Why was she so skittish? This was not the warm reunion he'd hoped for. "Come sit with me." He extended an arm.

Isabelle lifted her chin in that pert way of hers. She eyed him warily as she crossed the room to the chair Grant had occupied.

"Come here." Marshall patted the brocade duvet.

"This will do." She smoothed her skirt with her palms. Then she clasped her hands in her lap and looked vacantly around the room as though Marshall was not even there.

"I understand I have you to thank for my life," he said, adopting a business-like tone. "And Naomi's. There aren't words to adequately express—"

She cut him off with an irritated wave of her hand. "I didn't save Naomi's life. Miss Palmer had already shot you. She'd have had to reload to threaten Naomi. I just kept her from doing so."

What the devil was she irked about? Marshall cleared his throat. "Still, had it not been for your actions, I, at least—"

"Why did you do it?" Isabelle snapped. Her eyes flashed green ire.

A heavy uneasiness settled in his middle. "Why did I do what?"

Her chin trembled. "You're responsible for the death of the horse all those years ago, not Mr. Gerald."

Marshall jerked away from the accusation in her eyes. He felt like he was standing on the edge of a precipice, and that Isabelle was about to push him over. More than anything, he wanted her to look at him with love in her eyes again. He dug his hands into the mattress beside his hips and raised himself further, wincing at the piercing pain the movement elicited.

Isabelle's face was a stone mask.

He ran a hand through his damp hair. "I was thirteen," he said. "She was my father's favorite brood mare. I confused yew berries for juniper. It was a horrible, terrible accident. You have to believe that."

She crossed her arms under her breasts. "I believe it was an accident. But why did you blame Thomas Gerald? Why was he transported for your mistake?"

Marshall shook his head. "He was blamed because he's the one who fed the medicine to the horse. If you'd seen how devastated and furious my father was, I was horrified by what happened. I—" he stammered, "I was afraid of disappointing my father, of letting him down. It was a terrible shock."

Isabelle exhaled loudly. "What would he have done?" Her voice rose in pitch. "Docked your allowance?"

Her words stung like nettles. He wiped a hand across his forehead.

"Lest you forget," she said indignantly, "I knew your father briefly. He adored you. He went against your mother's wishes in blessing our marriage just to make you happy. You cannot tell me the punishment he gave you would have been worse than what happened to Mr. Gerald."

He flinched. "No, I never said—"

"No, you didn't say!" she yelled, not giving him an inch. "You didn't say for years and years. Even after your father died, you didn't do the right thing." She leaned forward, jabbing a finger toward him. "A single word from you could have fixed the whole mess, but you never did it. Never."

God, it was all going so wrong! He was supposed to be declaring his love, not scrambling to explain himself.

He reached toward her. She snatched her arm back and jumped out of the chair, then crossed to the window and leaned her head against the glass. For a long moment, heavy silence filled the space between them.

"I was a child, and I made a child's mistake. And I did try to set things right, Isabelle. After Father died, after the divorce, I tried. Legal channels are deathly slow. By the time his name was officially cleared, his time was up. I couldn't get word to Australia sooner than the end of his sentence." The old frustration and guilt swamped him. "Once he left, my men couldn't find him. But I tried. His name was cleared, Isabelle. Shall I show you the papers?"

Cold eyes pinned him to the bed. "It doesn't matter anymore."

"Don't act this way," he pleaded. "If I could take it all back, I would. You cannot know how the guilt has eaten at me for years. I am so damned sorry."

Her head snapped around. "You're sorry?" Her voice had become frighteningly quiet. "You felt guilty." Her lip curled, as though he was a distasteful specimen she was forced to examine.

Somehow, Marshall preferred her to yell at him. He licked his lips. "I'd hoped we'd have a pleasanter conversation today, Isabelle. About the future."

She turned away to look out the window again. "What future?" Her words fell like stones into a well.

She was leaving him.

His breathing became rapid and shallow. "Ours, darling." If only she would look at him. If he could make her angry, even, then they could hash it all out and make up. "I'll apply for a special license when we're back in town. We can marry as soon as possible."

When she looked at him again, it was like staring into the eyes of a stranger. The green irises were flat, devoid of any emotion whatsoever.

"I will not marry you, sir," she said in a bored tone. "You have a nasty habit of ruining people. You can clear names and print apologies all you want, but you cannot give us back the time we lost. I would be a fool to give you the chance to do it to me again."

She strode across the carpet to the door. Fear choked him, stealing his breath. His heart felt like it was standing still, about to die. Her hand touched the doorknob.

"Wait!" The word tore from his throat.

She paused, but did not look at him.

"I've made mistakes," Marshall said in a rush. He felt like he was drowning, thrashing to keep his head from going under. "But there are no more secrets now, Isabelle, I swear it. We can truly make a new start. Listen to me, darling." He swallowed. "This isn't how I imagined telling you, with me injured in bed and you angry, but it doesn't matter. I love you." He laughed softly. "I've always loved you, but I was too stupid to realize it. That's why it hurt so much before. But none of that signifies now. I love you, Isabelle, and I swear I'll do anything and everything within my power to make you happy."

He paused to take a breath.

She remained impassive. "Are you finished?"

Marshall's jaw went slack. He'd failed. He stared disbelievingly at the woman he loved more than life itself, the woman who was about to walk out of his world forever. He shook his head. "I love you," he whispered hoarsely, his entire being thrumming with yearning.

She twisted the knob and opened the door. Then she turned her head slightly so he could see her beautiful profile. "I love you, too," she said dully. "But it will pass."

* * *

The door closed with a soft click. She met Caro and Naomi on the landing and paused to greet her younger friend. The dowager duchess reached a hand toward her. "Isabelle . . ." the older woman began.

Isabelle blinked. She realized it was the first time in ages—perhaps ever—she'd heard her own name on her former mother-in-law's lips. Suspicion had her backing away almost immediately. What did the witch want now? Something inside raised a voice. *No more*, it said. *This ends.*

Caro's lips turned upward. Horns springing from her head would have looked more natural than a smile. "I want to thank you . . ."

Her words trailed away as Isabelle stared blankly at her, a deliberate, stupefied expression devoid of recognition. She continued to regard the woman quizzically until, finally, the color drained from Caro's face.

"Oh," Caro said in a small voice. "I see."

She fled down the stairs. Naomi gave Isabelle an anguished look before following her mother.

Caro's change in attitude, which once would have seemed a miracle, was no longer of any consequence. Giving her the cut direct was not the gratifying experience Isabelle could have hoped for. What Caro thought of or said about her no longer mattered.

Nothing did.

She'd spent the hours after the greenhouse in a kind of numb haze, scared out of her mind that Marshall was going to die. When it became apparent that he would not, the shock wore off, giving her opportunity to ruminate on all she'd learned.

The unfortunate truth was that Marshall Lockwood had stolen her life, Justin Miller's, and Thomas Gerald's. If she'd been in the convict's shoes, she would have wanted to shoot Marshall, too—and the only surprise was that it was not Mr. Gerald with the violent streak, after all, but his lover.

Before seeing Marshall today, she'd already determined not to marry him. She was furious. But then something happened in the injured duke's room.

The more she'd railed against him, the angrier she'd become—not at him, but at herself. The longer he attempted to explain away his actions, the more she couldn't believe she'd ever fallen for his flimsy veneer of honor.

And then, suddenly, there was nothing. He'd taken everything from her—her trust, her love, her respect—and showed it all for the rubbish it was. All the feelings she'd had for him, good and bad, were simply gone.

She returned to her own room and sat in a window seat overlooking the rose garden.

The gaping emptiness where her heart used to be terrified her. If she could just feel something, *anything*, it would be better than this nothing.

She blinked rapidly. A woman in her position should be weeping at the injustice of her lot right about now. Her eyes remained dry. She just couldn't muster the emotion needed to cry. There was simply nothing left.

* * *

At the sound of the sharp rap on the door, Marshall perked hopefully. But he realized a split second later that it couldn't be Isabelle. That was a man's knock. His spirits plummeted again.

He was not surprised when Alex Fairfax came in. He was not surprised by the man's perplexed expression. And from the instant he'd realized there was a man at the door, he'd fully expected the first words out of Alex's mouth.

"What happened?"

Isabelle's brother looked down at the bedridden duke with frank curiosity. There was no malice or vitriol in his expression or tone, only bewilderment. "When I saw my sister ten minutes ago," Alex continued, "she told me she was ready to leave. Her trunk is already packed. What happened, Monthwaite?"

Marshall breathed a humorless laugh. "I happened," he muttered. "I ruined everything with her when I was thirteen years old and every day since."

Alex raised a questioning brow. "Have you taken laudanum again, man?"

"I'll have the bank draft for her quarter million drawn up." A great weight pressed down on Marshall's chest. He blinked heavily. "If she ever needs anything more, anything at all . . ."

He was not expecting the sobs that suddenly shook him, great, racking sobs that protested a life without Isabelle.

When he opened his eyes to apologize, he was alone.

Chapter Twenty

A minuscule adjustment of the small, concave mirror beneath the specimen stage flooded the glass slide with light. Marshall carefully rotated the microscope head until the blurred image of pea roots sharpened into focus.

He examined the thread-fine structures for any sign of wilt. Finding no evidence of decay, he jotted a few notes before removing that slide and replacing it with a cutting from the stem of the same plant, one of his hybrids from Bensbury. The sample showed neat, regular cell walls, with none of the discoloration or deterioration associated with wilt.

Each specimen he scrutinized was healthy, despite the plant having grown in soil known to be contaminated with the disease. *Damnation, I think I've done it.* He'd have to grow a new generation of plants to be sure his hybrid was truly wilt-resistant, as well as ask some colleagues to check behind him by growing plants from his seeds. Hornsby would certainly help, he thought. A weak sense of satisfaction slogged its way through his mind, but it was too feeble to take hold and bloom into any kind of positive emotion.

He stepped unsteadily back from the microscope and reached for the glass of scotch that had become omnipresent in recent weeks. Finding it empty, he limped across the conservatory to where a decanter stood on a table. As he poured, the door opened to admit his mother. He grimaced and concentrated on filling his glass.

"There you are." Caro's brows drew together in a worried frown. "You've spent too much time cooped up inside; you're looking rather wan, dear. And you're losing weight. Now that you're a bit more mobile, wouldn't you like to get outdoors? I'm sure Naomi would be happy to walk with you, or you could ask a friend to join us here."

"I'm not asking anyone to Helmsdale to stroll with me while I convalesce." He greedily swallowed a mouthful of liquor, willing it to dull his senses more quickly.

"You're drinking too much," Caro said in a fretful tone. "Don't think I haven't noticed. You've got to take better care of yourself. You're behaving just like the first time—" Her mouth shut with a snap of her teeth.

Marshall laughed bitterly. "Go on, say it. Just like the first time I parted ways with Isabelle, you mean? Is it supposed to be easier to have one's guts turned inside out and stomped into the ground the second time? Does one become inured to the sensation?"

"Lord, son, you're drunk." Caro shook her head and tsked. "It isn't even noon yet. You must get a hold of yourself. This cannot continue."

His eyes roved the face of the woman who had given him life. Pleasant memories floated across his vision, of stories before bed and birthday dinners and time spent together in the garden. But they were all many years past. Caro had never learned to relent control of her children's lives to them as they matured. Pity washed over him, tempered by his weariness of dealing with her ceaseless interference. "You can't stand that we grew up, can you?"

Her eyes clouded. "I haven't the foggiest notion what you mean. Watching my children grow into adulthood has been the greatest joy of my life."

"I don't believe you."

She pinned him with an arch look. "And if one of you would make me a grandmamma before I die, my work will be complete."

His jaw tightened. Anger coursed through his veins, setting his hands to trembling. Scotch sloshed over the rim of his glass and across his fingers. "You cannot be serious!"

She strolled to the glass wall and looked out over the expansive parkland, now ringed with trees displaying vibrant gold and orange foliage. "Of course I'm serious. All women of a certain age want grandchildren."

He rubbed his eyes. Maybe he had been drinking too much. "You did everything in your power to separate me from Isabelle. I don't believe for one instant that grandchildren crossed your mind. We might have had a nursery full by now, but for you!"

She turned and huffed. "You still don't understand. For your sake, Marshall, I'm sorry she's gone, but I can't say I wish it were different. She was never the proper choice. Somehow, I seem to have failed to educate you when it comes to the importance of marrying a female of our class, a noblewoman of good breeding and character. Someone like Lucy."

His eyes narrowed and he stalked forward, dropping his glass beside the microscope. Halting in front of her, he looked down with a disgusted sneer. "Hear me now, and hear me well. You don't get a say about my life. My marriage was my own to handle, not yours. And what you did to us is unforgivable. Frankly, I don't know if I will ever not despise you for what you took from me. I hope it was worth it."

Caro swallowed. Her eyes slid down his face and chest.

"Mother." Slowly, she raised her fearful eyes to his again. "I have an unfulfilled promise to keep."

The color drained from her face and she quailed visibly. He gave her a toothy, ruthless smile. "I promised I would deal with you later, if you recall. Later has arrived."

She raised a brow and firmed her lips, but voiced no reply.

Marshall clasped his hands behind his back and straightened. "This is my decision. Because the divorce into which you wrongly manipulated Isabelle and myself resulted in her expulsion from society, it is only fitting that you endure a similar fate."

Caro gasped, stricken. "You can't do that!"

"I just did."

She raised her chin. "What if I refuse? You can't lock me away like a prisoner. I shall go to town as I see fit."

"Fine." Marshall threw his hands wide. "Go to town. You're right, I can't stop you. But," he said, raising a finger, "I can cut you off."

"You wouldn't dare," she hissed.

"Just try me," he ground out. "At this point, I'd really like to see you do that."

Caro's face went ashen. "How long do you intend to keep me here?"

Marshall shrugged. "I haven't quite decided. It took Isabelle three years to regain some degree of society." Caro staggered backward. "We'll start with a year," he declared. "Next September, then, we'll see where things stand. If you've behaved yourself out here, maybe I'll let you come back to town."

"But what about Naomi?" Caro asked. "You can't mean her to miss next Season."

"Aunt Janine will keep an eye on her until I'm back from South America. Grant will be in town in the spring, too. She'll be perfectly well cared for."

The light in Caro's eyes dimmed. She seemed to collapse in on herself as her shoulders slumped and her head drooped. For a woman as self-important as his mother, there was nothing worse he could do than render her useless. But when it came right down to it, that's exactly what she'd already made herself.

* * *

A week later, Marshall started back to town. With the expedition sailing in less than two months, he couldn't waste any more time rusticating. His leg was strong enough to support his weight without a cane most of the time, and Caro's attempts to change his decision about her exile at Helmsdale were becoming tedious.

He stopped to stay the night at David Hornsby's home before the final leg of the trip to London. His colleague met him with his typical air of being one drink shy of blindingly drunk. And yet, as usual, he managed to defy reason and speak coherently when they repaired to the library after supper to discuss the herbarium.

Marshall tapped his thumbnail against his teeth while Hornsby showed him the architect's proposed design. He listened with only half an ear as his friend pointed out the building's features and the layout of the various gardens that would surround the facility.

"'M thinkin' of a water garden," Hornsby slurred. "It'd go 'bout here." He jabbed at the plan. "Now, what do you think about a pagoda for a folly? Or a temple? Or would a mock ruin be more picturesque?"

Marshall shook his head, endeavoring to focus and catch up with the conversation. "Pardon?"

"Over here, look." Hornsby gestured to a rectangular area on the plan. "Maybe a rose garden. I've always liked yours at Bensbury—do you s'pose you could help with the herbarium's?"

Marshall cringed at the mention of the Bensbury rose garden, a brutal reminder of his failed courtship of Isabelle. When he squeezed his eyes closed, he saw her on the backs of his lids as she'd looked the night of Naomi's party, all rumpled, delectable female—soft in his hands and generous in her affections. And she'd needed him then, every bit as much as he'd needed her. *But she doesn't need you anymore.*

"Are you all right?"

Marshall cast an agonized look at his friend's red-rimmed eyes.

"You don't look well, old man." Hornsby gestured to a chair. Marshall fell heavily into it and rubbed his eyes. A moment later, Hornsby pressed a glass into his hand.

Marshall took a sip, but the alcohol made his stomach churn. He'd had his fill of overindulgence.

"A bit of bad luck," Hornsby sank into the chair across from Marshall and crossed his feet at the ankles. "Being shot, and all, I mean."

Marshall scoffed. He'd hardly given the shooting any thought, beyond the frustration it had caused him in moving about. The pain in his leg paled in comparison to the empty ache in his chest he wasn't sure would ever go away. Not this time.

But riding close behind it was the guilt he felt for Thomas Gerald, now floundering around in London, looking to rebuild his life. His young love, Sally Palmer, would return to Australia—as a convict this time. The woman had poisoned his horse, abducted his sister, and attempted murder. It had taken the weight of Marshall's influence to save her from the gallows. He couldn't help but pity the anguish Thomas must feel at losing her. Indeed, he could empathize all too well.

"If you don't mind my asking," Hornsby said, pulling Marshall from his thoughts, "what was all this about poisoned horses and whatnot? Not that I would expect a stupid journalist to get anything botanical correct, but something in the report in the paper struck me as off."

With his elbow propped on the arm of the chair, Marshall rested his forehead against his fingertips. He was exhausted and loathe to discuss recent events yet again. Nor was he particularly interested in Hornsby's drunken insights, which probably sounded more sensible in his addled mind.

The portly man clinked the decanter against his glass as he refilled his beverage. "Why don't you tell me? What happened all those years ago?"

Marshall raised his head to meet a surprisingly penetrating gaze. Hornsby's esteem for him would come crashing to earth when he heard the truth, but what did it matter? The pain of losing Isabelle had dulled his response to everything else. Losing the regard of someone like David Hornsby would not even register.

He shrugged and related the story of his father's ailing mare, and his desire to help induce her foaling. "I cooked up the medicine. Thought I'd used juniper berries. Thomas Gerald fed it to the horse, because she wouldn't let anyone else approach her. A short time later, her womb ruptured, and she and the foal died. Later, I discovered I'd made a dreadful mistake, and used yew instead of juniper."

Hornsby grunted. "Yew is nasty business."

Marshall nodded in agreement.

"However," Hornsby raised a finger, "as I suspected, you're completely mistaken about that mare's demise."

Marshall's eyes snapped to his face. "What do you mean?" His words were clipped. "I was right there in the stable when she bled to death."

"Well, that's jus' it." Hornsby took a long swallow of his drink before continuing. "Yew is deadly stuff, but it don't cause bleeding, old man—it stops the heart. If you don't believe me, we can pay a visit to Jeremiah Brodrip, a sheep farmer lives just down the way. He lost several of his flock to accidental yew poisoning this summer. And I tell you, Monty, there was no blood or anything like what you're talking about with that poor beast all those years back. C'mon, Monty, this is basic stuff. Surely, you know what's what here."

Marshall stared, stupefied, at his half-inebriated friend. "I . . . You're right. Huh." Suddenly, he felt cut loose, ungrounded. Everything he'd believed about this one wretched incident was wrong. "It was so sudden, so violent. The screaming and bleeding started seconds after Thomas gave her the medicine. I was so sure it was my fault."

Hornsby blew through his lips. "If you'd killed that horse with yew, she would've dropped dead without spilling a drop of blood. Sounds like your Thomas Gerald didn't feed her enough of it to do her in. What you've got is a foaling gone wrong, nothing more. Unfortunate about that Gerald person being dragged into all this, though he seems a shady sort anyway."

Marshall's gaze floated to the flames crackling in the fireplace. By slow, minute increments, the pain and guilt he'd carried for half his life began to fall away. He hadn't killed Priscilla and her foal, after all. For an exquisite moment, he was awash in relief.

I have to tell Isabelle, he thought. For an instant, he envisioned the warm smile she'd give him when she heard; he could almost feel the welcome weight of her in his arms when they embraced.

No, there would be none of that. The memory of her last words seared through him again like a red-hot poker. He couldn't share his news with her, because she despised him for what he'd done. She'd all but sworn to eradicate whatever love she may have felt for him.

He hastily excused himself, claiming a complaint in his wounded leg. In his guest room, he sprawled facedown across the bed while the same tormenting thoughts that had been eating at him for weeks resumed their relentless circuit.

Learning that he'd not been responsible for the mare's death was welcome news, but it did nothing to fill the hole in his life created by Isabelle's departure. While reason suggested their separation should have left two plenary individuals in its wake, this was not the case—at least not for Marshall. When Isabelle left, she'd incised out some fundamental part of his being, so that he was now less than he was when they'd been together.

Could she really stop loving him? If so, he envied her. For himself, Marshall could not foresee a diminishing of his own devotion. Further, he thought as he burrowed into the bedding, he didn't want his love to go away. Even if the object of it despised him, it was a way to keep her close, to remember what they had shared.

If only I'd known it sooner, if I'd told her sooner. The self-recriminations mounted as he drifted into an uneasy sleep. He listed them nightly, a perverse flock leaping through his mind, driving him into oblivion in the hope of escaping them. *I never should have listened to Mother. I should have made love to her a thousand times while I had the chance. I can't believe I ever doubted her. I should have come clean about Thomas Gerald straight away.*

Gerald was still an albatross of shame around his neck. As darkness blissfully brought him temporary release, he determined to find the man in London. He might never escape the torment over Isabelle, but at least he could free himself of that blot on his conscience.

Chapter Twenty-one

Bessie opened the door for Isabelle, admitting her to the rambling farmhouse she'd taken near the small cottage the two had previously inhabited. The home was modest, but more spacious than anything Isabelle ever thought she would have for herself. She handed off her shawl and gloves and rubbed her hands together. "So chilly out. You can feel winter coming in the air."

"Yes, ma'am," Bessie replied. "How was the committee meeting?"

Isabelle groaned. "Getting the ladies' auxiliary to settle on a charity to receive the proceeds of the Harvest Ball is like pulling hen's teeth. I nearly went mad listening to the bickering. When they'd narrowed it down to five, I thought it would come to blows. I finally said I'd give a thousand pounds to each if we could just pull the name of one out of a hat and conclude the meeting."

Bessie gasped. "Five thousand pounds! You're too loose with your money, ma'am," she chided. The servant clucked her tongue and shook her head.

Isabelle smiled ruefully. She understood Bessie's apprehension. When she'd lived with Isabelle before, she'd known her as Jocelyn Smith, and they'd been destitute. Isabelle had returned to the village with her true name and the unwanted burden of Marshall's money. Alexander had been quite firm on that point: take the money or marry. And since Isabelle had decided she would never marry, she took Marshall's guilt money. The least she could do was use it to help the less fortunate.

Bessie handed off Isabelle's outerwear to a passing maid. She'd taken to her new position of housekeeper like a duck to water. She kept the house running smoothly, leaving Isabelle with plenty of time to do as she pleased. Too much time, truth be told.

"The post is on your desk," Bessie said. She followed Isabelle to the sitting room where Isabelle did her writing. "There's calling cards, too."

Isabelle dropped into the elegantly curved wingback chair behind her oak desk. She pulled a penknife from the drawer and opened the envelopes.

The first one contained an invitation to Lady Chirken's birthday *fête*. The second, an invitation to join the Ladies' Society for the Improvement of Our Fallen Sisters, which, if Isabelle read between the delicately composed lines correctly, sought to provide assistance and training in new occupations to prostitutes. The next was a letter from Lily.

Isabelle scanned the lines in her friend's neat hand. "Ah!" she said. "Mrs. and Miss Bachman will be here in three weeks, Bessie. Please make a note to have rooms prepared."

She pulled the contents from the final envelope. When she unfolded the paper, a newspaper clipping fluttered to the desk. Isabelle sighed. "Still?"

The note was from someone she'd never met, asking would she please autograph and return the enclosed clipping.

Isabelle turned over the piece of newsprint, barely paying attention to the bold words: DK. MONTHWAITE SAVED IN HEROIC RESCUE, and the smaller words below, "Former wife preserves life of the duke and his sister; family calls her a heroine!"

In the weeks following Marshall's shooting, clippings identical to this one had poured into the Bachmans' London home and Fairfax Hall. She'd signed papers until her hand cramped and spent a small fortune on return postage.

Everyone seemed to want a piece of the cast-off wife who had saved her former husband and sister-in-law from a love-crazed murderess. Isabelle was touted as a heroine. Doors that had slammed in her face years ago were opened once again. She received invitations to parties, balls, charity events—and callers. People actually came to her door, seeking her company.

Inevitably, though, conversation turned to Marshall. People wanted to hear about the shooting or talk about his public apology. After a couple weeks, she'd had enough. Isabelle quit the Bachmans' home and returned to Fairfax Hall, and from there, traveled to the only place she'd ever escaped public scrutiny.

She scrawled her name across the newspaper clipping and stuffed it into an envelope. Then she picked up the five calling cards from the silver salver Bessie had brought her. She didn't recognize a single name. Isabelle tossed them back into the tray and made a disgusted sound.

The village was not the haven it once had been. As bothersome as she found signing newspaper clippings for autograph collectors, this was worse. She'd become an attraction. Perfect strangers invaded her home, hoping for an audience with the famous heroine.

If she was home, she simply refused to see the visitors. Then guilt nagged at her for disappointing people. She solved that problem by keeping herself busy. She threw herself into local charity work, traveling to schools and orphanages. She'd even been to Newgate and donated sewing supplies for the female prisoners.

Isabelle was tired. It would all blow over soon enough, but meantime, she wished people would just leave her alone. Most of all, she wished they'd stop talking about Marshall.

"What was that?" She squinted at Bessie.

"I said, ma'am, the painter came by to look at the nursery. He'd like to begin soon as possible, so he can finish before the weather turns."

Isabelle nodded. "Yes, all right. Good. He may start whenever he'd like."

Bessie wrung her hands at her waist.

Isabelle looked up from her papers. "Is there something else?"

"Begging your pardon. It prob'ly ain't my concern, but I was wondering why you're fixing up the nursery so nice." The older woman pulled her head backward so that the loose skin bunched around her cheeks and chin.

Isabelle tapped her fingernail against the desk. She closed her eyes. The old daydream came at once, a vision of holding a baby in her arms, rocking and singing while the little one cooed. But it wasn't her baby. Not anymore. The hollow ache in her chest bloomed into a staggering pain of loss. Isabelle wrenched her eyes open.

"I'll have nephews and nieces one of these days," she said quietly. "I'd like to be ready when they come to visit."

Bessie exhaled. "Oh, right. Nephews and nieces. Of course, ma'am. And might I say," she rushed, "it'll be a beautiful nursery. You have the nicest taste in colors, I always say."

"You always say that, do you?" Isabelle shook her head.

The mental picture came again: her baby, and Marshall kissing them both.

She pushed back from the desk. "Has Cook started dinner yet?" she asked as she walked briskly, trying to outpace the visions.

Bessie struggled to keep up. "I don't believe so, ma'am."

"Good."

Isabelle strode to the kitchen where her cook, a portly man, was about to decapitate a feathered pigeon.

"Stop!" Isabelle ordered. The man let out a high-pitched shriek and his knife clattered to the board.

Isabelle shooed him with a flick of her wrists. "Out you go, then. I'll see to myself tonight."

"Are you sure, ma'am?" Cook asked. "I was just about to braise—"

"That sounds excellent," Isabelle said, tying an apron around her waist. "I'll do it myself. Thank you."

The man grumbled as Isabelle evicted him from the kitchen. Then, as she did from time to time, she stood in the center of the room with her hands on her hips and took stock of her surroundings. It was a good kitchen. Perhaps not as fine as another she had cooked in, but it was clean and well-provisioned for a modest country household.

She stirred together wine and stock for the braising liquid and put the pot on to heat. Then she peeled several onions and began methodically chopping them.

As she sliced into a vegetable, the first tear slipped down her cheek. She liked to chop onions. When she worked with them, no one asked why she was crying.

* * *

". . . am prepared to offer a considerable sum for your services as translator, as I realize this has arisen at the last possible moment. The urgency of your immediate response cannot be overstated. Gratefully yours, *et cetera.*"

Marshall blew out his cheeks while Perkins finished jotting down the dictation. He looked out the window over Grosvenor Square. Crisp, dry leaves crunched under boots and hooves in the street below. The air was turning cold. In a few weeks, winter would fall upon England.

Brazil, though, would be a tropical paradise—warm and damp, teeming with undiscovered plant life. He'd wanted to do this for years, to really sink his teeth into some meaty botanical work. He was excited, he told himself as he stared dully out the window. There was nothing for him here. Brazil offered an opportunity to lose himself in his work. And he needed to lose himself in something, before he was lost forever.

"I'll send this right away, Your Grace," Perkins said.

"Tell the courier to wait for the reply," Marshall ordered.

He ran a hand down the side of his face. His cheekbone was more prominent beneath his palm than it had been a few months ago. Back when she might have loved him. Before she despised him, at any rate.

Perkins' papers rustled as the secretary prepared Marshall's letter. "One more thing." Marshall turned. "Please send Mr. Gerald in. I'd like to finalize his list of provisions for the horses."

"Of course." Perkins bent his neck before stepping from the study.

When the secretary had gone, Marshall glumly eyed the stack of paperwork awaiting his attention.

It was no easy task for a nobleman of Marshall's position to leave the country for six months. He'd wanted the expedition to last a year, but the howls of protest from his family brought an end to that notion. Grant would have the assistance of Marshall's various solicitors, bailiffs, stewards, and men of business to keep the Monthwaite estates and investments running smoothly. Still, his brother expressed apprehension at taking the reins from Marshall for even half a year.

He plunked into his chair and began going through his work with only part of his attention on it. Another part toyed with the idea that had taken hold of him some weeks ago. What if he never came back? Accidents at sea were not unheard of. They could encounter a French war vessel. There were diseases in South America, too, like yellow fever. As heir apparent, Grant would have to take over the dukedom permanently if something happened to Marshall. He was a smart, capable young man. He would adapt.

Grant would adapt, too, if he simply didn't come back for a year, Marshall thought petulantly. Or never. He could send word once he was there. No one could force him to return. And the work he could accomplish! Ignoring the other work demanding his notice, he jotted down a few notes as to what he could say to explain a permanent leave of absence.

"Oh, there you are," Naomi said breezily as she strolled in, as though Marshall hadn't been chained to his desk for the last month.

Marshall flipped his notes over. "What is it?" he asked without looking at her.

"Nothing, really." There was a soft rustling of fabric as she settled into the chair across the desk. "I'd like to spend some time with my brother before he sails to the other side of the world."

Marshall cleared his throat and very carefully affixed his signature to a purchase order. "I don't have any time to give you just now."

She took no notice of his dismissal. "It's such a shame you won't be here for Christmas. It's always such a jolly time watching you and Grant try to out-eat each other. Now poor Grant shall have to dispatch the lion's share of the goose all by himself. I fear his stomach will burst, and then where will that leave Mama and I? Oh, well," she sighed, "I don't suppose that's any of your concern, now is it?"

Marshall pressed his lips together and resolutely kept his eyes on his work. If he ignored her, she would leave.

Several minutes of silence passed. Marshall became engrossed in a report of Hamhurst's autumnal crop yield, and truthfully forgot his sister was still in the study.

"I wonder if Isabelle will prepare Christmas dinner herself or if she'll have a cook do it."

Marshall startled at Naomi's voice. He slapped his hand against the desk. "Are you still here? I told you I have work to do."

Naomi shrugged. She held her hand out at arm's length, examining her manicure. "I haven't prevented you from working, have I?"

Marshall made an annoyed sound at the back of his throat and attempted to put his mind back on the report.

Naomi hummed tunelessly.

Marshall closed his eyes and took several deep breaths. He reminded himself how grateful he was Naomi had not been harmed when she was abducted. When he remembered that harrowing trial, it sapped the worst of his temper.

"I had a letter from Miss Bachman today," Naomi announced.

Marshall's guts twisted at the name of Isabelle's friend. In what marked the greatest display of cowardice he had ever exhibited, he'd refused to see Lily Bachman when she'd come looking for him a week after Isabelle left. At that point, he could barely hold himself together. He didn't have the fortitude to withstand another of Miss Bachman's withering diatribes, no matter how much he undoubtedly deserved it.

"Oh?" he said in a neutral tone. "I trust she is well?"

"I believe so, yes. She tells me she's going to visit Isabelle this week."

Heat crawled over his shoulders and neck. Why wouldn't she go away and leave him alone? "How about that," he said noncommittally.

"She related an amusing anecdote," Naomi said. "It seems Isabelle found herself trapped in the middle of a squabbling committee of ladies who could not decide on a cause for their charity event. So Isabelle promised a thousand pounds to each of five causes, just to make the women be quiet and end the meeting." Naomi let out a silvery laugh.

Marshall felt like the air had been punched from him. "Did she really?" he managed to drawl.

"Isn't that just like Isabelle?" Naomi shook her head from side to side. "Generous as the day is long, but won't put up with anyone's nonsense." She laughed again. "It reminds me of the time she—"

Marshall's fist crashed against his desk, sending papers flying. "Enough!" he roared. "Get out!"

Naomi flinched as though he had struck her. Then her eyes filled with tears and her chin trembled.

Marshall immediately regretted yelling at her.

She scrambled out of her chair and backed away from him. "You've been monstrous ever since she left. I used to feel sorry for you, but I don't anymore." Her mouth twisted with hurt and anger.

Marshall stood, his temper rising again. "If my society doesn't suit, I can pack you off to Helmsdale to keep Mother company."

"I'm glad you're running away to Brazil." Naomi fumbled with the doorknob behind her. "You're an idiot." She wrenched the door open. "Isabelle is better off without you," she shot, "and we will be, too." She turned on a slippered heel with a flourish of her skirts, and slammed the door behind her.

Marshall stood at his desk, staring at the door. He flexed his hands, opening and closing them into fists at his side. As much as he'd like to take offense at Naomi's remarks, he couldn't. He was an idiot. He was a bad-tempered brute who made his sister cry. And Isabelle was better off without him. About that, and so many other things, Naomi was absolutely right.

Chapter Twenty-two

Isabelle sat on a wooden bench in the little garden behind the house. Despite the cold morning, the sun shone warm on her face. The pages of her book gleamed a soft white.

"Ma'am!"

She looked up from her reading. Bessie leaned out a window with her hands cupped around her mouth. Isabelle smiled and shook her head. The woman would never be a prim housekeeper like the stuffed shirts the titled class employed, but Bessie's earthy ways suited Isabelle just fine.

"What is it?" she called back.

"There's a gentleman here to see you."

"Who?"

"He asked me not to say. He says it's a surprise."

Isabelle's smile faltered. Marshall? Her heart slammed against her ribs. She gulped. "Show him to the parlor," she instructed. "Tell him I'll be right there."

She marked her page and closed the book, then pressed the backs of her fingers to her mouth.

Marshall had come to her. At last. She'd gotten past her anger, but it didn't change the fact that he couldn't be trusted again. *Could he?* The question clanged in her mind over and over as she walked to the house.

She removed her bonnet and briefly considered changing into something more presentable. No, she decided. This was her home. She would meet him on her terms. She patted her hair, then opened the parlor door.

A man stood with his back to her. His broad shoulders filled a camel coat. A white neck cloth peeked over the collar, and a bit of sunned neck showed in the space between the cravat and his clipped, sandy-colored hair.

At the sound of the door, he turned. His hazel eyes crinkled as a broad grin split his face.

"Justin?" Isabelle clapped a hand to her mouth and staggered back against the door. Her eyes widened in stunned disbelief at the vision before her. Her dear friend had been missing for so long, without a word—but here he was, in her parlor!

"Hello, Isa." He cocked his head to the side in that disarmingly charming way of his. "How are you, darling?"

Isabelle threw herself into his outstretched arms. He grabbed her to his chest in a strong hug. She laughed and laughed while joyous tears poured down her face.

"Oh, my God," she murmured. "You're home. I thought I'd never see you again."

He gave her a tight squeeze and grunted. Then he dropped a kiss on her forehead and pushed her back to arm's length.

"You look wonderful, Isa. Tell me how you've been keeping yourself."

Isabelle wiped her face with a handkerchief. She sniffed loudly. "How have I been?" she said through her smile and tears. "Are you serious?"

She gestured to a chair. Justin sat, crossing his right ankle to his left knee. Isabelle sank to an adjacent settee.

"You heard about the divorce."

Justin's smile fell. He nodded and looked at his shoes.

As happy as she was to finally see her friend, a myriad of questions that had plagued her for years came bubbling to the surface. She tucked her legs up against her side and leaned toward him. "Where were you?" she asked softly. "I faced the entire House of Lords. My name was shredded in the papers. I lived in exile, Justin."

He made a clucking sound, and a wretched expression crossed his face. "I'm so sorry you had to face that alone, Isa. I should have ignored his threats and stayed close."

Isabelle's brow furrowed. "Whose threats? Marshall's?"

"Yes, at least," he gave a half-smile and jerked his head to the side, "I thought so. Now I'm not so sure."

Isabelle's head reeled. "I don't understand."

Justin raised his hands. "I'm hoping you can help me clarify a few things. We'll get to that. I thought you'd like to know where I've been the last several years."

"That's a bit of an understatement," Isabelle said.

"I went to America," Justin said. "It was made clear to me in no uncertain terms that I could either expatriate myself or suffer fatal consequences."

Isabelle startled. "Marshall threatened to kill you?" Her brow furrowed. "That doesn't sound like him at all." Then she remembered how he'd pounced on Viscount Woolsley when he'd asked Isabelle to become his mistress. Maybe he would have been capable of threatening Justin, when he thought he'd been intimate with his wife.

"See for yourself." Justin produced an envelope from his pocket and handed it to Isabelle. The corners were bent and the edges worn. The broken wax seal was brittle with age, but bore the unmistakable imprint of the Monthwaite crest.

Isabelle scanned the unsigned note, which indeed bore a very threatening message. Something about it though wasn't right. And then it came to her.

"But Justin," she said, looking up, "this isn't—"

"Da da!" squealed a little voice.

A very small girl wearing a light blue dress took several toddling steps through the parlor door and across the rug before falling to her knees. She resolutely pushed herself up again. Her tiny, rosebud lips pursed in a determined scowl as she half-ran, half-fell toward Justin.

For an instant, Isabelle thought she was daydreaming again, imagining the precocious child.

"There's my girl!" Justin said in a happy tone. "All clean now?"

Isabelle's jaw dropped in surprise.

Justin slid from the chair to the floor, his legs sprawled wide. He held his hands out to the little child. She gurgled a laugh when he snatched her up and lavished kisses on her plump cheeks.

"Hello, ma'am."

A pretty, dark-haired woman about Isabelle's age followed the baby into the room and made an awkward curtsy.

Isabelle's questioning eyes flew to Justin. He smiled and shrugged. She stood to greet the newcomer. "Mrs. Miller, I presume?"

Justin clambered to his feet with the small child in his arms. "Isa, this is my wife, Mrs. Rebecca Miller."

"How do you do," the woman said in an unfamiliar accent. She curtsied again and wobbled, clearly unaccustomed to such gestures.

Isabelle clasped her hand. "I'm so pleased to meet you, Mrs. Miller," she said. "Please don't curtsy, I'm not the queen." She smiled warmly, hoping to put the woman at ease. Instead, Mrs. Miller's face flushed pink up to her brunette hairline.

"And this," Justin hoisted the little girl around to face her, "is Belle."

Isabelle leaned forward, bringing her face level to Belle's. The little girl had round, rosy cheeks and a tiny nose. Her eyes were a startling hazel and they peered fearlessly at Isabelle.

"She has your eyes, Justin," Isabelle murmured.

The girl's hair was a wispy, honey brown fringe on the top of her head. Isabelle lightly stroked the feathery hair that felt like silk under her fingers. "Hello, darling."

Belle extended a small hand with bits of fuzz stuck to it and grabbed Isabelle's nose in a strong grip.

"Ow!" Isabelle yelped in pretend pain.

Belle gave an open-mouthed laugh, revealing eight miniature, pearly white teeth in her gums.

Tears stung Isabelle's eyes. "Justin, she's perfection."

She looked up to his face, which beamed with pride. "Isn't she?"

"Did you really name her for me?" she asked.

"No," Justin deadpanned. "She's named for my other friend Isabelle."

Isabelle wrinkled her nose. She turned to his wife. "Please, Mrs. Miller, sit down."

Mrs. Miller sank onto the sofa and smoothed her simple cotton dress with her hands. "Call me, Rebecca, ma'am."

"Of course," she acquiesced. "But you must call me Isabelle."

Bessie arrived with tea. Little Belle crawled around the floor, always staying close to her mother and father. She pulled up on her mama's skirt, balancing precariously on small, booted feet.

"How old is she?" Isabelle asked as she poured for everyone.

"A year last month," Rebecca answered, stroking the girl's head fondly.

An unexpected sadness crept over Isabelle as she watched the mother and daughter's loving interaction. "I wish I'd known you were coming," she said, blinking away her despondency. "I'm having the nursery painted. I'd have done it sooner—"

Justin cut her off with a wave of his hand. "We wouldn't arrive on your doorstep unannounced and expect to stay with you. There's a fine inn in the village that will suit."

"The George?"

"That's the one," Justin answered. "Do you know it?"

Isabelle raised her teacup and chuckled. "Yes, I'm familiar with the establishment. It's a good inn." She sipped her beverage. "I do hope you'll stay here, though. It won't be any trouble at all."

Rebecca and Justin exchanged a silent communication. Isabelle envied their obvious closeness.

"All right, then," Rebecca answered. "Thank you so much for your hospitality, ma'am."

"Dearest, you must not bestow any honorific upon Isa whatsoever," Justin chided his wife. "You should have seen the way she abused me the one and only time I called her Your Grace—and she was a duchess!"

Isabelle rolled her eyes at his teasing, but then she caught the uneasy expression on Rebecca's face. The subject of Isabelle's divorce had clearly made the woman uncomfortable. For that matter, Isabelle thought crossly, she'd never discussed it with Justin; he'd disappeared before it ever transpired. Yet, here he was, teasing her about it like he used to tug her braid.

She felt her temper rise. How could he have let so many years elapse without a single word of communication, and then come waltzing back with his American wife and child to pop in for tea as though it were nothing?

"Why didn't you write?" The words came out more bitingly than she'd intended them to do. Justin slowly lowered his teacup. "When the baby was born?" Isabelle said, moderating her tone. "Or when you married? I would have liked to have known. Or that you were in America—or alive, for that matter."

Justin flinched. "I'm sorry." All the gaiety he'd shown at their reunion evaporated. His shoulders slumped a fraction. He sighed heavily. "Isa, believe me, I've argued with myself since the second I set foot on American soil, wondering if I was doing the right thing. I know it can't have been easy for you. We visited my parents first thing when we got back. Then we went to Fairfax Hall. Alexander told us how awful the trial was."

Isabelle's jaw tightened. She didn't like to think of her brother discussing the particulars of her personal life with anyone, even if it was Justin. He hadn't been here. What gave him the right to know these things now?

"Part of me wishes I'd never left," Justin continued. "I don't know that the two of us could have stood a chance against the Lords, but at least it would've been two, and not just you." His mouth twisted in a bitter expression. Isabelle knew he felt guilty for leaving her alone to face Marshall's accusations.

"Well," Isabelle demurred, "if you hadn't gone, you wouldn't have met Mrs. Miller." She smiled and nodded toward the woman. "And sweet Belle wouldn't be gracing my home with her presence."

The baby pawed at her mother's face, oblivious to anyone else. A fresh pang of longing shot through Isabelle like an arrow. She turned on Justin again. "But why didn't you write at all?"

He leaned forward, resting his forearms on his knees; his head drooped between his shoulders. He raised his eyes to her hurt gaze. "When your mother-in-law came to Hamhurst, she made those horrible accusations. She said she sent for your husband, and she demanded I leave at once. I didn't want to go, Isa, I swear. But I feared staying in the house would make things worse for you. So I decided to wait at a nearby inn. Figured between us, you and I could convince Marshall of the truth."

Justin's fingers clenched and released. "The next evening, there was a knock on my door. Two big fellows. After that, I don't remember anything, until I woke up on a ship already at sea, with a lump on my head, a broken nose, and that letter stuffed in my pocket."

Isabelle's hand flew to her throat. "My God, Justin!" She grabbed his arm. "Are you all right?"

He chuckled. "I am now. It was a long time ago." His expression sobered. "All along, I planned to turn around and come right home, despite the threats. When we arrived in Boston, though, the captain gave me this." He produced another missive and handed it to Isabelle.

The Monthwaite ducal seal had stamped this one, too. Isabelle smoothed the creases out of the paper and began to read. And promptly felt as though she'd been slammed into a wall.

"Me?" Who hated her so much? Her voice raised an octave; there was a hollow ringing in her ears. "Why? What did we ever do to deserve this?"

Rebecca took a porcelain figurine away from the baby. "Isabelle, it's all right now. Everyone is safe. Justin, do something, for mercy's sake."

Her friend took the letter and its unthinkable words away.

"I just don't understand." she said. "Threaten me harm if you so much as contacted me? This is unreal."

"Now you know why I didn't write," Justin explained. "I didn't want to believe Monthwaite would actually hurt you. It just didn't seem like anything he was capable of. But I couldn't take a chance, Isa. I wasn't willing to risk causing you harm."

"How is it you are back now?" Isabelle asked. "If you were told never to return under pain of your death and mine . . . ?"

Justin exhaled a laugh. "It's a curious thing. Two months ago, I received a letter from Monthwaite. The third and final epistle in this saga."

"Two months?" Isabelle's eyes drifted to the window. For Justin to have received the letter two months ago, Marshall must have sent it after Isabelle left Bensbury.

He pulled another letter from the interior pocket of his coat. As he unfolded the paper he said, "He apologized profusely for accusing us of . . ." Justin's face reddened and his eyes cut to his wife.

"He said what I knew all along," Rebecca announced stoutly, "that Justin hadn't done anything wrong. Or you, ma'am," she added.

Belle twisted around in her mother's arms. She lunged toward Isabelle, who took her from Rebecca and jostled her on her knee. The little girl gurgled in delight.

Isabelle bent her neck to breathe in Belle's scent. Her hair smelled faintly of powder. All the upset of the last few minutes faded and the world receded to a hazy background. She could have happily held her friend's child for the next twenty years.

"Isa?"

Justin's voice pulled her from her blissful daze. "Hmm?"

"Can you look at this letter? This is what I wanted to ask you about. The handwriting doesn't match the others. I thought perhaps this most recent letter was a forgery, but the bank draft was good, so it seemed safe."

"Those first two aren't Marshall's hand," Isabelle said simply. "He did not write those threats. I'm stunned that anyone would, but I knew at once it wasn't Marshall. He would never kill in cold blood. And he most certainly would never threaten me so."

Calm certainty spread through her as she spoke. Marshall might be capable of horrible blunders, but he was no murderer.

He frowned. "A secretary, maybe?"

Isabelle snickered. "Really, Justin, how many gentlemen do you suppose have their secretaries scribe their criminal communications? No, Marshall neither wrote nor dictated those."

Justin extended the third letter. "How about this one?"

She recognized his distinctive hand in the salutation. "That's Marshall, definitely."

"Then who wrote the first two?" Justin mused.

Isabelle blew her cheeks out. "If I were a betting woman, I'd put my money on the dowager. She's gone to excessive lengths over the years to punish me for overstepping my station and marrying her son." She rolled her eyes. "Obviously, whoever wrote those wanted you to think they were from Marshall. She has easy access to his stationery. I don't think anything would have actually come of these threats, but even thinking to write them is ghastly."

Isabelle lapsed into a brooding silence, pondering the depths of her mother-in-law's malice. Justin seemed to detect her mood and merely handed her Marshall's letter, as Belle slipped to the floor to try walking again. Rebecca serenely picked up her daughter and took her outside.

Eventually, Isabelle began to read. Marshall's smooth voice spoke the missive in her mind. A shiver coursed down her spine.

My dear Mr. Miller,

I cannot imagine how you will receive this letter, but please believe that I approach you now humbly, with the deepest sorrow and regret for the turmoil you have experienced on my account.

Circumstances have led to the renewal of my acquaintance with Mrs. Lockwood, my former wife. Through a series of communications, I have determined that I was in the most egregious error when I accused her and yourself of wrongdoing. The pain this realization has caused me cannot be overstated. I have begged her forgiveness, and I must beg yours, as well.

It would be trite of me to assume that a few words dashed upon parchment would suffice for the years of separation from your family, friends, and homeland you have endured. While I sincerely hope you have made a satisfying life for yourself in America, I would like to extend an invitation for your return to England. I trust the enclosed bank draft will prove sufficient for your expenses. Renew your ties with family. Take up old friendships again. There is one friend in particular, dear to us both, who would welcome you back with open arms; certainly there are others.

The unfortunate circumstances surrounding your departure from England are beyond regrettable. I alone shoulder the full responsibility for your exile. Therefore, I extend the full measure of my support by any means necessary to facilitate your repatriation or whatever else you may desire.

Yours,

Monthwaite

Isabelle swallowed. *Dear to us both.*

Marshall would have found Justin regardless; this she did not doubt. He was a true gentleman, and he brought Justin back. For her. For Justin, too, of course, but he had her in mind. *There is one friend in particular, dear to us both . . .*

She missed him so much. He haunted her waking thoughts. He dwelt in her dreams. He made love to her in those dreams, sometimes tenderly, sometimes urgently, always passionately. She daydreamed about the children they might have had, but when she opened her eyes again, her arms were empty. But not her heart. It was always full of pain and longing. The longing was her constant companion. It never went away.

"Isa?"

Isabelle opened her eyes. Justin knelt on the floor in front of her. "Are you all right? You look faint."

He picked up one of her hands and lightly slapped her wrist.

"Everything's gone wrong," she whispered.

"Monthwaite?"

Isabelle nodded miserably.

"Did he suitably atone for the divorce?" he asked.

"He had an article printed in the paper."

Justin whistled. "Sounds serious."

"It was," Isabelle answered. "But I don't know if I can trust him. He hurt both of us—"

"But he's made up for it," Justin pointed out. He patted her cheeks. "You still look pale."

She shook her head, trying to clear her thoughts. "There was someone else."

Justin's face darkened. "Another woman?"

Isabelle shook her head. "No, there was another man whose life Marshall ruined."

"Ruined is a strong word." Justin lifted her chin with a finger. "You suffered, Isa. I did, too. But I wouldn't say my life was ruined." One side of his mouth pulled up in a lopsided smile. "To be sure, it's taken some unexpected twists, but I'm happy. And it turns out he didn't even send me packing to begin with—his mother did, and we already knew she was a harpy."

Isabelle's shoulders jostled with her exhaled laugh.

"I do note," Justin said, "that he takes responsibility, even though his mother sent threats in his name. Very stand-up of him. And," he raised a finger, "when Monthwaite learned of his mistake, he made it up to both of us, didn't he?"

She nodded again.

"You loved him then," Justin said quietly, "when you were an eighteen-year-old girl. You still love him." It wasn't a question, and Isabelle didn't try to deny it.

"Do you know whether he's remedied things with this other man?" Justin asked.

Isabelle's fingers tightened around Justin's. Her brow furrowed. "He has," she admitted. Her lower lip trembled. "Oh, Justin. I think I made a mistake."

* * *

"Good God! Justin Miller!"

Isabelle looked up and Justin awkwardly turned on his knees. Lily stood in the door in a royal blue traveling costume, her fingers paused in the act of untying her bonnet. She looked from Justin to Isabelle, and back to Justin again.

"My word, are you proposing?"

Justin barked a laugh. "I don't think my wife would thank me if I did." He hauled himself to his feet.

"I wasn't expecting you until tomorrow. Justin was trying to keep me from fainting," Isabelle explained, rising to take Lily's hands in greeting. "It was something of a shock to find him in my parlor," she said in an over-bright voice. "He brought his lovely wife and daughter, too. They've gone for a walk. I'll have them called in, shall I? Mrs. Miller is *American*, Lily. Our Justin went and married an American!"

Lily raised a lace-gloved hand. "Isabelle," she said in a stern tone, "the prospect of meeting Justin's wife and child fills me to the brim with rapture, I assure you, but there's something I have to tell you first."

The commanding edge to her voice brought Isabelle's frenetic recitation to a halt. The firm set to Lily's mouth aroused a queasy feeling in Isabelle's middle. "What is it?"

"I had a note from Naomi yesterday afternoon, and I left as soon as I could to reach you."

Pure, unadulterated fear sprang up in her very blood, coursing through every inch of her. "Marshall. What's happened to him?"

"He's leaving tomorrow," Lily said. "He's going to South America."

Isabelle shook her head, not understanding. "His expedition. I already knew about that."

"It's supposed to be only for six months, but Naomi found notes indicating he never intends to return."

The final bit of color drained from Isabelle's face. "Tomorrow?" she whispered harshly. The full meaning of Lily's information pressed down on Isabelle like a load of stone. A life without Marshall. Forever.

"Isabelle!" Lily snapped. "Listen to me."

Isabelle lifted her head from where it had fallen against Justin's shoulder.

"It's time to come clean," Lily said. "Naomi and I have been keeping an eye on you two, hoping you'd come 'round on your own. It appears you're both bull-headed ninnies who would rather be miserable and alone for the rest of your natural lives, rather than simply put the past behind you and move on." She drew a deep breath and lifted a brow.

Isabelle had seen her take such a tack with others, but she herself had never felt the full brunt of Lily Bachman's ire. It was not a pleasant experience.

"Buck. Up. You love Marshall. He loves you. And if you don't do something about it right this instant, I shall be subjected to your insufferable malaise for the rest of my days. Spare me that fate, and do the right thing." She glanced at the clock on the mantle. "If you aren't already too late to get there before the ship sails."

Isabelle grabbed Lily in a fierce embrace. "Thank you."

"Don't thank me," Lily said in a softer tone, "go. Go!" she insisted, shooing Isabelle out of the parlor.

As she dashed for the stairs, Isabelle heard Lily behind her: "And just where in the blazes have you been all these years?"

Isabelle's fingers shook as she changed into a traveling costume. She had to get to Marshall. She had to tell him she'd forgiven him, that she loved him, even if he wouldn't take her back. But she couldn't allow that possibility in her mind. Everything would work out. She just had to get there.

Chapter Twenty-three

Isabelle gracelessly stumbled out of the carriage Lily had loaned her. The footman caught her with a steadying hand under her elbow.

She took a few steps, her bunched muscles protesting and cramping. They'd stopped only to change horses. Her blue-gray traveling gown was hopelessly rumpled. She felt sticky all over from her long confinement.

Now that she was at the London docks, trepidation tugged at her skirts. The sights, sounds, and smells were overwhelming. The docks teemed with activity, and dawn had scarcely broken. Large men lugged crates and trunks up gangways. Raucous laughter erupted here and there, punctuating the ceaseless, dull roar of hundreds of voices.

The water of the Thames was scarcely visible from Isabelle's vantage point. From where she stood, the river was a forest full of branchless trees with sails instead of leaves. Ships crowded the docks and waited in the river. Somewhere nearby, the hulks were anchored in the middle of the river—whole ships full of convicted thieves and murderers.

Even at this hour, prostitutes lurked at the fringes of activity, calling out to passing men. At the mouth of an alley, a man lay face down in a pool of vomit, a bottle of gin clutched in his hand. Isabelle couldn't tell whether he was dead or alive, and no one else seemed to notice or care.

She shivered. This was no place for a lady. Reason shouted at her to climb back into the safety of the carriage and send the footman for Marshall.

This time, though, she had to let her heart take the lead. She had hurt him when she'd left, and she had to be the one to reach out and find him. She selfishly wanted to see the look on his face when he saw her.

He wouldn't ever see her, however, if she remained planted next to the carriage, gawking at the bustling activity. He would be gone, forever beyond her reach, if she didn't start moving.

With a shaking hand, she pulled from her reticule the paper Lily had given her. On it was the name of Marshall's ship.

"*Adamanthea*," she muttered. She looked at the ship closest to where she stood. The name painted on the hull was *Siren's Call*. Isabelle scowled and took a few steps. A hand clamped around her upper arm. She shrieked.

"Wouldn't you like me to go with you, ma'am?" Lily's footman asked. "Miss Bachman would have my head if any harm came to you."

Isabelle nodded gratefully. Together, they plunged into the morass of humanity moving across the docks and quays.

She allowed the footman to do most of the talking, asking for directions to Marshall's ship. The first several brutes he questioned claimed ignorance. Another sent them toward the East India Company's private docks. Yet another seaman sent them back in the direction from which they had just come.

The sun was fully above the horizon now. Isabelle stomped her foot and let out a strangled cry of frustration. She had come all this way at a breakneck pace to find Marshall, and now she was going to lose him forever because she couldn't locate his bloody ship.

"Excuse me," she called out to a nearby man holding a horse by the bridle, carefully guiding the animal through the crowd. He didn't notice her. Isabelle tapped his shoulder. "I'm looking for the *Adamanthea*," she said. "Do you know where it is?"

The man turned, revealing a weathered, hard face. Isabelle sucked in her breath. Thomas Gerald tugged the brim of his cap. "Indeed I do; I'm headed there m'self," he said amicably. A flash of recognition crossed his face.

Isabelle backed away, looking over her shoulder for the footman.

"Please," Gerald extended a staying hand, "me and His Grace have settled our differences. Why," he said, pulling himself erect, "I'm going with him to South America as master of the horse." He smiled proudly.

Isabelle returned his smile weakly. It seemed they had made their peace after all. And more, the former convict could help her find Marshall.

"Where's the ship?" Isabelle asked Thomas. "I have to see the duke."

"Two ships down," he answered.

Isabelle wheeled around to see where he pointed. She tsked in annoyance. "We passed it," she said to the footman.

"Come on, then. I'll walk with you." Gerald gently tugged on the horse's lead.

A dockhand stumbled into the horse, dropping a crate against its haunch. The already nervous animal reared up on its hind legs, flailing to escape. "Whoa now!" Gerald struggled to calm the horse. "Go on ahead," he called over his shoulder. "I'll be a few minutes here."

Isabelle plowed through the crowd, not paying attention to whether Lily's footman followed. Marshall was close. She had to find him, had to see him. The thought looped through her mind like a mantra, driving her forward.

Two guards stood at the foot of the gangplank. One of them put his arm across her path as she tried to step onto the ramp. "Stop there, miss."

She huffed with impatience. "I'd like to board the ship, please."

The great brute merely smacked his lips and shook his head. "Yer got papers to show me?"

Isabelle sniffed. "Papers? Why on earth do I need papers? I'm here to see the Duke of Monthwaite."

"If yer ain't got papers," the guard replied, "then you got no bidness on this 'ere ship. Off you go, then."

Isabelle gave first one guard, and then the other, her most dazzling smile. "Surely it's nothing to you if I just step aboard for a moment. His Grace would not want you to bar my way."

The other guard spat on the ground near her feet. "His Grace don't want no thieves or whores on 'is ship. On your way."

Isabelle's mouth dropped open. "Why you despicable—" She set her jaw and lifted her chin. She had not come all this way to be insulted into defeat by two unwashed ruffians. "You seem to have mistaken my identity. I am neither thief nor whore, and I'm done discussing the matter." She took a step forward.

"Right, then," said one of the guards. Each man roughly grabbed hold of one of her arms and began dragging her away from the ship.

"Let me go!"

Lily's footman argued with the men, to no effect.

Marshall and another man emerged on the *Adamanthea*'s deck. "Marshall!" she called. Her voice was swallowed in the bustling din; he did not look her way. He and his companion began walking across the deck with their backs to Isabelle.

She desperately twisted in the grasp of the large guards.

"Gawd, she's a wild one," one of the men said. "Where's a charley when we need one?"

Marshall was about to round the prow of the ship. If Isabelle lost sight of him now, she might never see him again. She gathered her breath and screamed his name. He turned. His brows snapped together when he spotted the ruckus taking place near his ship. Then he saw her, and his lips parted.

She nearly cried in relief. He'd seen her. It would be all right now.

Marshall strode the length of the deck and paused at the top of the gangway. The breeze tousled his hair. He wore no jacket over his ivory shirt and camel waistcoat, in spite of the cold morning. His brown breeches fit like a second skin. He was the most beautiful sight she'd ever seen.

"Hold," he called. A single word in his commanding baritone was all it took to get the guards' attention. "She can come up."

Isabelle schooled her features into regal composure and arched a brow at her captors. They released her arms.

Her eyes were locked onto Marshall as she climbed the ramp to *Adamanthea*'s deck. Butterflies buffeted her stomach. She wanted so much to smile or laugh, but his fierce expression kept her on tenterhooks.

Marshall's lips were drawn into a tight line, his guarded features betraying nothing. Was he not pleased to see her?

Maybe she shouldn't have come. He didn't want her anymore—she could see that now. She'd hurt him too badly. Too much time had passed.

Despite her uncertainty, her feet carried her forward. She stopped in front of him. Her hands twisted in the cord of her reticule, two white knuckled fists.

"Isabelle." He nodded once. His pulse flicked beneath the skin of his throat. She longed to cover that place with her mouth.

She swallowed. "Hello, Marshall." Whatever happened, she had to try. If he told her to leave, she would. But she could never live with herself if she didn't try.

Without a word, he took her elbow and guided her across the deck. Sailors stepped out of the way as they passed.

They descended narrow steps into the belly of the ship. He opened a door and gestured. She stepped past him into a neat, small cabin. A bunk was built into one wall. A desk was nailed to the floor against the opposite wall, with a single wooden chair in front of it. His trunk stood open near the bunk. She glimpsed his shaving articles nestled atop a stack of snowy nightshirts.

"What do you want?" he asked, closing the door. He stood with his feet planted wide, his arms crossed across his chest.

She took a deep breath. It was now or never. "You."

Marshall flinched.

Isabelle laid her hand on his arm. His muscles tightened beneath her fingers. When she glanced up, he was looking at her hand.

"I saw Mr. Gerald," she said. "Did you really give him a position?"

His jaw hardened. "I needed a competent master of the horse, and he just so happens to be the finest hand with horses I've ever seen. Is that why you've come—to discuss Mr. Gerald?" She detected a note of hurt in his voice, and his piercing eyes bored straight into her core. "This ship sails in two hours," he said. "I'm extraordinarily busy."

"No." Isabelle gripped his arm. "No, of course I haven't come to discuss Mr. Gerald. I came because . . ." Her courage began to flag.

He arched a brow, and she caught the faintest hint of a smile at the corners of his lips.

"I love you," she blurted. She turned away and tossed her reticule onto the bed.

Marshall crossed the cramped cabin in a couple steps. He turned the chair around and sat down, crossing his ankles. "This sounds more interesting than Thomas Gerald," he drawled.

Isabelle bit her lip. She sat on the edge of the bed with her fingers curled around the side rail. "I've been perfectly miserable these last few months. I thought I could be happy on my own, but I'm not."

"You're respectable again," Marshall pointed out. "I hear you have the ladies' committee well in hand."

Isabelle started. "Ah," she raised her brows, "Naomi. Who must've had it from Lily. They've been conspiring behind our backs, you know."

"I find I am not surprised in the least."

"Justin came home," Isabelle said. "He showed me the letters he received."

"Mother again." Marshall gave her a pained look. "She's staying in the country, perhaps for a very long time."

Isabelle winced. "I'm sorry it had to come to that."

Marshall blew his cheeks out. "So am I, but I couldn't allow her to continue unchecked. What might she do when it comes time for Grant to marry, or Naomi?"

It was a bitter thing for a son to have to punish his own mother, but

Isabelle didn't want him brooding now. "You did the right thing. Thank you for bringing Justin home."

He shrugged. "I couldn't let him spend the rest of his life fearing to return to England. He didn't propose?" he asked mildly. "I thought you'd come to tell me you were marrying Miller."

"What?" she gasped, amazed he could ever think such a thing. "No, darling, Justin brought his wife and child with him." She wrinkled her brow. "It's never been like that between him and me. You know that."

He smirked. "Not really," he said, cutting his eyes to her. "Logically, yes, but if I hadn't been so damned jealous of your relationship with him I never would have taken my mother's word for what happened in the cottage that day."

"Jealous?" Isabelle said, bewildered. "You never said anything before. I shouldn't have invited him while you were gone, Marshall. I know that now. I ask your forgiveness for doing so. Truly, though, I never would have done if I had any inkling you'd object. I thought you understood how things were with Justin."

He leaned back and raked his hands through his hair. "I know. And I did try not to let my emotions overrule my sense. I was insecure. I wanted you so much, but Mother would hear nothing but that you were only after the title and money. When she found you with Justin, it was easy to believe the worst." He lowered his head into his hands and groaned. "I did so many things wrong," he muttered miserably.

"So did I," Isabelle said wistfully.

She crossed the room, crouched in front of him, and took his hands. Marshall's pained gaze tore her heart. "I never told you back then that I loved you. I should have, but I didn't think you wanted to hear it."

Marshall's fingers squeezed around hers. "Did you?"

She nodded, and felt the knot she'd been carrying in her middle for months begin to unwind. "I've loved you since before we married. And I'm afraid that no matter what I do, I shall love you until the day

I die. So you see," she said with a half-smile, "I find myself in quite a predicament."

Suddenly she was in his arms. They were standing, with her full length pressed against his. His mouth came down on hers, tenderly at first, but rapidly becoming more demanding. Isabelle felt like the light of the sun pulsed between them, bright and hot and unquenchable.

Marshall dragged his lips away from hers. He stroked the hair above her temples and brushed his lips against her forehead. "So many mistakes," Marshall said, repeating his self-incrimination. "I should have told you I loved you in that inn. I should have told you a thousand times before you left me. I know why you did. I would've left me, too."

Isabelle laughed softly, leaning her forehead against his chin. She pulled back in his arms and tilted her head so she could look him in the eye. "You'll stay now, though, won't you?"

Marshall smiled sadly and stroked her cheek with a knuckle. "No, my love, I won't stay. I have to go."

Isabelle recoiled. Her mind reeled, refusing to accept what he was saying. Not when she loved him, and he loved her.

"But," he said, touching the tip of her nose, "if you'd like, I will delay sailing for a few weeks—long enough to get invitations out and guests to town. How does South America strike you for a wedding trip?" His lips turned up in that sly, boyish smile of his, the one she loved best of all.

She flung her arms around his neck and raised up on her toes to kiss him. It was an awkward kiss, more teeth than lips for the smiles they each wore.

He scooped her into his arms and carried her to the bunk, where he gently set her down on the wool blanket. Then he straightened, made quick work of the buttons on his waistcoat and tossed it aside. His shirt soon followed and joined it on the floor.

Her breath caught at the sight of him. Heat stirred her blood. He stretched out beside her on the bunk. Their arms wound around each other as he delivered kiss after scorching kiss.

Marshall began working the buttons on the back of her dress. Isabelle's breath left her in a whoosh as moisture pooled between her legs. She was desperate to feel him. Isabelle tugged first one sleeve, and then the other, pulling her arms back through the material. Marshall shimmied her skirt up so it bunched around her waist. When Isabelle's arms were clear, she lifted them, and Marshall pulled the frock over her head and tossed it to join the heap on the floor.

Their eyes locked together, and Isabelle thought she would die if she couldn't have him. She quivered all over with the force of her wanting. Her eyes never leaving his, she stripped out of her chemise and stockings while Marshall made short work of the rest of his clothes.

She had one delicious glimpse of his glorious, naked self before he grabbed a folded blanket from the foot of the bed and shook it open. He turned and covered her in one smooth motion; the blanket billowed then settled over them.

Isabelle traced her tongue up the side of his throat, relishing the light, salty tang of his skin and his spicy, masculine scent. She didn't care how forward or wanton she might seem. Theirs was a mutual hunger, a soul-deep yearning that went beyond lust.

Marshall groaned and captured her mouth in a heavy kiss. Their tongues danced and stroked. Isabelle clutched his neck with frantic need.

He dragged his mouth across her cheek and then propped himself up on his elbows. Sheltered by his large body, Isabelle felt safe and warm and . . . home.

Marshall's heavy erection pressed against her thigh. Isabelle parted her legs and made a whimpering sound. Marshall moved to cover her there with a hand, stroking and parting her folds. "I have to have you now," he said in a strained voice.

"Yes," Isabelle said. Her breath was already coming fast. "Me, too. I need—"

And then he was in her, and she gasped at the pleasure. Her nails dug into his back as she clutched him as tightly as she could, even squeezing the muscles around his staff—which resulted in an earthy grunt of approval from Marshall.

He withdrew and drove in, burying himself to the hilt. Her taut nerves jumped in response. He moved in slow, long strokes, claiming her with his body. "You're mine," he rasped. "My Isabelle."

She hugged her arms around his shoulders, near to crying with joy and the force of her passion, oblivious to everything but the heat between them. "Yes," she whispered.

She *was* his. She loved him. She'd loved him since she was eighteen years old. She'd loved him through divorce and exile and everything life threw in her path. She'd loved him through it all.

Marshall rose onto his knees and lifted her thighs to receive him even more deeply. The blanket fell around his hips. His fingers dug into the globes of her buttocks. She pressed her feet into the bed, willing their flesh to meld together into one.

His eyes were hazy but intense upon her as she neared her climax. "You're so beautiful," he said. He drew a deep breath and shook his head. Isabelle knew he was holding back.

"Don't stop," she said. "Come with me."

His mouth dropped open, and Isabelle closed her eyes. She felt him shift over her, moving higher, while maintaining their joining.

The change in position had the base of his shaft dragging against her tight bud with every stroke. Everything below her navel clenched. It was all she could do to hang on and ride the pounding waves of pleasure he brought her with every driving thrust.

"Love you, Isabelle," he said between heavy pants.

"Love you so much," was her breathless reply.

Their sweat-slicked skins slid together with sinful ease, every movement ratcheting her tighter and tighter until . . . "Aaah!" she cried. Her heels pressed into the mattress and the force of her orgasm arched her off the bed, lifting Marshall just as his own climax had his fingers digging into her hips, holding them tight together while he poured into her womb.

When they were spent, Marshall held her close for a moment, then disengaged from her arms. He dropped a kiss to her damp brow and hastily dressed to inform the captain they would not sail just yet.

He paused in the doorway and gave her a sated smile. "I must warn you," he drawled, "the only reason I proposed is because we need another cook. This is a working expedition, after all. No lazing about like a pampered duchess."

Joyous mirth bubbled up inside Isabelle and spilled out in a gale of silvery laughter. She tossed a pillow at his head, which he easily caught. He brought it back to the bed and leaned over. He planted his hands on the mattress on either side of her. She loved the feeling of being surrounded by him.

"However," he said, his eyes full of rekindling passion, "you'll spend most of your time right here, assisting me in the very important endeavor of producing an heir."

She rose to meet him as another wave of desire fell across her. "That," she said, smiling wickedly and curling her fingers around the back of his neck, "is an occupation I shall be glad to have."

About the Author

Like all good Southern girls, Elizabeth Boyce fell in love with the past early on, convinced the bygone days of genteel manners and fancy dresses were only an air conditioning unit shy of perfection. Her passion for the British Regency began when she was first exposed to that most potent Regency gateway drug, *Pride and Prejudice*. She's remained steadfast in her love of the period ever since. Those rumors of a fling with ancient Greece are totally false—honest.

Elizabeth lives in South Carolina with her husband and three young children. She loves to connect with her readers, so keep in touch!

E-mail: *bluestockingball@gmail.com*

Blog: *http://bluestockingball.blogspot.com/*

Facebook: *http://www.facebook.com/AuthorElizabethBoyce*

Twitter: *https://twitter.com/EBoyceRomance*

A Sneak Peek from Crimson Romance
From *Once an Heiress* by Elizabeth Boyce

CRIMSON ROMANCE

HISTORICAL

Once an
Heiress

Elizabeth Boyce
Author of *Once a Duchess*

Chapter One

Lily Bachman squared her shoulders, lifted her chin, and drew a deep breath. Behind the study door was another dragon to slay—or perhaps this one would be more like a pesky dog to shoo off. Whatever the case, one thing was certain; in that room, she'd find a man after her money. He was the fourth this Season, and it was only the end of March.

She smoothed the front of her muslin dress with a quick gesture, and then opened the door.

The Leech, as she dubbed all of them, halted whatever nonsense he was blathering on about and turned at the sound of the door opening, his jaw hanging slack, paused in the action of speaking. Her father sat on the sofa, situated at a right angle to the chair inhabited by the would-be suitor.

"Darling." Mr. Bachman rose. "You're just in time. This is Mr. Faircloth."

Lily pressed her cheek to his. "Good morning, Father."

Mr. Bachman and Lily were close in height. He was of a bit more than average height for a man, while Lily was practically a giantess amongst the dainty aristocratic ladies. She stuck out like a sore thumb at parties, towering over every other female in the room—just another reason she detested such functions.

The man, Mr. Faircloth, also stood. He was shorter than Lily and lacked a chin. The smooth slope marking the transition from jaw to neck was unsettling to look upon. He wore mutton-chop sideburns, presumably an attempt to emphasize his jawline. They failed miserably in that regard, serving rather to point out the vacant place between them where a facial feature should have been.

"My . . ." Mr. Faircloth wrung his hands together and cleared his throat. "My dear Miss Bachman," he started again. "How lovely you look this morning."

Lily inclined her head coolly. She settled onto the sofa and folded her hands in her lap. Mr. Bachman sat beside her and gestured Mr. Faircloth to his chair.

Mr. Faircloth cast an apprehensive look between Lily and her father. "I'd thought, sir, that you and I would speak first. Then, if all was agreeable, I would speak to Miss . . ." He lowered his eyes and cleared his throat again.

Good, Lily thought viciously. He was already thrown off balance. She knew from experience that when dealing with fortune hunters and younger sons, one had to establish and maintain the upper hand.

"When it comes to my daughter's future," Mr. Bachman said in a rich baritone, "there is no such thing as a private interview. Miss Bachman is a grown woman; she's entitled to have a say in her own future. Would you not agree?"

Mr. Faircloth squirmed beneath the intense gazes of father and daughter. "Well, it's not how these things are usually handled, sir, but I suppose there's no real harm in bucking convention just this—"

"Mr. Faircloth," Lily interrupted.

The man swallowed. "Yes?"

"I don't recognize you at all." She raised her brows and narrowed her eyes, as though examining a distasteful insect. "Have we met?"

"I, well, that is . . . yes, we've met." Mr. Faircloth's head bobbed up and down. "We were introduced at the Shervington's ball last week. I asked you to dance."

As he spoke, Lily stood and crossed the room to her father's desk. She retrieved a sheaf of paper and a pen, and then returned to her seat. She allowed the silence to stretch while she jotted down notes: name, physical description, and first impression. *Younger son*, she decided, *a novice to fortune hunting*. She glanced up with the pen poised above the paper. "And did I accept your invitation?"

Mr. Faircloth gave a nervous smile. "Ah, no, actually. You were already spoken for the next set, and every one thereafter." He pointed weakly toward her notes. "What are you writing there?"

She leveled her most withering gaze on him. "Are you or are you not applying for my hand in matrimony?"

His jaw worked without sound, and then his face flushed a deep pink. "I, yes. That is why I've come, I suppose you could say."

"You suppose?" Lily scoffed. "You're not sure?"

"Yes." Mr. Faircloth drew himself up, rallying. "Yes, I'm sure. That's why I've come."

So there is a bit of spine in this one, after all, Lily thought. "That being the case," she replied, giving no quarter in her attack, "it is reasonable for me to keep a record of these proceedings, is it not? You are not the first gentleman to present himself."

Mr. Faircloth sank back into himself. "I see."

"Tell me, what prompted your call today?" Lily tilted her head at an inquisitive angle, as though she were actually interested in the man's answer.

Mr. Faircloth cast a desperate look at Mr. Bachman.

"That's a fair question," her father said. Lily loved many things about her father, but the one she appreciated more than anything was the way he treated her like a competent adult. Most females were bartered off to the man who made the highest offer, either through wealth or connections. When he spoke up for her, supporting her line of questioning, Lily wanted to throw her arms around his neck and hug him. Later, she would. Right now, they had to eject the newest swain from their home.

Mr. Faircloth grew more and more agitated with every passing second. He fidgeted in his seat and finally blurted, "I love you!"

Lily drew back, surprised by the tactic her opponent employed. She waved a dismissive hand. "Don't be ridiculous."

"It's true," Mr. Faircloth insisted. "From the moment I saw you, I thought you were the most beautiful woman at the ball. Your gown was the most flattering blue—"

"I wore red," Lily corrected.

Mr. Faircloth blinked. "Oh." He rested his elbows on his knees, his head drooped between his shoulders.

He was crumbling. Time to finish him off.

"Let's talk about why you've really come, shall we?" Lily's tone was pleasant, like a governess explaining something to a young child with limited comprehension. "You're here because of my dowry, just like the other men who have suddenly found themselves stricken with love for me."

"A gentleman does not discuss such matters with a lady," Mr. Faircloth informed his toes.

"A *gentleman*," Lily said archly, "does not concoct fantastical tales of undying affection in the hopes of duping an unwitting female into marriage. Tell me, sir, which son are you?"

"I have two older brothers," he said in a defeated tone.

Lily duly made note of this fact on her paper. "And sisters?"

"Two."

"Ah." Lily raised a finger. "Already an heir and a spare, and two dowries besides. That doesn't leave much for you, does it?" She tutted and allowed a sympathetic smile.

Mr. Faircloth shook his head once and resumed his glum inspection of his footwear.

"I understand your predicament," Lily said. "And how attractive the idea of marrying money must be to a man in your situation." She tilted her head and took on a thoughtful expression. "Have you considered a different approach?"

The gentleman raised his face, his features guarded. "What do you mean?"

She furrowed her brows together. "What I mean is this: Have you considered, perhaps, a profession?"

Mr. Faircloth's mouth hung agape. He looked from Lily to Mr. Bachman, who sat back, passively observing the interview.

"It must rankle," Lily pressed, "to see your eldest brother's future secured by accident of birth, to see your sisters provided for by virtue of their sex. But do consider, my dear Mr. Faircloth, that younger sons the Empire 'round have bought commissions and taken orders, studied law or medicine, accepted government appointments. The time has come," she said, pinning him beneath her fierce gaze, "for you to accept the fact that yours is not to be a life of dissipated leisure. Instead of hoping for a fortune to fall into your lap, your days would be better spent pursuing a profession."

Mr. Faircloth wiped his palms down his thighs. "Miss Bachman, you've quite convinced me."

She blinked. "Have I?"

"Yes," he said. "I am well and truly convinced that marriage to you would be a nightmare from which I should never awake until I die. Sir," he turned his attention to Mr. Bachman, "I see now why you offer such a large dowry for your daughter." He stood. "It would take an astronomical sum to make the proposition of marriage to such a controlling, unpleasant female the slightest bit appealing."

Lily's mouth fell open. "Why, you—"

Her father laid a restraining hand on her arm. Lily exhaled loudly and pinched her lips together.

"Thank you for your time, Mr. Bachman." Mr. Faircloth inclined his head. "Miss Bachman." He hurried from the parlor. A moment later, the front door closed behind him.

"Well!" Lily exclaimed. "Of all the sniveling, puffed up—"

"You wore blue," Mr. Bachman cut in.

"I beg your pardon?"

"The Shervington's ball. You wore blue, just as Mr. Faircloth said." He stood and crossed to his desk, where he poured himself a brandy from a decanter.

"Did I?" Lily murmured. "I could have sworn I wore red." She tapped a finger against her lips.

"No, darling," Mr. Bachman said with a sigh, "you wore blue. I'm quite certain, because your mother fretted that the color washed you out and no gentleman would notice you."

"Ah, well," Lily said. She rose and briskly rubbed her palms together. "It doesn't signify. One more Leech gone."

Mr. Bachman's chest heaved and heavy, graying brows furrowed over his dark eyes. "My dear, you cannot continue in this fashion. You know I'll not force you to marry against your will. But marry you must, and it *is* my desire that your marriage elevate this family's status."

Lily straightened a pile of papers on the desk as he spoke; her hands paused at this last remark. Indignation mingled with hurt slammed into her like a physical blow. She idly slid a paper back and forth across the polished desk and kept her eyes studiously upon it as she recovered, hiding the force of her emotions behind a casual demeanor. However, she could not fully suppress the bitterness in her voice when she spoke. "Fortunate, then, that Charles died. A mere ensign and son of a country squire would not have provided the upward mobility you crave."

Mr. Bachman's glass boomed against the desk. "Young lady, guard your tongue!" Her eyes snapped to his mottled face. His own dark eyes flashed rage, and his nostrils flared. "Had poor Charles returned from Spain, I would have proudly and happily given you in wedlock. Indeed, it was my fondest wish to unite our family with the Handfords."

A humorless laugh burst from Lily's lips. Turning, she twitched her skirts in a sharp gesture. "A fact you made sure to educate me upon from the earliest. I spent the whole of my life with the name of my groom and date of my wedding drilled into my head."

It was an unfair accusation, she knew, even as it flew from her mouth. Yes, she had been betrothed to Charles Handford since time out of mind, but for most of her life, it was simply a fact she'd memorized, along with the color of the sky and the sum of two and two.

There'd been plenty of visits with their neighbors, the Handfords, but Charles was ten years her senior and rarely present. Her earliest memories of him were his visits home from Eton and Oxford, or later, leaves from his lancer regiment.

Their betrothal only became more relevant as her twentieth birthday neared, bringing the planned summer wedding that was to follow on its heels—an event postponed when Charles' regiment could not spare him, and which was never to be when he died that autumn.

The silence stretched while her father regained his composure. Gradually, the angry red drained from his face. "Now, Lily," he said in a more moderate tone, "I'll not be portrayed as some chattel dealer, looking to hoist you off without a care for your feelings. Since last year was your first Season—and you just out of mourning—I did not push the issue. I still wish you to make your own match. The only stipulation I have placed is that the gentleman be titled—either in his own right or set to inherit. Surely that is not too onerous? There are scores of eligible gentlemen to choose from."

"I don't wish to marry an *aristocrat.*" She dripped disdain all over the word. "They're a lot of lazy social parasites, with a collective sense of entitlement, just like that last one—"

Mr. Bachman's brows shot up his forehead. "Lily!"

She ducked her head. "I'm sorry," she muttered, abashed. "My mouth does run ahead of me—"

"And it's going to run you right into spinsterhood, if you don't mind yourself."

Heat crept up Lily's neck and over her cheeks.

"Now, dear," Mr. Bachman continued, "poor Mr. Faircloth certainly *was* here because of your dowry. It's big on purpose, and no doubt about it. But he also knew what color gown you wore to a ball last week. Do you know the last time I noticed a woman's gown?"

Lily shrugged.

"Thirty years or more," Mr. Bachman proclaimed, "if, in fact, I ever noticed to begin with." He lifted her chin with a finger. Lily raised her eyes to meet her father's softened expression. "You are an exceedingly pretty girl—"

"Oh, Papa . . ."

"You *are*. The way society works, however, renders it almost out of the question for the right kind of man to come calling, even if he thinks your dress *is* the most becoming shade of blue. Your dowry clears a few of those obstacles." He took her hand and patted it. "Now, let us be done quarreling and speak of pleasanter things."

Lily nodded hastily.

She happened to disagree with her father on the issue of her dowry. To Lily's mind, the "right kind of man" would want to be with her, fortune or no. She thought of her dearest friend, Isabelle, Duchess of Monthwaite. Even though she and her husband, Marshall, went through a horrible divorce—reducing Isabelle to the lowest possible social status—they still found their way back together. Marshall didn't allow Isabelle's reduced circumstances to keep them apart, once they came to terms with their past.

For the thousandth time, Lily wished Isabelle was here. But she and His Grace were in South America on a botanical expedition-cum-honeymoon. They'd be home in a couple months, but oh, how time dragged when Lily so needed her friend's advice.

Fortunately, Isabelle's sister-in-law, Lady Naomi Lockwood, would soon be in town. She'd written to Lily that her mother, Caro, would be sitting out the Season to remain in the country—a singularly odd choice, Lily thought, considering the dowager duchess' responsibility to see Naomi wed. Instead of her mother, Naomi would be chaperoned by her spinster aunt, Lady Janine.

Lily would be glad to see their friendly faces. She didn't get on well with tonnish young women, and there was always the suspicion that men were only interested in her money. Lily often found herself lonely in the middle of a glittering crush.

"Are you attending?" Mr. Bachman said.

Lily blinked. "I'm sorry, Papa, what was that?"

"I asked," he repeated patiently, "if you've decided on a project."

Lily's mood brightened. *This* was something she would enjoy discussing. "I have."

"Excellent!" Mr. Bachman sat in the large armchair behind his desk, the throne from which he ruled his ever-expanding empire of industry. He moved the chair opposite the desk around to his side. "Have a seat, dear."

Despite the tempest that had just flared between them, Lily felt a rush of affection for her dear father. Since she was a girl, he'd shared his desk with her. When she was young, he'd held her on his lap while he spoke to her about things she didn't understand then—coal veins and shipping ventures; members of Parliament and government contracts.

At the time, it all blurred together into Papa's Work. As she grew, she began to make sense of it all.

She understood now that all her life, he'd treated her as the son he never had, heir apparent to the name and fortune he'd made for himself. Never had he indicated any doubt in her capability or intelligence on account of her sex. He took pride in his daughter's education, and emphasized mathematics and politics, in addition to feminine accomplishments such as drawing and dancing.

Just before they'd come to town this Season, Mr. Bachman presented Lily with a unique opportunity. He desired she develop a sizable charity project. He would fund her endeavor, but Lily had to do the work to bring her plans to fruition. She jumped on the proposal, glad for an occupation beside the *ton's* vapid entertainments.

Mr. Bachman rummaged through a drawer and withdrew a sheet of paper covered with Lily's neat writing.

"So, here is the list of ideas you began with. What have you settled upon?"

Lily pointed to an item halfway down the page. "The school for disadvantaged young women," she said. "I should like to keep it small for now. Girls would receive a sound education, plus some accomplishments that would enable them to take positions as governesses, ladies' maids, companions, things of that nature."

Mr. Bachman cupped his chin in his hand and listened with a thoughtful expression while Lily enumerated her ideas for the school. When she finished, he slapped his fingers on the desk. "Marvelous, my dear."

Lily swelled with pride at her father's approval.

He took a fresh sheet of paper and jotted a note. "I'm putting my solicitor at your disposal. The two of you can select an appropriate property for purchase. Meanwhile, you also need to secure a headmistress, who can, in turn, hire the staff. You'll need tutors, a cook, maids . . ."

As the plan came together, Lily's confidence in the project soared. There was nothing she could not accomplish once she knew how to approach a problem.

She kissed her father's cheek at the conclusion of their meeting.

"Just think, m'dear," he said on their parting.

"What's that?"

"When you marry one of those lazy aristocrats, he'll have scads of free time to help with your work." He winked and patted her arm.

Lily scowled at his back. He seemed to think a man in need of her dowry would also, in turn, look kindly upon her efforts to care for those less fortunate than themselves. She snorted. Such a man did not exist.

Find out more about *Once an Heiress* when you visit
http://www.crimsonromance.com/crimson-romance-ebooks/
crimson-romance-book-genres/historical-romance-novels/once-an-heiress/.

Also Available

In the mood for more Crimson Romance?
Check out *Once an Innocent* by Elizabeth Boyce at
CrimsonRomance.com.